Mint Juleps, Mayhem, And Murder

**Center Point
Large Print**

Also by Sara Rossett
and available from Center Point Large Print:

Magnolias, Moonlight, and Murder

**This Large Print Book carries the
Seal of Approval of N.A.V.H.**

Mint Juleps, Mayhem, And Murder

Sara Rosett

CENTER POINT PUBLISHING
THORNDIKE, MAINE

This Center Point Large Print edition
is published in the year 2010 by arrangement with
Kensington Publishing Corp.

The text of this Large Print edition is unabridged.
In other aspects, this book may vary
from the original edition.
Printed in the United States of America.
Set in 16-point Times New Roman type.

ISBN: 978-1-60285-825-1

Library of Congress Cataloging-in-Publication Data

Rosett, Sara.
    Mint juleps, mayhem, and murder / Sara Rosett. — Center Point large print ed.
        p. cm.
    ISBN 978-1-60285-825-1 (lib. bdg. : alk. paper)
    1. Motherhood—Fiction. 2. Avery, Ellie (Fictitious character)—Fiction.
    3. Air Force spouses—Fiction. 4. Large type books. I. Title.
    PS3618.O844M56 2010
    813'.6—dc22
2010018948

To the AFRC spouses at Robins Air Force Base.

Chapter
One

I flinched as a rifle shot fractured the air.
"Good lord, what was that?" Mitch's aunt
jumped and nearly dropped the slice of peach pie
she was transferring to a plate.

"Hunters," I explained, gesturing to the woods
behind our backyard. "The neighborhood backs
up to a state wildlife area. We hear them quite a
bit, especially since deer season opened early this
year." I kept my voice casual, but that shot had
been awfully close, much louder than usual. I
tensed, waiting for more shots, but the only
sounds I heard were the low murmurings of voices
punctuated with an occasional laugh from the fifty
people gathered in our backyard for the annual
Avery Family Reunion.

"Oh dear, I'd love a slice of that chocolate cake,
too, but I really shouldn't," Mitch's aunt said as
she surveyed the spread on the dessert table.
Mitch's family was from Smarr, a small town outside of Montgomery, Alabama, and they were a
true southern family—they overflowed with
charm and friendliness and they knew how to
cook. None of the new-fangled sugar substitutes,
low-calorie, or low-fat recipes for them. *The more
butter and sugar, the better,* seemed to be the
family motto, which I certainly couldn't argue

with, since I have an affinity for sweets myself, particularly chocolate. "Here, I'll split a piece with you," I said, trying to cover for the fact that I wasn't sure if this was Aunt Christine or Aunt Claudia. Or maybe . . . Aunt Claudine? No, that wasn't right. As she cut a slice in half, I caught Mitch's gaze and mouthed the words, "Aunt Christine?"

He gave me the thumbs up, broke away from the men by the grill, and headed across the yard toward us. "Hi, Aunt Christine," Mitch said as he gave her a peck on the cheek, then ran his arm around my shoulders to give me a quick hug. "How's Grandpa Franklin doing in this humidity?" he asked her. "Would he be more comfortable inside?"

"I'm sure he would be, but he'd never admit it. He refuses to let anything slow him down. I do try to keep him hydrated," she said, holding up a bottled water dripping with condensation. "I'd better get back to him."

We watched her roly-poly figure waddle away. "She takes good care of your grandfather," I said. "She's never been married?"

"Nope, but I hear she's got a boyfriend. Aunt Nanette says the Walgreen's pharmacist is a real hottie for a sixty-year-old and keeps asking Aunt Christine to dinner. They're both metal detector enthusiasts. They met at a treasure hunt."

"You have the most interesting family," I said.

Mitch glanced at me questioningly, and I said, "Don't get defensive. I've got a few quirky types in my family tree, too. I'm the one with the aunt who recycles stray paper clips and used staples. Last time I visited, she'd collected enough to fill a large coffee can. She also makes masks from dryer lint. Cake?"

He shook his head and I devoured the last bites of the rich chocolate and creamy icing. Mitch's healthy eating habits were annoying at times, but right now I was glad to finish off the cake myself. "You know, a few bites won't hurt you."

"I've learned never to come between you and chocolate," he said, the skin around his dark eyes crinkling as he smiled.

I licked the last trace of crumbs from the fork. "Wise man. Now, since I'm fortified with chocolate, I need a refresher on that crash course you gave me on your relatives." The avalanche of Avery relatives had begun at breakfast this morning and I still hadn't sorted out all the names and faces. Mitch's military assignments had kept me from getting to know the whole Avery clan. I nodded to the picnic tables covered with red-and-white checked cloths where the aunts had gathered at the back of the yard in the shade of the loblolly pines. "Aunt Nanette is the one with the Afghan hound at her feet, right?"

"Yes. If you run out of things to talk about, ask about her new Mini Cooper."

"Really? I saw the black one with the British flag on it in the driveway, but I figured it belonged to one of your cousins. She seems more like a Cadillac type."

"Nope. She's an Anglophile who's into sporty cars. And don't forget to pet Queen," Mitch said. "If Queen likes you, Aunt Nanette will, too."

"Oh, who's that—the man with the stubble and the phoenix tattoo on his forearm? I couldn't figure him out."

"None of us can. That's my Uncle Bud. You'd never guess that he's one of the most successful real estate brokers in Alabama, would you? He still lives in the double-wide he's lived in for the last twenty years. Aunt Nanette says he doesn't just pinch pennies, he makes them beg for mercy." Mitch lowered his voice and leaned closer to me. "Don't tell anyone, but I know he sponsors one of the baseball teams in Smarr. No one else in the family knows. If it got out, it would ruin his reputation as a miser."

One of the young cousins threw open the screen door from the house and galloped across the lawn toward Mitch, her pigtails flying and our ringing cordless phone clutched in her hand. The second before the door eased closed, Rex, our rottweiler, who has a seriously scary bark but a sweet disposition, slipped outside. I'd figured keeping him inside during the reunion was a good idea. It was crazy enough in the backyard without him, but he took off, running in huge, looping circles. Queen hesitated for a second, then shot after him. I glanced at Mitch and he shrugged. "We might as well let them wear themselves out. No way we're going to catch them now."

"Thanks, Madison," Mitch said as he took the phone. He listened, then his posture changed from normal and relaxed to taut. He tilted the phone away from his face. "It's Abby."

I could tell from his face that something was wrong. My heart seemed to tumble in my chest, then drop sharply. Abby was another military spouse and my best friend. My thoughts flittered from her to her husband, Jeff, then to their son Charlie. "What is it?" I asked.

Mitch put his hand on my shoulder. "She's fine. They're all fine. It's Colonel Pershall. He's at the E.R."

"Colonel Lewis Pershall? Your squadron commander?" His words didn't make sense. Colonel Pershall couldn't be more than forty. He was a towering giant of a man. He was a sturdy, broad-shouldered black man with a barrel chest and, oddly, one of the softest-spoken people I knew. Mitch said Colonel Pershall never raised his voice at the squadron. He didn't need to. Mitch enjoyed working for him more than anyone else he'd ever worked for.

"Okay, let us know if you need anything. All right. Here's Ellie." He handed me the phone.

11

Abby's shaky voice came over the line. "Oh, Ellie. It's so terrible and I'm sorry to call you during the reunion. I completely forgot about it."

"Don't worry about that. What's going on?" I asked.

"It's touch and go right now," Abby said. "Someone tried to strangle him, Ellie. That sounds strange to say out loud, but that's what they said happened. He'd finished a round of golf. Another golfer found him unconscious in the parking lot beside his car."

I wasn't sure if I'd heard correctly. I turned away from the chatter and laughter. "Did you say strangled?" I asked as I pressed the phone closer to my ear.

"Yes. I know, I can't take it in either, but that's what the doctors are talking about—oxygen deprivation and jugular veins and lots of other words I don't understand, but it's serious."

"How's Denise?"

"Shocked. She's not saying anything. Just sitting there. They come and talk to her and she nods, but that's about it."

"That's not like her at all," I said, thinking of the woman who hadn't been afraid to shake things up at the squadron coffees by daring to ask what the spouses wanted out of their spouse club. The thought that we didn't have to continue to meet once a month and organize fundraisers nearly caused a revolt from some spouses. Sometimes traditions die hard.

"I know," Abby said miserably. "Jeff and I were at the park and we saw the security police pull up to their house." Abby lived in base housing at Taylor Air Force Base and we'd spent several afternoons this summer at that little park situated in base housing, watching Livvy, Nathan, and Charlie clamber up and down the slides. "I went over to check on Denise. The only way I can think to describe her is shell-shocked. She was in a daze. I had to get her purse for her before she left for the hospital. It was like leading Charlie around. Jeff took Charlie home and I came up here to be with her. I'm rambling, aren't I? I think I might be in shock, too."

"No, it's okay. You're at the North Dawkins Medical Center?" I asked. North Dawkins was the city located outside Taylor's gates.

"Right, no E.R. on the base anymore, remember? I don't know if he'll be moved up to Atlanta or not. I'm going to stay until Denise's family gets here."

"We can get away for a while later tonight and come by. Do you need anything?" I asked.

"No. Denise and Lewis are the only ones who need anything. They need prayer. The outlook isn't good. They're not giving Denise much hope."

We said good-bye and I turned back to look around the yard, amazed that people still chatted, the sun still beat down. A blue jay called sharply from the trees above me, then swooped away. Nothing had changed. At least, not for us. I prayed a quick, rather incoherent prayer for Denise and Lewis and took a step toward the house, feeling like I should do something.

I stopped. There was nothing else I could do. Mitch touched my shoulder again. "Are you okay?" he asked, his face concerned.

"Yes. No. Oh, I'm okay, but poor Denise and Colonel Pershall." I couldn't even imagine what Denise was going through. "It's just . . . news like that . . . it's almost unbelievable. I mean, this is North Dawkins, Georgia. People don't get attacked and . . . and *strangled* in North Dawkins. And at a golf course? Was he on base, do you think?" There was a nice course on base.

He shrugged. "I don't know. He liked to play eighteen holes on Saturday and for the last few weeks he'd been playing there. He was determined to birdie sixteen, called it his nemesis, but I suppose he could have been at one of the other neighborhood courses around here." We didn't live in a golf course neighborhood, but there were a few of those scattered around the area.

Mitch had barely finished his sentence when someone slapped him on the shoulder, nearly knocking him over. "Uncle Kenny! How are you?" Mitch asked, and I could see him slip into host-mode, despite the worry he felt.

Uncle Kenny adjusted his University of Alabama baseball cap as he said, "What do you think about the team this year? Did you hear about the new running back? I think we've got a real shot at the SEC West."

I stood by and listened, but wasn't able to contribute much to the conversation. My thoughts were still with Denise and Colonel Pershall. I put the slim phone in my shorts pocket and pulled my thoughts back to the scene in front of me. Abby would call if anything changed. Right now, I had to concentrate on the reunion.

I tried to remember what I'd learned about Uncle Kenny and Aunt Gwen during last year's reunion. I knew they'd cornered the market on roadside boiled peanut stands. They loved the Crimson Tide and were extremely competitive. The volleyball game at the reunion last year had been as hard fought as an Olympic match with Uncle Kenny and Aunt Gwen captaining the two teams. I also remembered that Mitch said they'd wanted to paint the trim on their house crimson earlier this summer, but regulations in their subdivision had forced them to limit the crimson to their front door. I was too shaken to figure out how to work any of those topics into the conversation, so I was relieved to see Mitch's mom, Caroline, walk up with a droopy Nathan snuggled into the crook of her arm.

Caroline was an interesting mixture of reticence

and southern charm. She could fold a fitted sheet so that it looked like a flat sheet and that fact alone intimidated me. She wore the same Avery Family Reunion T-shirt we were all wearing, but on her it looked stylish. She'd gathered the hem of the shirt and fastened it through a clip above her trim hip. The clip matched her heavy silver earrings, which set off her silvery-white hair that swung against her jawbone as she swayed back and forth to keep Nathan dozy. Despite the heat, she looked as fresh as she did when she stepped out of the car this morning at the end of our driveway, carrying her famous peach pies and homemade rolls.

"Are you okay, Ellie? You look a little pale."

I followed Mitch's lead and said, "I'm fine. We just got a call with some bad news about a friend in the hospital." I left it at that. There was no need to trouble everyone at the reunion with the terrible news.

"That's a shame. I hope there's a quick recovery."

"Thanks, I hope so, too. Looks like Nathan is ready for a nap." There's nothing like my kids to keep me grounded and in the moment. I ran my hand down his limp, plump arm. Lately, he'd been boycotting naps, but he needed one today.

"Would you mind if I put him down?" Caroline asked, and I said not at all. Then she said, "Thank you so much for hosting the reunion this year. Everything's been lovely. With the remodel, there's no way we could have done it."

"Glad we could help out. It was nothing."

I heard what sounded like a snort from Mitch and leveled my gaze at him, but he kept his attention fixed on Uncle Kenny, who was saying, "The secret to winning at croquet is all in the order of play . . ."

"Nonsense," Caroline said. "I know how much work this is and you've pulled it off beautifully." Uncle Kenny noticed some of the guys setting up a game of horseshoes and went to join them. Mitch fell into step beside me as Caroline and I walked back to the house. One of Mitch's cousins-in-law, Felicity, nearly ran over us as she marched across the grass.

"Felicity," Caroline called, "I haven't seen Dan. Where is he?"

"Gone. He's never around anymore. I should have known better than to assume he'd skip his jog during the family reunion."

"Oh, so that was him I saw trotting down the driveway earlier? I thought it was you, Mitch," Caroline said. "You boys always have looked so much alike—same dark hair and eyes. And, you're both tall and lanky."

"I was going to run with him, but I'm not feeling one hundred percent." Mitch rubbed his hand over his stomach. "I know I couldn't keep up with him in this humidity." Unlike in so many conversations I'd had today when I had no clue about who was being discussed, I actually knew Mitch's

17

cousin Dan. He and his wife, Felicity, had arrived yesterday and spent the night at our house. Almost everyone else, including Mitch's parents, had driven in earlier in the day.

"I knew we shouldn't have left Aunt Christine's potato salad in the sun so long," I said, but Mitch waved his hand and said, "It's nothing like that. Too much food, probably."

"Are you boys enjoying catching up with each other?" Caroline asked. Mitch said they were and Caroline turned toward me. "They got in more scrapes growing up. Have you heard about the time they hid on the roof all afternoon to avoid Summer?" Caroline asked, referring to Mitch's younger sister.

"That was the time you called the police when you couldn't find them?" I was glad Nathan was too young to pick up any details of his dad's misdeeds.

"Amazing that I can laugh about it now, isn't it, Mitch?" Caroline said.

"It's amazing I can even talk about it," Mitch countered. "Besides one heck of a sunburn, I couldn't sit down for about a week."

"Dan's not nearly as much fun now," Felicity said crossly. "Unless you're discussing the new spin class or weightlifting, forget it. You might as well be speaking a foreign language to him." With her brows lowered and jaw clenched, she reminded me of the dark thunderhead clouds I'd seen as a kid in the Texas panhandle.

Actually, comparing her to a thunderhead was a bit incongruous, since she was petite and skinny. Correction, she wasn't just thin, she was toned. There was barely an ounce of fat on her, except maybe in her cheekbones above her pert nose and pointed chin. With curly brown hair cropped short in a boyish style, she looked every inch the athlete she was. A fitness instructor at a gym in Montgomery, she taught Pilates, spinning, yoga, aerobics, and a scary-sounding class called Killer Boot Camp. Felicity continued, "Sorry he talked so much last night about his metabolism."

"Well, he is training for a triathlon," Mitch said mildly.

Felicity rolled her eyes. "I get that at work all day. Workouts and fitness are the last things I want to talk about at home."

A squeaky voice called out, "Felicity! Felicity! Watch me!" Livvy, in her pink ruffled swimsuit, waved frantically at us from the wading pool.

I said, "Sorry she's been pestering you so much." Five-year-old Livvy had taken an instant liking to Felicity. Felicity had hardly stepped through our front door before Livvy was dragging her by the hand down the hall to show off her stuffed animals. She'd practically been Felicity's shadow all day. I was glad Livvy's shyness had vanished, but I didn't want her driving Felicity crazy, either.

Mitch and his mom continued up the porch steps

and into the house while Felicity and I stopped by a group of birch trees to watch Livvy. She dog-paddled around the tiny pool, then checked our reaction. "Great job," Felicity shouted as she leaned against the tree trunk. One of Livvy's cousins splashed into the pool and drew her attention away from us. Felicity said, "She's not pestering me. Actually, it's given me an excuse to get away from Jenny."

I was thankful that only one of Dan's freshly divorced parents had been able to come to the reunion. His dad was somewhere in Indiana, running a weekend seminar for corporate managers. "If Jenny says the word *green* one more time, I'm going to scream," Felicity continued. "Her whole save-the-earth thing is driving me crazy. I can't believe she gave up a great job to start a 'lifestyle cleansing' business."

Jenny's announcement that she'd quit her job as a CPA and started a business that helped companies and individuals become more ecologically friendly had caused a stir this morning. She'd even bypassed wearing the family reunion T-shirt because it wasn't made with pesticide-free cotton and nontoxic dye. Felicity said, "I've always known she was weird. I mean, she actually *likes* jigsaw puzzles. That told me something right there. Anyway, she was raking in the dough. Why would she quit a job like that? This whole divorce thing has brought out—"

The crack of a rifle shot split the air again. Felicity and I both flinched. She said, "How can you stand that?"

That rifle shot had been even closer than the earlier one and it seemed to come from a different direction. The shots were usually far away, but that sound seemed to come from the direction of the neighborhood, not the woods. My heart jumped into high gear. "They're not usually that close," I said nervously, but the shot hadn't seemed to spook anyone else. There were a few curious glances, but most people carried on with their conversations.

Bill, Mitch's dad, stood up and shouted for attention. He was the complete antithesis of Mitch's mom. His family reunion T-shirt was already rumpled and the hem hung crookedly over his faded cutoff denim shorts that trailed a few white strings. Beat-up boat shoes completed the look. His reflective sunglasses flashed in the sun as he rubbed his hands together in exaggerated anticipation and announced, "I think it's time for the games to begin." I went to set up the croquet game with Mitch, who had emerged from the house.

Uncle Kenny jogged up, holding the croquet mallets like a bouquet. "Are you in the game, Ellie? Winner gets another piece of peach pie."

"Let us get it set up, first," I said as I pushed a wicket in the ground.

"Here," Uncle Kenny took a few wickets from me, "I'll help. You'll be on my volleyball team later, right? Gwen's still giving me a hard time about losing last year."

"Sure, Uncle Kenny. I'm not exactly a stellar player," I warned. Winning was what it was all about for Uncle Kenny.

"You can serve it over the net. We lost last year because of Vera's net balls, but that won't happen again. You just get it over the net and I'll take care of the rest."

I positioned the last wicket and surveyed the setup. "I hope I don't crumble under the pressure. Now for the badminton net."

Tradition held that games, croquet, badminton, horseshoes, and volleyball, were the order of business until sundown. At least I didn't have to worry about setting an agenda. The reunion pretty much ran itself. Everyone knew the schedule and I knew better than to try and change things. In fact, changing anything was the last thing I was interested in. Right now I was still so thrown by Abby's news that I could barely get the net taut. Felicity helped me while she kept an eye on the gate, watching for Dan's return, which is probably why she was the one who said, "I think that lady's looking for you, Ellie."

I turned and saw my neighbor Dorthea hurrying in my direction, her bad hip frustrating her progress. I'd never seen her move so quickly and rushed to meet her. "Dorthea, what's wrong? Here, sit down." Under her floppy walking hat, her lined face was flushed to the color of her new cherry red convertible, and her gray hair was plastered to her forehead. She walked every day at a methodical pace and I'd never seen her this out of breath.

She gripped my arm and pulled me toward the gate. "No time. You've got to come now. You and Mitch. Someone from your family reunion has been shot. I don't know who, but he's wearing the shirt you're all wearing, so I came to get you. I saw it all as I came up that steep hill in the new area. He'd jogged past me just a few minutes before. I still can't believe it. He was at the top. I heard the shot, he shuddered, then collapsed."

Chapter
Two

I heard sirens in the distance and looked at Dorthea with raised eyebrows.

"Already called nine-nine-one," she wheezed. "There was a contractor at one of the houses. He had a phone . . ."

Mitch ran across the lawn. "The new area, you said?"

She nodded and I was relieved to see that she didn't look quite as flushed. "At the top of the rise on the new road, near that two-story house with the veranda."

Mitch nodded. "I'll go check," he said and sprinted off. The sirens grew louder, then cut off abruptly.

It had to be Dan. My gaze flew to Felicity. She'd frozen in place, a badminton racket held at an odd angle, her eyebrows squished together. "Shot?" she said impatiently, then rolled her eyes. "He probably pulled a muscle. Serves him right." She dropped the racket and followed Mitch at a jog.

I wanted to follow her, but glanced back at the pool where Livvy was still splashing. Aunt Nanette waved me toward the gate. "You go on, Ellie. I'll watch the kids." She pulled a chair into the shade by the pool and the Afghan hound flopped down beside her. Aunt Claudine disengaged Dorthea from my arm and said, "Let's get you inside so you can cool off, dear."

Bill and Aunt Gwen were striding purposefully across the grass. He had his keys in his hand. "Ellie, show us where they are. Is it far? We can take my car. I'm parked on the street. Gwen's coming with us."

I swallowed, remembering Mitch had mentioned that Gwen had been a nurse before she and Uncle Kenny started their own business. "Good idea," I said as we hurried to the front yard.

The front door burst open and Aunt Jenny hurried down the steps. "Where's Dan? He's hurt?"

"Come with us," Bill shouted as he unlocked his Saab. Aunt Gwen and Aunt Jenny clambered into the backseat and I hopped in the front. I barely got the door closed before he pulled away from the curb and followed the street around to the pond. "Turn at the end of the street," I said as he tapped the brakes at the stop sign and accelerated up the road that had once been a gravel path. I glanced back and saw several cars were following us.

We passed a smattering of houses in various stages of construction. "Take the next left." I'd walked through this part of the neighborhood so many times that I knew each house, each vacant lot that flew by the windows now as Bill accelerated up the road's steep incline. I could see Felicity running up the slope and, beyond her at the top of the rise, a cluster of people. A fire truck and an ambulance angled beside each other at the curb.

We arrived moments after Felicity reached the small crowd. "You'll have to back up, ma'am," a firefighter instructed me as the paramedics raised a gurney and wheeled it to the ambulance. I couldn't see much because of the group around the gurney, but I caught a glimpse of a tall, dark-headed man on the gurney. The phalanx of cars pulled in behind us and various aunts, uncles, and cousins emerged.

Felicity stood frozen, a perplexed look on her face. She wasn't even winded from her sprint. "He's really hurt?" she whispered.

Aunt Gwen walked briskly over to the ambulance and spoke to a paramedic. I put my arm around Felicity's shoulders, while I looked for Mitch. I spotted him and saw his face was flushed from the run, but under that brush of color, his skin was pasty, like Livvy's complexion when she had the flu. Our gaze connected and I got that weightless feeling in my stomach like I'd just topped the peak in a roller coaster and was careening toward the ground. Aunt Gwen came back. "Come on, honey, we're going in the ambulance." She disengaged Felicity from me and steered her toward the ambulance where Aunt Jenny already waited. Everyone scrambled into their cars. The ambulance and fire truck pulled away and, like a receding tide, the rest of the cars followed them down the street, which left me and Mitch standing alone in the street.

"How bad is it?" I asked Mitch.

"I don't know. He didn't look good. There wasn't time to ask the paramedics anything." Mitch rubbed his hand over his mouth.

It had to be bad, if Mitch was so shaken. Mitch was my rock, hardly anything fazed him, but he looked frightened. I caught his free hand and held on tight. A couple of people who lived farther up the street in the freshly completed houses on this block told us to give them a call if we needed anything. I recognized them from my nightly walks. North Dawkins, Georgia, was the kind of place where people waved and said, "Evening," when you passed them. It was one of the things I loved about the South. The people were friendly and I could tell they were sincerely concerned for us.

I looked around the edge of the street where the crowd had been when we first arrived. "Well, maybe it's not as bad as you think. I don't see any blood at all."

Mitch took his hand away from his mouth and said, "He wasn't shot. I don't know what happened, but he wasn't bleeding."

"What? Then why did Dorthea say that?"

A man stepped into the street beside us and said, "Because that's what we thought happened." He was middle aged with a grizzled beard and wore a sweat-stained T-shirt, dirty jeans, and heavy work boots. He adjusted his baseball cap, embroidered with the words "Magnolia Homes," and held out his hand. "Larry Masters. I'm a contractor." He shook hands with both of us, then gestured to the unfinished houses behind us. "These two are mine. I was in that one," he said, pointing to the one farther down the street.

The house was almost complete, but didn't have any landscaping or grass. "I was in the garage, checking on a delivery—we've had some trouble with people stealing—copper wiring, appliances, stuff like that—when I noticed the guy jogging by. I waved and he raised his hand. He took about ten more steps—he was even with this house here," Larry said, pointing to the house behind us, "when

I heard a shot and the guy just collapsed. It was instantaneous. Both of us, that older lady and I, we both thought he'd been shot. She was still a ways off." He waved down the road. "I called out and told her I had a phone and I'd call nine-one-one. She didn't come up the hill, just yelled she'd get the family, then turned around and went back the way she'd come.

"I grabbed a couple of drop cloths out of my truck—for the bleeding, you know—while I called nine-one-one. It was all I had, but when I got to him, no blood. Not a scratch. He was out cold."

"Maybe it's heat exhaustion," I said, feeling relieved. "The shot you heard must have been hunters."

"I thought so, too, until I saw this." He turned and led the way through the dirt yard and past a pallet of bricks to the house. He climbed the porch steps and said, "Mind your step. No railing yet." He walked onto the wide porch and pointed to a hole in the siding. "We put this siding up yesterday. This bullet wasn't there."

Tips for Busy, Budget-Minded Moms

Morning Rush Hour
Getting everyone ready and out the door in the morning can be a hectic time. Take five to ten minutes the night before to prep for the next day:

- Choose clothing. Lay out everything that will be needed down to shoes and socks, even jewelry and accessories. Kids, especially toddlers, love to do things themselves and if their outfits are ready to go, they can dress themselves.
- Pack lunches. Cut time in the kitchen in half by putting dry and nonrefrigerated items like juice boxes, chips or crackers, fruit, cookies, and prepackaged pudding in lunch boxes the night before. In the morning, simply make a sandwich and add any refrigerated items like yogurt or cheese sticks.
- Prep for weather. Eliminate hectic searches for rain gear or cold weather gear. Store umbrellas, raincoats, mittens, and hats in a set of plastic storage drawers or plastic bins in your coat closet so you can grab what you need as you leave.
- Don't lose your keys. Place a basket or row of hooks beside the door. If you always drop your keys off in the same place when you walk in, you won't be searching countertops and coat pockets when it's time to head out the door the next morning.
- Keep a chart. If each day of the week brings a different set of activities, make a chart with days of the week across the top and each family member's name down the side. List which days of the week they need to

remember gym clothes, musical instruments, and school library books. Post the chart on the refrigerator or on the door to your garage. A quick check of the chart will let you know if everyone has everything they need. As your children grow, you can shift responsibility to them. Grade school kids can check the chart themselves and be responsible for remembering what they need.

Chapter Three

I looked back at the street. Despite the low, black plastic fencing enclosing the yard to prevent runoff, some dirt had escaped and covered the street. I could still see the footprints in it where everyone had gathered around the paramedics as they treated Dan. It was directly in front of us. "But this means the shot came from inside the neighborhood, not the woods," I said, trying to take it in. "That's why the last shot was so loud. It was close, much closer than normal."

Mitch had been kneeling down, examining the bullet lodged in the siding. He nodded as he stood up. All three of us turned and scanned the neighborhood. Larry said, "He's one lucky guy. Passing out probably saved his life." He looked at the opening in the line of trees across the street.

"There's a lot of places a rifle could have been fired from." The lots directly across from this house were empty. The land sloped down from what would eventually become the backyards to the valley where the majority of Magnolia Estates was located. The neighborhood was a mix of finished houses, cleared lots, houses under construction, and thick stands of forest on lots that hadn't yet been cleared. From our vantage point, I could pick out the pond and the new road that cut through the swath of woods behind our house in the base of the small valley. Originally, that section behind our house was slated for development, but after the discovery of an abandoned graveyard, a small family cemetery, development had shifted to the area where we stood farther up the hill.

"It could have come from anywhere," I said, surveying the patchwork of brown and green land spread below us.

"Probably kids messing around," Larry surmised.

Mitch said, "Maybe," then turned to Larry. "You'll leave the bullet hole alone? I think we should call the police. Just in case."

My thoughts skipped back to Dan and a fresh wave of worry descended. "We should get to the hospital," I said.

"You folks go on." Larry pulled out his cell phone. "Give me your number. I'll call the sheriff.

My nephew's a deputy. I'll get in touch with him and give him your number, if he needs it. I'll be here all day anyway."

"I'm sure he'll be okay," I said as the hospital's glass doors swished open. I wasn't sure of anything, but Mitch looked so worried. We'd walked home, checked on the kids, then driven to the hospital.

"I know," Mitch said, but there was no conviction in his voice. He scanned the signs. "WAITING ROOM B. This way."

I shivered as the chilled air enveloped us. My sweaty T-shirt stuck to me like a second skin. I tried to ignore the stridently clean smell. Hospitals were one of my least favorite places. "He's young and he's in great shape," I said, trying to distract myself as well as Mitch. He'd been silent on the drive over. I knew he was so worried about Dan that he wasn't paying attention to anything else.

"Right." He paced down the hall quickly, his gaze on the floor.

I pulled him to a stop. "Mitch, you're always the one saying not to borrow trouble. Don't assume the worst."

He focused on me and I felt like I had his attention for the first time since Dorthea burst into our backyard. The corners of his lips turned up slightly. "So you're saying I need a dose of my own advice? Don't worry?"

"Yes," I threaded my arm around his. "At least until we know what's going on."

As we walked down the hall, he said, "All right, but I want you to remember this moment the next time you're about to accuse me of being too laid-back. I can worry with the best of them. That would be you, in case you're wondering."

"Yes, sadly, that's probably the truth," I said, but I was smiling because Mitch looked slightly better. The deep line between his eyes was gone and he'd lost that preoccupied air.

We entered the waiting room, which had been taken over by the Avery family. There were three other people who weren't relatives gathered in one corner and they looked slightly bewildered at the Avery throng dominating the room. I knew exactly how they felt. The Avery family could be a bit . . . overwhelming. Aunt Gwen and Uncle Kenny were playing gin rummy in one corner, Mitch's dad paced back and forth in front of the windows, and Uncle Bud's voice carried to the door as he and Aunt Christine talked about a property renovation he was doing. Two of Mitch's cousins were resolutely flicking through magazines and there were a few more relatives milling around a coffeepot. The atmosphere was one of determined chitchat.

"I don't see Aunt Jenny," I said.

"Me either. I'll see if Dad's heard anything."

I squeezed Mitch's arm and went to sit beside

Aunt Christine since Uncle Bud had vacated his chair and moved over to the group around the coffeepot. "Any news?" I asked.

"I'm afraid not," Aunt Christine said, nervously running her hand over the stitching on the arm of the chair. She shifted and looked at the door. "They came for Jenny a few minutes ago. We should know something soon." She went back to rubbing the armrest. "He's their only child, you know."

"I know," I said and forced down the surge of anxiety that bubbled up inside me. "How about a cup of coffee?" I stood.

"No caffeine for me, dear, but thank you. High blood pressure. The doctor told me to cut that out of my diet and I'm sure my blood pressure is already up now."

"Well, how about some water? There's got to be a vending machine around here somewhere."

"That would be nice." I had a feeling she didn't care about the water but knew I wanted something to do besides sit in a waiting room.

I nearly collided with Aunt Jenny in the doorway. "He's going to be fine!" she shouted and relief swept through the room like a fresh breeze. Suddenly everyone was standing, talking, hugging. "It was sunstroke," Aunt Jenny announced over the chatter. "Very serious, but they got him here quickly enough that he's going to be fine." She gripped my hand. "We have to thank your neighbors, if they hadn't seen him—" She swallowed and wasn't able to continue.

I squeezed her hand. "But they did."

She drew in a deep breath, regained control, and nodded. "They want to keep him overnight, but he's going to be okay."

"I'm so glad." I caught Mitch's gaze and we smiled across the room. He looked more like his old self again, relaxed and happy.

I slipped out the door and found a vending machine on another floor. Aunt Christine had probably forgotten about the water, but I sure could use some now. I was on my way back, balancing several ice cold bottles of water, when I caught sight of a silhouette I recognized, curly dark hair and curvy figure. "Abby," I called. How could I have forgotten about her call? The scare with Dan had wiped everything else from my mind.

I hurried down the hall to catch her before she turned a corner. "Abby," I called again, and this time she turned toward me. She looked dazed and stared at me a moment before she said anything. "It was sweet of you to come, but you can't talk to Denise now," she said in a monotone, like she was repeating words she knew she should say. There wasn't any emotion, any warmth connected with them.

"How's Colonel Pershall?"

"He didn't make it."

I was so shocked, I couldn't form any words. It couldn't be true. The burly, strong man I knew couldn't be gone, just like that. We stepped to the side of the hall to let a group of people pass and Abby said, "I know. It's unbelievable. I've been wandering around, waiting for her to get finished with the police."

"The police?" I asked, leaning against the wall.

"Yes. It's a murder investigation now."

I could barely get my mind around the fact that he'd died. I noticed condensation was forming on the chilled water bottles and soaking into my already drenched shirt. I set them down on a small table and brushed at my shirt distractedly. "Who would do something like that? Everyone liked him."

"Well, not everyone. He made some people mad in the squadron. You know, Henry was pretty upset that he didn't get that class."

"But that's nothing. People get passed over all the time."

"I know, that's only an example. I'm just saying Colonel Pershall didn't play the game and some people didn't like it." Abby rubbed her forehead. "Maybe it was some random crazy person."

I frowned. "If I were bent on random violence, I don't think I'd pick him. He was so large and sturdy."

"That's probably true. I'm sure that fresh-faced

detective in there will put everything he has into it. It's probably his first case."

"Was it Detective Waraday?"

"Yes, how did you know?"

"It's not his first case. He investigated Jodi's disappearance." I'd met the detective over a year ago when heavy rains washed out an abandoned graveyard near our subdivision and revealed a collapsed casket with two sets of human remains. "But aren't the security police from the base involved?" I asked. "You said something about them."

"They came to notify Denise. Colonel Pershall wasn't on base when it happened. He was over at Five Pines."

The neighborhood golf course was in one of the housing developments scattered around North Dawkins. It wasn't inside the city limits, so the case fell into the jurisdiction of the sheriff's office. "The security police came to Denise's house. They said the sheriff's department had notified them."

"Yeah, they'll probably work together on the case. I'd better get back to Mitch's family." I explained what had happened with Dan as I picked up the water bottles, feeling almost guilty that our situation had turned out so well. We walked to the elevator and Abby pushed the button.

"When Denise is through talking to the police, I guess I'll take her home and wait for her sister to get here. She's driving up from Tampa."

As the doors opened and Abby stepped inside, I said, "Call me if you need anything, okay?"

"Sure. And I'll tell Denise you were here."

The doors slid closed and I continued down the hall. I had to tell Mitch. He'd be devastated.

He met me in the hall with his phone in one hand. The strained look was back on his face. "I just got a call from Jeff," he said, then took in my face. "You know?"

I nodded and wrapped my arms around him, sweaty water bottles and all. "I'm so sorry, Mitch. I saw Abby in the hall and she told me."

He squeezed me close and we didn't say anything for a few minutes. Then the hall filled with people swirling around us. Uncle Kenny slapped Mitch on the back and said, "Come on, let's get back to your house. I've got a croquet game to win." Absorbed into the current of Avery relatives, we were swept out of the hospital and back to our house.

I yanked a croquet wicket from the ground and shook off the mud and grass clinging to it before placing it back in the storage case.

After the scare with Dan yesterday, everyone had returned to our house and finished off the desserts. As he predicted, Uncle Kenny won the croquet game, but I think it was because no one took it quite as seriously as he did. Well, except for Aunt Gwen. She came in second. Later, the women helped me clean up the kitchen and wash the serving dishes while the men cleaned grills and loaded picnic tables and chairs in pickups. By sundown the reunion had broken up. Some people had to drive back home that night to teach Sunday school the next morning. Others, including Mitch's parents, had left this morning after breakfast. After Dan had spent the night at the hospital, Felicity and Aunt Jenny had checked him out and headed back to Alabama. We'd said good-bye to them at the hospital.

So the reunion was over and all my planning and worrying over picnic tables and grills and paper plates seemed so insignificant in comparison to what Denise was going through now. I couldn't stop worrying about her. Maybe it was because of the scare with Dan and the visit to the hospital. It made the trauma more real to me.

The drama with the bullet in the siding added to my anxiety. Larry had relayed the information to us that the sheriff's department had removed the bullet from the siding and they didn't need to speak to us now. Larry said they thought a misguided hunter had accidentally strayed out of the wildlife area. When Mitch passed that news on to me, I'd looked at him in disbelief. He'd said, "It happens. The thrill of the hunt and all that."

"But I thought people used tree stands around here," I said.

"They do, but some people track their game, too."

I wiggled the striped croquet pole out of the ground and placed it in the case. Livvy had convinced Kenny to leave the croquet set out yesterday. This afternoon, I'd found Livvy and Nathan swinging mallets around within inches of each other's heads. I'd relocated them to the swing set where they split their time between arguing over the swings and tossing sand out of the sandbox.

"Mom, Rex is in the pool again," Livvy yelled.

I turned to see Rex standing in the middle of the kiddie pool. I sighed. Really, I couldn't blame him. It was terribly hot and he did have a fur coat, but I really didn't want the dog *and* the kids swimming in the same pool. I shooed him out and he shook, flinging drops of water that made the kids squeal. He settled down on the grass, looking for all the world like he was grinning at his own cleverness.

As I carried the croquet set to the storage shed at the back of the yard, Mitch came in right behind me, carefully maneuvering the long pole of the extension trimmer through the door. He'd been trimming low-hanging branches, one of his favorite activities. I glanced out the door of the storage shed through the open gate to the front yard. I was relieved to see the trees still had branches on them.

Mitch tended to get carried away when he was trimming and he'd reduced some bushes to mere stumps. Limbs were stacked neatly at the curb, and leaves and twigs littered the driveway.

"Did it feel a little awkward to you at the hospital today?" I asked as I zipped the cover over the croquet set.

Mitch picked up the leaf blower and an extension cord. "Awkward? You mean they all couldn't wait to get out of here?"

I half-shrugged. "No, I can understand that. Who wants to linger at a hospital? I doubt any of them will remember this reunion fondly. Did you get a weird vibe between Dan and Felicity?"

"Not really," Mitch said as he turned away to plug in the extension cord at the wall outlet.

"Yesterday in the street, when she realized he was hurt, she looked so shocked and worried, but today she seemed to be mad at him . . . well, not mad, but there was a definite coolness between them."

"Felicity's always been that way. She can hold a grudge forever. She was mad at me for weeks after that fender bender in the high school parking lot," Mitch said. "She's still upset about the triathlon thing. Just because he almost died is no reason for her to let up on him. At least, that's the way she'd see it."

I shoved the croquet set onto the storage shelves and turned to him. "High school? You knew her?"

"Yeah, didn't I tell you?" Mitch asked, looking genuinely puzzled. "I've known her for years."

"And you didn't mention this before now?"

Mitch braced the blower against his hip. His voice had a distinctly choppy, irritated tone as he said, "Well, no. I didn't think it mattered. It was a small town. Everyone knew everyone else. In the interest of full disclosure, I'll tell you now that I took her to get ice cream once back during our sophomore year, but then I crushed the fender of her brand new Accord on a rainy morning and she was so mad at me that she started flirting with Dan. They've been fighting ever since." Mitch picked up the rolled extension cord and pointed it at me as he said, "So that's how I know she can hold a grudge." He strode out of the storage shed, unfurling the extension cord.

I realized my mouth was open and closed it. Wow. I hadn't expected that *at all*.

A popping sound came from outside the storage shed and I headed for the door, glancing out the window into the backyard. The kids were in the sandbox, looking around. Apparently, they'd heard it, too, and they were fine.

I reached the open door and saw Mitch pacing back and forth across the driveway, alternately clasping one hand in the other, then shaking it out. The blower was on the driveway. The aroma of hot plastic and a whiff of smoke wafted toward me. "Mitch, what happened?"

He examined the palm of his hand as he said, "It short-circuited."

"Are you okay?" His thumb and part of his palm were red, but not blistered.

"I'll be all right," he said as he strode into the storage shed and used his other hand to disconnect the plug from the outlet. "Looks like we need a new blower."

"Try not to look so delighted," I said. For Mitch, any excuse was a good excuse to visit the huge home improvement store. I wasn't a big fan of shopping myself and didn't understand the lure of a store that stocked plumbing supplies and lumber, but Mitch could spend hours in one.

Faintly, I heard the sounds of the song, "Who Let the Dogs Out?"

I saw my cell phone, the display bright, where I'd left it on a small table on the patio. I leveled my gaze at Mitch. "Very funny. What if I'd been with an organizing client? That sound wouldn't be professional, would it?"

Mitch had changed the ringtone on my cell phone last week from a plain vanilla ring, which I preferred, to a pitiful elevator music impersonation of "Don't Worry, Be Happy." He thought the gag was hilarious, especially since Nathan kept saying, "Make it sing again, Mom," during my entire conversation.

"Sometimes things aren't so funny the second time around," I said.

"Oh, come on. It's kind of appropriate, don't

you think? One of us is always asking if Rex is outside," Mitch said.

"I'd better get it." I left Mitch whistling the tune as he turned on the water hose to douse his hand. "Two can play at that game," I muttered under my breath as I sprinted across the lawn and caught the phone before it went to voice mail.

It was Denise. "Ellie, I think I need . . . well, I don't really know how to put this. Can you come over?"

"Of course."

Chapter
Four

I parked on the street in front of the rancher in base housing with the nameplate that read, LIEUTENANT COLONEL AND MRS. PERSHALL. Lieutenant Colonel had been his full title, but people with that rank were usually referred to as just "colonel" in conversation. I hurried up the sidewalk, thinking about Denise. On the phone she'd sounded rattled and almost frail, which was so different from her usual confident demeanor.

She opened the door with a spray bottle of cleaning solution in one hand and a crumpled paper towel in the other. "Ellie, thanks so much for coming." She looked drawn and tired. A large, black T-shirt with the squadron's emblem engulfed her down to her jean-clad knees. I recognized the shirt. Mitch had several like it and wore them under his flight suit. Denise was a tall, statuesque woman, but the shirt swallowed her. Colonel Pershall had been a big man. Just looking at the shirt hanging loosely on Denise made me sad.

"Sure. I'm glad you called me. I'm so sorry." I gave her a hug. The words didn't seem like enough, but she hardly seemed to hear them.

She wasn't wearing her contacts. Instead, she had on an outdated pair of glasses with huge lenses and circular red frames. Her short hair, normally smoothed across her forehead and tucked behind her ears, was pulled straight back with two haphazardly placed barrettes and was flat on one side and crinkling into frizz on the other.

I handed her a rectangular pan. "It's frozen lasagna."

"Thanks. Come on in," she said as she led me through the small but comfortably furnished living room with chairs in warm reds and browns. One of the throws she'd knitted was tossed over the arm of the squashy leather couch. The vacuum stood in one corner, its cord still connected to the outlet and the smell of lemon furniture polish hung in the air. "Let's go back to the kitchen. One more cabinet and I'm done in there." Colonel Pershall and Denise didn't have children and the house seemed extremely quiet to me compared to the constant background noise of toys, kids' television shows, and the never-ending high-pitched query of "Mom?" that filled our house.

A small galley kitchen ran along the front of the house. The sink overlooked the front yard and there was a door to the carport at the far end of the kitchen. With white cabinets, white tile floors, and white Formica countertops, the kitchen could have felt sterile, but Denise had added splashes of red, including a red and chrome dinette set, red canisters, and red and white gingham curtains. She put the spray bottle down, placed the lasagna in the freezer, then opened the fridge. "What can I get you to drink? Soda? Tea?"

"Nothing, thanks."

"You've got to have something. Everyone who comes over has to have something. We were hosting a party next weekend, so I'm stocked and I have to get rid of it. Wine spritzer? Flavored vitamin water? Plain water?" Her voice was as tense as those unbreakable wires that hold new toys in their boxes, the kind we can never seem to get open on Christmas morning. I noticed the flats of canned sodas and bottled water beside the door to the carport and said, "Sure, I'll have a water. Plain is fine." Poor thing. She couldn't even open the refrigerator without being reminded of how her life had changed. "Did your sister make it to town?"

"Yes, she's at the store, getting more cleaning supplies." Denise handed me a Fiji water bottle, opened one for herself, then picked up the spray bottle and doused one of the cabinets at the far end of the kitchen. "I'll be finished in a minute," she said as she waved me into a chair at the table. She attacked the cabinet with the paper towel, scrubbed it down, then moved on to the door that led to the carport. I hadn't noticed until she sprayed the door frame, but it was covered with a fine black powder. The paper towels were smeared with black when she tossed them in the trash. "I had no idea fingerprint powder was so hard to clean up," she said as she dropped into the chair across from me. "The house is coated in it. I haven't even gotten to the upstairs yet."

"I think there are professional cleaning crews you can hire to help with that type of cleaning," I said as I fiddled with the water bottle lid.

"No. I'd rather do it myself. It helps. Gives me something to do with my hands." She took off her glasses and rubbed the bridge of her nose. I thought she might cry, but she replaced her glasses and squared her shoulders. "Ellie, I need you to do something for me." Her voice sounded more like her usual self-confident tone. "The police had some very pointed questions for me yesterday and today. I'm their favorite suspect."

"Are you sure?" I asked. "They've got to be looking at all kinds of possibilities at this point."

"They did ask if anyone had anything against Lewis, any grudges, but it's all so insignificant.

There's nothing for them to pursue. There's always a couple of people upset about *something* in the squadron. Sour grapes, nothing more." She sipped her water, glanced at me, then focused her gaze on the green leaves bobbing outside the kitchen window. "I think Lewis was having an affair."

I froze, my water bottle poised in the air. "What? Why?"

"I need you to help me find out if it's true."

I put the bottle on the table and leaned forward. "But he wouldn't—" The idea of Colonel Pershall having an affair was such a stretch for me that I had a hard time forming a coherent sentence. I tried again. "I mean, that doesn't seem like him. You were so close."

Denise switched her gaze to me. "We were, but we weren't always like that. We had our share of hard times." She shifted and sighed. "Lately, he's worked late quite a bit and he acted . . . secretive, that's the only way I can describe it. I asked him a few times how things were at work and he'd give these vague answers. Normally, it wouldn't have bothered me. There's all sorts of stuff he can't talk about, but this time something seemed off."

She tipped the water bottle up for a drink, then sat silent for a moment before saying, "Last week, he called me as I was on my way out the door to the commissary at about six-thirty. He said he wouldn't make it home for another hour or two." She took another quick swallow of water. "I drove by the squadron on my way home and glanced at the parking lot. I wasn't checking up on him." She half-laughed and shrugged. "It was kind of an automatic thing, looking for his car in his parking space."

I nodded. As squadron commander, Colonel Pershall had his own parking space and it would be easy to see if he was parked there, since the parking lot emptied at four-thirty, the time the military closed up shop. Colonel Pershall's restored red 300ZX didn't exactly blend in with the shrubbery either, so it would be easy to see.

"It wasn't there, so I expected him to be here when I got home. He wasn't. I phoned him and asked him if he was on his way home, but he said he was still at the office. Then when he finally got home, I could smell perfume on his clothes, a musky scent."

"And you didn't ask him about it?" Even as I asked the question, I wondered what I would have done in her place. Would I have confronted Mitch? Look at my reaction to the news that Mitch had dated Felicity. I'd been surprised but hadn't asked Mitch any more questions.

Denise looked miserable. "No. I was so astonished and then I wasn't sure what to do." She reached across the table and gripped my hand. "Please help me with this, Ellie. I thought he really loved me. Now I'll never know, unless I pursue this."

"You don't have to pursue anything. Let the police look into it. Did you tell them about it?"

She released my hand, grabbed her empty water bottle, and stood up. "If he was having an affair, then I'll have an even better motive, at least in their eyes." She paced to the other end of the kitchen. "Their line of questioning was already going in that direction. I don't want to give them any more ammunition."

"They'll probably find out on their own. It would be better for them to hear your suspicions from you. And it may not be—probably isn't—true."

"No." She punctuated her sentence with an effortless toss of her water bottle. It arced and landed dead center of the recycling bin. "You're the one to help me out."

I recognized that look. Every squadron commander's wife had to either have or develop quickly the skill of drafting help. Denise had never been shy about recruiting volunteers to help with various programs. Of course, she went about it in a revolutionary way: she asked what the wives wanted the squadron spouse club to do, then focused our goals on those things. That's why we had a book club and a supper club now and no bake sales. Usually, she was savvy enough to match a person's interests with projects they had genuine enthusiasm for. She'd asked Abby and me to coordinate the summer playgroup and we'd loved the idea.

I wasn't nearly as excited about this task. Since I obviously wasn't going to talk her into going to the police, I tried another approach. "Why call me? Sounds like you need a private investigator." A pile of mail tilted on the table. I stacked it, squaring the edges.

She put her hands on her hips and fixed a level gaze on me. "You're the only one I know who's got experience with the police."

"Thanks a lot. You make me sound like a hardened criminal."

She grinned faintly. "You know I didn't mean it that way. But you have dealt with Detective Waraday, right?"

Reluctantly, I nodded. I was sure if he found out Denise was asking me to help her, Waraday would be less than thrilled. He'd found my involvement in the last case odd and slightly suspicious.

"Has anyone from the OSI been in touch with you?" I asked.

"Honey, I'm pretty good with acronyms, but during these last few hours, I couldn't tell you if someone from NASA had been here."

"The Office of Special Investigation," I explained. "They investigate crimes on military bases and I think they'd be involved in something like this."

Denise pulled a stack of business cards out of the pocket of her jeans. "Yeah, here's someone from the OSI. Special Agent Kelly Montigue. I remember her now. She said they would coordinate their investigation with the sheriff's office. I did get the feeling that Detective Waraday was taking the lead. He asked most of the questions. That other time, you found several things he missed, didn't you?" Denise persisted.

Now it was my turn to shift uncomfortably in my seat. "Well, technically it was the crime scene investigators who missed those things and they were searching an immense area—"

Denise interrupted me. "But you *did* find stuff they'd missed. And I trust you. I don't know any private detectives and I'm not going to pick one off a Google search or out of the phone book. This is Lewis's reputation."

She sat down again and pulled the stack of mail and a small, flat package toward her. "Yesterday's mail," she said with a beleaguered tone. "Do you mind if I open these while we talk? I'm so scattered right now, I'm afraid I'll put this somewhere and forget about it for weeks."

"Of course not."

She pulled the tab on the package. When she tilted it, a large coin fell into her hand. I could tell it was a squadron coin from the coloring. About the size of a fifty cent piece, the coin had the squadron patch, a brown hawk on a blue and yellow shield, on one side and an engraving of the squadron's refueling jet on the other side. Mitch had one just like it. In fact, everyone in the squadron had one.

Coin checks were a military tradition that Mitch had to explain to me when I became a military spouse. He had to keep his coin "on his person" at all times because anyone in the squadron could call for a "coin check" at any time. If you couldn't produce your coin, you had to buy drinks for everyone who produced their coin. Mitch had quite a collection of squadron coins now because he got a new one at each squadron he'd been assigned to and after all our moves, that added up to many coins. Sometimes people had them made for special occasions, like retirement, or to give away as a thank you. Mitch received one when he found a general's lost bag after a flight.

Denise handed me the coin and flexed the package open. There was nothing else inside. "Lewis must have lost his coin somewhere around base," Denise said, checking the postmark. "Yep, it was mailed from the post office on base."

I turned the heavy coin over in my hand. "That was nice of someone."

Denise said, "He probably slapped it down on the bar at the O Club, then walked off and left it. That would be just like him. He never was good at picking things up." She blinked, then seemed to mentally shake herself. She tossed the package in the trash, then attacked the stack of envelopes. She slit each one, then began pulling out the bills and credit card offers and handing them to me so quickly I could hardly keep up. "Help me sort these, will you?" she asked. I set the coin down on the table and grabbed at the papers she was shoving at me. I'd become her secretary, but I didn't mind. If sorting papers helped her out, then that's what I'd do.

She stopped abruptly when she opened a sheet of plain white paper. "No." She quickly folded it back into thirds, then crumpled it in her fist and tossed it across the room. "I cannot deal with her today," she said, her voice shaky.

"Denise, what's wrong?" I asked. Her mercurial change frightened me.

"Those letters are vile. I can't—not today—" she broke off as her eyes watered. She pushed her glasses up onto her head and covered her eyes with one hand.

I moved slowly across the kitchen, watching her, but she remained seated with her hand over her eyes, her mouth working as she tried not to give in to tears. I picked up the ball of paper, then grabbed a few paper towels and handed them to her as I sat back down. She nodded her thanks and went to work dabbing at her eyes and blowing her nose while I smoothed out the crinkles in the paper. It was a handwritten note.

Forty days.
Almost six weeks without my husband and it's your fault. I'm going to make sure you never forget what you did to Ryan. He's dead because

of you. Dead! You're the reason I don't have a husband. I hate you. You'll never have any peace. I'll make sure of it. You don't deserve to live in your perfect little house with your perfect lawn and edged sidewalks. Do you know who cut the lawn and edged the sidewalks at my house this week?

Me. *Because Ryan's dead. Because* you *sent him to his death. You deserve to be dead, too.*

I dropped the letter on the table, not wanting to touch it. "Whoa." It was so full of vitriol that I wondered how my hands hadn't been scorched from touching it.

Back under control, Denise balled up the paper towel and said, "She's sent a letter each week. They get angrier every week."

It wasn't signed, but I knew the name Ryan. I sat back in my chair, stunned. "Carrie Kohl wrote this?"

Denise nodded, then executed another flawless throw. Her wadded paper towel landed in the trash, no rim.

Carrie's husband, Ryan, had been on the last Mideast deployment when he'd been in a wreck. It hadn't been a case of insurgent violence. Only bad weather and bad driving were to blame. Ryan had died two days later at a hospital in Germany. Mitch hadn't been on that deployment, but he'd heard that the truck ran off the road and flipped. Ryan's death had rocked the squadron and the community. The air force was a fairly safe assignment, at least compared to some of the other branches of service. Although, it seemed the front lines had shifted and anyone, anywhere, could be a target. But, overall, the types of jobs airmen did were usually lower risk than the jobs of marines or army members. To have someone die on deployment was fairly rare in the air force and the outpouring of support for Carrie from the squadron and the community was intense. There had been a huge memorial service attended by hundreds of people who didn't know Ryan. Food, cards, and letters poured in. People set up Web sites for family and friends to post memories and express support.

"Fragile little Carrie Kohl wrote this? Wow, I'd never have thought she'd write something like this. I mean, she cried nonstop for what was it? About three weeks?"

She'd sobbed throughout the memorial service and seemed as delicate as a wilted flower. She was always leaning on someone, her mom or dad or one of the other squadron spouses, her big brown eyes red and puffy behind the wispy hair that was constantly falling over her face.

Denise shrugged. "I don't know. It doesn't seem like her, I know, but she's been mailing them to Lewis. She's disconnected herself from us. I haven't seen her since she began sending the letters about a month ago. I've called her. She never picks up. Same story when I've stopped by her house."

"I haven't seen her either. I called her and offered to help out with anything—food, hanging out with her, whatever she needed, but she said she'd call me if she needed anything. I haven't heard from her since." Looking at Denise's ravaged face, I felt a spark of anger at Carrie for her brutal words. "Why would she do this to you and Colonel Pershall? The whole squadron, practically the whole town, stood by her and offered to do anything to help her. We know it's terrible and want to help. Why would she lash out like this? There are plenty of people who'd mow her grass for her or whatever she needs."

"Lewis said to let her be angry, that she needed someone to be angry at. 'I can absorb it,' he said."

"Maybe he couldn't." I thought about what had happened to Colonel Pershall. A cold feeling of dread replaced that flare of anger I'd felt at Carrie's harsh words. "You have to show this to Detective Waraday. Do you have the other letters?"

Carrie was a small woman, but if she caught Colonel Pershall by surprise . . . My thoughts immediately skittered away from that conclusion because I didn't want to think that someone I knew would do something so terrible. But the letter indicated that she wasn't quite as weak and helpless as I'd thought.

Denise shifted in her chair, looking slightly uncomfortable. "Lewis threw them away, said they were nothing but her working through her grief." She looked away at the spotless white linoleum. "I pulled them out of the trash."

"So you've got them. That's good. That will give Waraday another avenue to pursue."

"I shouldn't." She looked almost guilty.

"What? Why not?"

Denise fiddled with the empty envelopes, then said, "Because she is—was—a spouse in our squadron. I'm supposed to be looking out for her, helping her. That's the basic principle of the spouse club."

I knew Denise took her duties as the commanding officer's wife seriously. To her, the spouse club was more than a social club or a way to wield influence. She wanted the spouse club to be something that supported the wives, not something they dreaded or avoided. "Carrie's a spouse, but that doesn't mean she's not responsible for her actions," I said. "Your job isn't to protect her. The spouse club is here so we can help and support each other, you said that yourself in the first meeting. This isn't helping or supporting you and you're not helping Carrie by keeping it a secret. Obviously, she's got a massive amount of rage and anger inside and she needs to deal with that. You have to give this to Waraday. These are threats."

"You're right, of course," she said grudgingly.

"It still feels very wrong." With a sigh, Denise got up and opened a drawer. She removed several white sheets of paper from under the phone book, then dropped back into her chair and reached for the phone.

I put a hand on her arm. "Before you do that—can you think of anyone else who'd want to . . . harm Colonel Pershall? I know they probably asked you this before, right?"

"Yes, they did, and I couldn't really think of anyone besides Carrie and I didn't want to tell them about her. Everything else is so insignificant."

"I heard Henry Fleet was pretty upset with him."

She flicked her hand dismissively. "Promotion squabbles, nothing more." Her face went still and she said, thoughtfully, "Rich Barnes. He's always been jealous of Lewis." She shook herself and sat up straight. "This is absurd."

I'd picked up a notepad she kept by the phone and jotted down the three names—Carrie Kohl, Captain Henry Fleet, and Colonel Rich Barnes. I underlined the last name.

"Colonel Barnes knew Colonel Pershall for a long time, right?" I asked.

"Yes, they went to flight school together. Same class at the Academy. Rich always looks at everything like it's a competition. He hated it that Lewis made colonel before him. He'd never say it to my face, but he thinks General Crabtree played favorites when he recommended Lewis for the squadron commander billet. What Rich doesn't want to admit is that Lewis worked his butt off and Rich is lazy. So, you see, nothing. There's really nothing out there except for Carrie and the . . . other woman."

"Possible other woman. You don't know for sure," I said. "Right?"

"No, I don't know for sure, but it's the only thing I didn't know about his life."

A humming sound came from her purse on the kitchen counter. She replaced her glasses, found her cell phone, and looked at the screen. "It's from his phone." She pressed a few buttons, her face a mixture of dread and anxiety. "I had his cell phone calls forwarded to my phone. It's a text message. From her."

Tips for Busy, Budget-Minded Moms

Morning Rush Hour—Advanced Maneuvers
A little time on Sunday afternoon or evening can take prepping for the work/school week to the next level and give you even more free time during the week.

- Prepare snacks/side items/desserts for the entire week. Grab a box of plastic zip-top bags and a variety of snack items like animal crackers, pretzels, and chips. Put a serving of the items in the bags and store them in a large basket or bin. When it's snack time or time to pack lunches, you'll already have individual portions ready. And, you'll have the bonus of knowing you're saving money because you're buying the cheaper, larger size of the snack items and repacking them individually yourself.

- Prep clothes for the whole week. A set of hanging shelves is an easy way to divide clothes for the week. For kids, label the shelves with the days of the week and they can dress themselves.

Chapter Five

"Her? How do you know it's from a woman?"

Denise didn't answer right away. Instead, she read the message aloud, "Back in town. Meet at four?"

She gazed into space for a moment, then punched in a message.

"What are you doing?" I asked, amazed at the assumptions she was making.

She read over her message, then hit send. "I said yes to the meeting, but said I'd lost the address." She carefully placed the phone on the table, which was now covered with envelopes, bills, the squadron coin, and the notepad and a pen. "I recognized the number from our phone records. Did you know you can pull those up online? Lewis called it several times during the last few days."

"But how do you know it's a woman? It could be anyone, someone from the base, a business."

Denise watched the phone as she said, "I called it last night. No answer, just a voice mail message, no name." Her gaze shifted to me. "It was a woman. She sounded familiar, but I can't place the voice."

"Denise, this isn't the smartest thing to do. You shouldn't pursue this by yourself—"

"That's why I asked you to help me."

The phone vibrated, shimmying a few inches closer to the squadron coin before Denise snatched it up. "It's in North Dawkins, somewhere along Tarlton," she said, naming one of the busiest streets in town that was crowded with big box stores and restaurants. And a few hotels. I hoped it wasn't one of the hotels.

Denise stuck her phone in her purse, pulled out her keys, then stopped to jot a quick note for her sister on the notepad. I stood up during her flurry of activity. There was only so much I could say to try and talk her out of this. Even though she worked hard to erase those lines of structure that had separated her from the squadron spouses, she was the squadron commander's wife. I wasn't going to push it too far. I wasn't going to be able to talk her out of going. I could see that.

She paused at the door to the carport, her purse

on her shoulder. She'd switched her red-rimmed glasses for sunglasses. "Well? Are you coming with me? I'm going whether or not you're with me."

"I know." I picked up my purse and followed her outside.

Another car whipped around Denise's hulking SUV as she rode the brake, counting off addresses under her breath, oblivious to the frustrated drivers behind us. She swung into the left turn lane and made a U-turn. "I missed it. It's got to be behind us because now we're in the seven thousands."

I gripped the armrest and cringed as another car swerved around us. The clock on the dashboard read five minutes until four o'clock. Denise gripped the steering wheel and leaned slightly forward. Even if we found the address, I didn't see how we'd identify the mystery woman because there was so much traffic. We crept past a strip mall set back into a huge parking lot behind banks of landscaped medians. "It's got to be right around here," Denise said, twisting in her seat.

"I don't know . . . I only see a car wash and that new Italian restaurant."

"Wait! I bet it's back there." Denise slammed on the brakes and turned quickly into the small paved lane by the restaurant.

"It's a storage place?" I asked. "That seems . . .

odd." A heavy-duty fence encircled the low building. The entrance was an automatic security gate of wrought iron with a keypad.

She double-checked the address. "This is it," she said doubtfully.

We waited ten minutes in silence, with Denise checking her phone every ten seconds or so. I shifted, trying to unstick the back of my shirt from my shoulder blades. The humidity had been climbing steadily and despite the cool air blasting out of the air conditioner, I felt as if I was glued to the leather seats. Finally I said, "Denise, I think we should go."

She gripped the steering wheel. "No, look."

A white SUV rolled to a stop at the security gate, the tinted window powered down, and a lean, tan arm reached down to punch in the code. I could see a bit of a tank top and the swish of a black ponytail as the woman arched over to reach the keypad. I leaned closer . . . it looked like . . . no, it couldn't be.

"That's Amy Yuyuan," Denise said and I could tell she was as surprised as I was.

We looked at each other for a moment, then watched the SUV roll through the now-open gate and park on the other side of the fence near one of the storage units at the front of the complex. Amy was a fairly new member of the squadron's spouse club. Her husband had been transferred to Taylor last winter. Thoughts were flying through my mind, mainly that she had three kids, twin boys under a year old and a three-year-old daughter. She didn't make it to a lot of squadron events, probably because she was so busy with the twins. She was ten, maybe fifteen years younger than Colonel Pershall. What was she thinking? What had *he* been thinking? And how had she had the time or the energy?

"Do you think . . . she and Lewis . . ." Denise couldn't finish the sentence. She looked angry.

"No. It's probably a coincidence," I said. "And it's a strange place to meet. She probably needs something from their storage unit." Amy's SUV idled. I hurried on, trying to think of a reason she'd be here at this exact moment, waiting around the parking lot. "She lives on base, right? Those houses, even officers' quarters, are tiny, so I could see how they'd need extra storage space."

Denise nodded, but I could tell my words didn't help. The driver's door of the SUV opened and Amy hopped lightly down from the seat. It was actually a pretty good sized drop for her, since she was all of about four foot five. She was wearing a tight tank top, shorts, and flip flops and she had her phone to her ear. She scanned the small parking area, then checked her watch.

Denise's phone vibrated in her hand and she dropped it. By the time she'd scrabbled around the floorboard, it had gone to voice mail. Denise put it on speaker. Amy said, "Hi. I'm here. Are you going to make it? I can wait a few minutes, but then I have to go. We can reschedule, if you like."

"I don't know, Denise. She sounds pretty businesslike."

"Business. Right," Denise said, her face set. "What kind of business would she have with my husband? And she always wears too much of that musky perfume." She opened the door and was marching across the asphalt before I could say anything else. I reached over, turned the SUV off and clambered down, pocketing the keys.

Denise reached the gate. Amy saw her and hurried over to open it. Right now, that didn't seem like such a good idea. Denise was pretty mad and I would have felt better with solid metal separating the two women. I sprinted across the parking lot, slipped inside the gate, and walked into an invisible wall of musky perfume. The gate rattled closed behind me. This had to be worse. Now we were all locked in here together.

"Hi, Denise," Amy said. Denise had never stood on ceremony—she insisted we all call each other by our first names. I glanced between the two women and realized Denise was so furious that she wasn't even able to speak. Amy totally missed the hostility aimed at her. She checked her watch as she said, "That's weird that you're here, since he wanted to keep it such a secret, but whatever. Hey, Ellie. I guess the cat is really out of the bag now. I've only got a few minutes. I've got groceries—"

"The cat is out of the bag?" Denise's screechy voice shocked Amy to a halt. She took in Denise's clinched fists and angry face. "What's wrong, Denise?" she asked cautiously.

"That's all you can say?" Denise stepped toward her. I hurried over and practically wedged myself into the space between them. Amy quickly took a few steps back. "Denise, I think there might be a tiny mistake," I said. Amy didn't look guilty. In fact, she hadn't looked a bit anxious until she took in Denise's angry face.

"There's no mistake. I know what it all means, the late nights, the messages, his clothes smelling like your perfume," Denise said, inching closer with each word.

Before she could say anything else, I jumped in. "Amy, you were expecting Colonel Pershall today?"

She frowned, looking from me to Denise. "Yes. He wanted to see the bike again," she spoke cautiously again. "He said you'd be mad and, wow, he was right. I can see why he didn't want to tell you about it." She glanced quickly at me with widened eyes as if to communicate, *help me here*.

"Bike?" I asked.

"Here, you can see for yourself." Amy spun the combination lock on one of the storage unit doors. She unhooked it, then heaved the door up, revealing a jumble of packing boxes, tools, and furniture. She pushed a box out of the way and pointed to one side. "There it is, over in the corner."

"But that's a Harley," Denise said in a tone that some people would have reserved for tarantulas or black widows. Her tense muscles uncoiled. She gazed at the gleaming bike, bewilderment replacing her anger. "A motorcycle?"

Amy twisted the combination lock and shrugged, almost apologetic. "Colonel Pershall said you wouldn't like it, but Cody never rides it anymore. We sold mine when I got pregnant the first time and now that we've got three kids, it seemed like a good idea to sell his, too. We thought we'd use the money to buy a fort for the backyard. You know, the wooden kind with a slide."

Her voice died away as Denise inched through the boxes and furniture. When she reached the bike, she ran her hand over the smooth metal. "I would have fought him all the way on this. They're so dangerous. Just one mistake and it could all be over."

Amy swung the dial on the lock again, looking uncomfortable. "Yeah, he was pretty sure you wouldn't like it, so he said he'd try to change your mind before he bought it. That's why I was so surprised to see you."

When Denise didn't move or respond, Amy looked at me with raised eyebrows. I signaled for her to follow me a few steps away. When I explained what had happened to Colonel Pershall, she said, "He's dead? Dead? No way." When my expression didn't change, she said, "Oh my god. That's awful—no wonder Denise is acting so strange. We've been out of town—just got in a few hours ago. I called Colonel Pershall because he looked at the bike last week and wanted to see it again this weekend. I told him that if I made it back in time I'd call him and we could meet here like we did last week."

"So he'd already seen it?"

"Yeah. He met me here one night after work."

So that explained the sneaky disappearance after work and it was no surprise he'd come home smelling like her perfume. I was sure I'd smell like it, too, after being near Amy for a while. She continued, "He loved it, absolutely loved it, but didn't want to upset Denise."

Denise came out of the storage unit. She blinked in the bright sunlight and shaded her eyes. "Amy," she said, her voice weak and strained, "I'm so sorry . . . I had no idea."

"I know. Ellie just explained. I can't tell you how sorry Cody and I are about what happened with Colonel Pershall. Is there anything we can do?"

"No, I need to apologize for yelling at you. That was inexcusable."

"Don't worry about it," Amy said as she rolled down the storage unit door and clipped on the lock. "You take care and let us know if you need anything. Don't worry about this at all. Here, I'll let you out," she said and ushered us back to the gate.

"Would you mind driving us back? I'm a little unsteady," Denise said.

"Not at all."

We climbed in the oversized SUV. Denise leaned against the car door and stared out the window. She didn't say anything for most of the drive and I was so busy concentrating on navigating the huge SUV through the traffic that I didn't attempt to draw her out. I'd adjusted to driving my new minivan, which we'd bought after I said a reluctant good-bye to my trusty Jeep Cherokee. Compared to this beast, my minivan felt like a sports car. I spun the wheel and turned onto the long magnolia-lined drive that led to Taylor Air Force Base. As we neared the gate, I fished in my purse for my ID card. "Denise, I need your ID," I said.

She started. "Right." She handed it over and I pulled even with the uniformed security officer behind his bulletproof shield. Security was changing on the base. Instead of the military's security police monitoring the gates, the military had contracted out some of those jobs and now I was just as likely to see a contractor in a security guard–type uniform as I was to see a member of the military police in fatigues. He scanned the cards, wished us a good afternoon, and waved us through.

The transition onto the base brought Denise out of her reverie. "Ellie, what is wrong with me, thinking that Lewis could do something like that?"

I picked my words carefully as I eased off the accelerator. Speed limits were low on base and I certainly didn't want to get a ticket. "Denise, I can't imagine what you're going through right now. I don't think you should beat yourself up about this. I won't tell anyone what happened and Amy—she's so scattered right now—I don't think she picked up on what you initially thought was going on. She thought you were mad about the bike, nothing else."

I pulled into Denise's carport and felt like I'd brought a ship into dock. I put the SUV in park and leaned back, relieved I'd made it in the small space without dinging or scratching anything.

"And I would have been, too." Denise's voice was almost wistful as she removed her sunglasses and gazed at the neat rows of trash cans and recycling bins. "What I wouldn't give to be arguing about buying a motorcycle with him right now."

"I know." I made a move to get out of the SUV, but she was motionless, lost in thought. "Ready to go in?" I asked.

Still staring through the windshield, she said, "Ellie, I wasn't completely honest with you earlier."

"About what?"

"I *did* suspect Lewis was having an affair, I really did. And I didn't want it to be true. But there's something else I'm worried about. I know my thinking is warped to say this, but I'd almost hoped he *was* having an affair because then it would make everything else not seem so bad."

"Everything else?" I asked. What could be worse than the situation she was in right now?

She dropped her gaze down to her fingers, which were clamped around her sunglasses. She swallowed hard and I realized she was fighting off a wave of tears. In a barely audible voice she said, "About a year ago I decided I wanted a divorce."

I sputtered, "But—you and Colonel Pershall— you were happy." She might as well have said she decided she wanted to jump off the Empire State Building to see if she could fly. A crazy statement like that would make as much sense as what she'd just said.

She nodded and unhooked her fingers so she could press at the corners of her eyes. "We were. We really were, especially lately. But a year ago . . . well, you know that cliché? 'We drifted apart.' There's a reason it's a cliché—there's some truth to it. People do change. Lewis was enmeshed in work and I found myself drifting through the days looking for something to do. I wanted to make a difference, do something significant. It seemed to make sense at the time. We didn't have kids and we hardly ever spent any time together. We were living separate lives anyway."

I thought back over the last year. I'd never seen any indication of a problem or strain in their marriage, but now that I thought about it, I hadn't seen them together all that often.

Denise rubbed her fingertips under her eyes to erase the smudged mascara. She sighed and said, "So, I did what all those women's magazines recommended. I empowered myself. I opened a bank account in my own name and made sure I had a few credit cards with only my name on the account. I made copies of all our financial paperwork and put it in a safety-deposit box. I researched divorce attorneys, even consulted with a few."

"What happened? Did Lewis know?"

"Yes. His reaction was so far from what I thought it would be. I thought he'd be fine with it. I mean, I knew he'd be stunned, at first, but then I thought he'd realize it was best for us." She picked up the sunglasses and polished them with the hem of her T-shirt.

"But that's not what happened?"

"No, far from it." She was actually smiling slightly. "He hadn't realized I was so unhappy and he said he'd do anything to make things right between us. He agreed to counseling and told me to go for it—really do what I wanted. That I didn't even have to be 'the commander's wife' if I didn't want to. That's when I threw the spouse club open to big changes. And I had . . . I guess you'd call it an epiphany. I can't go into the details, but I realized that I could do what I wanted, make a difference, and I didn't have to break away from Lewis to do it. He could be part of it. By then I *wanted* him to be part of it."

"Is that when you began taking knitting orders?" I asked. Denise knitted the most beautiful sweaters I'd ever seen. She used incredibly soft wool in colors so rich that she had orders from almost every spouse in the squadron. Abby, my acting personal shopper, had advised me to have Denise make a crimson sweater for the holidays. Abby didn't need to talk me into it—I loved the beautiful colors and textures Denise used for her projects.

"That was part of it, but other things changed, too." She put down the sunglasses as she said, "My feelings . . . it's hard to describe. You're not going to believe this, but I started taking golf lessons—that probably says it all. I wanted to surprise Lewis. I knew he loved playing and I figured it would be something we could do together."

She went silent and I didn't know what to say. I didn't have any words to comfort her. Eventually, she said, "All those big plans I made for a divorce weren't even in my thoughts anymore until this morning."

"And now you're worried about how it's going to look," I said.

"I know it's not going to look good. And there's no way to hide it. No one else knows, except for the lawyers I talked to, of course. But all the information is there for them to find—the searches I did on my computer about how to prep for a divorce—it's all there in my search history. I don't know how to remove it and I'm afraid that if I tried, I'd look even guiltier."

"I think it's hard to completely remove anything from your computer," I said as I flicked through the keys on her key ring.

"It doesn't matter. The new bank accounts and credit cards can't be removed. It's only a matter of time until they're uncovered," she said.

She was right. I knew the detectives would keep pressing until they found the information she was worried about and then they'd wonder if she'd chosen murder over divorce.

Her voice broke into my thoughts. "So you can see why I thought it would simplify things if Lewis was having an affair. It didn't make sense to me that he would do that after we worked so hard on our marriage, but it would have made it more understandable for me to be looking into a divorce. I didn't want to believe he was, but . . ."

"Now you're back where you were."

"Prime suspect."

"Are you sure about that?"

"Yes. I'm sure. Who else do they have? Somehow I don't think they'll take anyone on that list we made very seriously." She shoved her sunglasses in her purse with a resigned sigh as she added, "Just spats and anger, typical sour grapes stuff that commanders have to deal with every day. None of those people have a good motive."

"I don't know. I think they'll take Carrie's letters seriously."

She half-shrugged and moved to get out of the car. "Not as seriously as they'll take a wife who wanted a divorce and has no alibi. I can't prove that I drove over to Wool Works yesterday afternoon."

She did have a point, but I kept that thought to myself. I didn't want to bring her further down. I handed her the keys and followed her into the kitchen. I wanted to make sure her sister was back before I left.

"Don't you have a receipt? I know you'd never come out of a knitting store empty-handed."

That made her smile briefly. "You're right. I would have bought something. I was actually going there to pick up a special order, some alpaca yarn in the most gorgeous shades of aqua, cobalt, and navy. I'm making a scarf for my sister. But they were closed. I thought I could get there before they closed, but MaryAnn had to leave early and she closed up at noon that day. I drove back home."

"Well, what did you do the rest of the afternoon?" I asked.

"I knitted."

"Of course." What else would she be doing? If she wasn't taking care of squadron spouse business, then she was usually knitting.

She tossed her purse on the counter and pointed through the doorway. "Right there in the living room, and believe me, if I'd known I was going to need an alibi I would have called someone, or asked someone over, or gone for a walk, but you know me, once I get into a project, I can't stop. I did show Detective Waraday the throw I finished," she stopped and suddenly laughed. "You know what? I just realized how funny that is. 'Here, Detective, here's my alibi.'" She was laughing harder now and I smiled along with her, but I didn't think it was quite as funny as she did. Half laughing, half gasping for breath, she said, "I gave the man a throw as an alibi."

It was kind of funny when you thought about it, but it wasn't *that* funny. Okay, this was not good. Denise was losing it, laughing, but on the verge of tears, too. She drew a long breath and I relaxed as she seemed to get a grip on herself. She dropped down at the kitchen table and I handed her a bottled water. "Do you think your sister is back from the store?" I asked.

She sipped the bottle, then listened, "Yes, she's back. I can hear the TV upstairs. She always has the news on."

Denise set down the bottle and picked up the

page of names we'd left when we'd rushed out the door. "We have to see where these people were on Saturday. It's hardly anything, but it's all I've got at this point."

"I don't think we need to do that, Denise."

"Yes, we do." The paper wrinkled in her tight grip. "If you don't help me, I'll do it on my own."

She'd certainly showed her determination earlier. She would have walked out that door without me, no hesitation.

And look how she came back, deflated and devastated, my conscience whispered. She was obviously going to pursue this with or without me. She was too emotionally fragile to do this on her own.

"Let me take a look," I said and she handed me the paper.

Chapter
Six

I skipped over Colonel Barnes's name. I didn't have any connection to him. He didn't live in our neighborhood and even if I did see him at some squadron function, a lieutenant colonel was well above Mitch's rank of major, and I couldn't think of any reason I'd have to speak to him. But Denise was looking at me with such hope in her gaze that I said, "Well, I do know Henry's wife, Megan. She won four hours of free organizing last spring at the squadron raffle."

In between diaper changes and carpool duty, I had a part-time organizing business called Everything in Its Place. "I haven't seen her much since Tyler was born, but she joined the stroller brigade—that's a workout group in my neighborhood—last week so I could talk to her and see what they were doing on Saturday. Carrie hasn't had much contact with anyone, so she'd be harder to talk to, but Abby lives close to her on base, so I might get Abby to go with me to see her." Hadn't Abby said something about inviting her to the supper club?

"Wonderful! That's a start."

"But you have to promise to call Detective Waraday and give him the letters from Carrie."

"I will," she said reluctantly.

"All right ladies, time to cool down for a stretch."

I parked my stroller beside Megan Fleet and she murmured, "Thank God. I haven't been this exhausted since I gave birth."

"I know. The first few workouts are real killers, aren't they?"

The sound of a rifle shot cracked through the air and I flinched, half-ducking before it registered that the sound was far away, not like the one on the day of the family reunion. Megan stared at me, puzzled. "You okay?"

I stood up straight. "Yeah, just a little jittery," I said as I pulled off my baseball cap and wiped my damp forehead before more sweat dripped off my eyebrows and ran into my eyes. The humidity was intense even at ten in the morning, despite the trace of a breeze. I'd been doing the stroller brigade workout for almost two years, but I was still beat at the end of each session. It had gotten easier, but the combination of cardio and toning still challenged me, partly because Tina, the leader, showed us different levels of intensity for each section of the workout.

"Mom, can we go play now?" Livvy asked impatiently. I unhooked the straps that held Livvy and Nathan in the double stroller. At five, Livvy was one of the oldest kids in the group and looked like a giant compared to the toddlers making their way unsteadily around the neighborhood playground, the starting and ending point of the workout. I felt a bit sad as I watched her swiftly climb to the top of the play fort. Only a few days and she'd start kindergarten.

Tina called out, "Extend your right leg behind you for a good calf stretch. Take your time. You need it after those hills."

I gripped the handle of the stroller and leaned into the stretch, thinking about Megan and Denise. I realized I'd missed Tina's prompt to switch to the other leg, which was typical of today's workout. I couldn't keep my "mind in my muscle" as Tina was always reminding us to do. I'd been thinking about Denise and Colonel Pershall's death.

Denise's dramatic shifts in attitude yesterday had been a bit extreme. I switched to arm stretches and decided that there probably wasn't a "normal" reaction when your spouse is murdered. With that awful situation, any reaction she had was legitimate. And if talking to Megan could help Denise, I'd do it.

We finished with several deep cleansing breaths and then all hit our water bottles. The group usually didn't break up right away. I drifted toward the park benches with Megan.

"Wait, you dropped something," I said as I picked up a pale blue blanket that had fallen out of her stroller's basket. "I remember you knitting this during one of the spouse coffees," I said, handing it to her.

"That's a stretch—saying I knitted it." She stuffed it back in the basket and parked the stroller. "I had to rip out so much and have Denise fix it. In the end, I gave up. She finished it for me." She disengaged Tyler's car seat from the stroller base and walked with me over to the park benches. I could see his tiny pink toes kicking above the edge of the car seat. She plopped down on the bench and laughed. "In fact, I cleaned out all my knitting stash and threw it away the next day. Henry came in and found me tossing everything in the trash. I told him I was so frustrated that Denise had to finish the blanket for me and I was never knitting again. By the time I described how she put the needles back in their plastic bag—she was almost reverent about it, do you remember? Anyway, by then, I'd cooled down and felt a little foolish for tossing everything. I'd spent a small fortune on yarn alone. Henry talked me into keeping everything.

"Do you knit?" she asked as she rocked Tyler's car seat with her foot. "I've still got all my needles and yarn packed away. I stuffed everything in those bins in the garage you helped me organize. I thought I might eventually try knitting again, but I don't really have any desire to knit, not to mention any time. Do you want my leftover yarn and needles?"

"No. Thanks, though. I tried knitting before Livvy was born. I've got everything, needles, yarn, and those little stitch markers. I actually completed a very simple pink baby blanket." Normally, organizing is about as crafty as I get, but I'd loved the soft, beautiful yarns. I'd started a scarf next, but had never finished it. I'd been too busy after Livvy was born to pick it up again. I made a mental note to give it another try. I had Denise around now, too, to help me when I got stuck, so I really should make another attempt.

"Hey, how's the storage system working out?" I asked.

"Good. It's about time for me to get out those bins where we put the bigger size clothes and see what Tyler can wear now. That was a good idea to put them away until he grew into them. It freed up a lot of space in his room."

"I'm glad it's working for you." Unlike some of my organizing clients who wanted me with them at each stage of the project, Megan only needed me to get her started on the right track. She'd completed the project on her own. "So do you like the workout?" I asked.

"I don't think *like* is the right word. I *need* the workout," she said as she adjusted her white-blond ponytail. "I gained thirty pounds with Tyler and I've got to do something to get rid of the weight. I look like a cow," she said, rocking the car seat with her foot.

I glanced down at the car seat. Tyler waved his fat fists and stared at the alternating pattern of sun and shade that flickered over us as the wind gently brushed through the tall loblolly pines overhead. He had a patch of brown flyaway hair that stuck up an inch from his scalp and make him look like he had a Mohawk. The wind teased at the tuft of hair.

"You look great. How old is Tyler now? Six months?" Megan wasn't overweight, or even *slightly* overweight. She looked normal, healthy.

"Yep, six months last week," she said. "I've been working out and watching what I eat, but I've only been able to lose twenty pounds. No matter what people say, breastfeeding doesn't make you skinny again." She patted her stomach.

"I've still got ten pounds to go and it's all right here. I hope this workout combined with weight workouts at the gym will get me back in shape. I suppose I should be glad that I've dropped the weight I have. It's amazing that I've been able to lose anything, considering I'm surrounded by food all the time," she said dryly.

"Really, you look great." Megan had a part-time business baking cakes. The squadron had ordered one for the last spouse coffee, a three-layer chocolate concoction, and it had been delicious. Megan hadn't eaten even a bite of it. Her willpower blew my mind. Pass up a three-layer *chocolate* cake? Unthinkable.

"Thanks, but Caroline Corriday's wearing a bikini now. Her son was born two weeks after Tyler," Megan said, naming the star of a popular TV crime drama. "I saw it in *People*."

I bit my tongue to keep from saying what I really wanted to say. Megan looked really good, considering she'd had a baby six months ago and that those images in the media of moms who regain their pre-baby body in a few weeks have given us a warped idea of what's normal. But I didn't feel like I knew her well enough to be that honest. Instead, I took a breath, one of those deep ones that Tina was always instructing us to take, and shifted my attention to why I really wanted to talk to her.

"So how was your weekend?"

"Let's see, nothing very exciting happened. Henry finally left on Saturday morning, thank God. I can get so much more done when he's not under my feet." A few fussy cries came from Tyler and Megan spun a rattle attached to the car seat handle.

"Really?" I asked.

She rolled her eyes. "Yes. He's forever talking about how hard work is, how essential he is to the squadron, blah, blah, blah. I'm sure you hear it all, too."

I never *liked* it when Mitch left and opened my mouth to say so, but Megan chattered on, "I mean, it really is so much easier when they're gone, isn't it? Less laundry, fewer dishes, and I don't have to listen to his jabbering about squadron politics, which I'm completely sick of, let me tell you." She gave the rattle an extra hard spin.

I was afraid she was going to tell me about it in detail. I hurriedly said, "So Henry's TDY. Where's he going?" TDY was the military acronym for Temporary Duty, which meant that Henry was out of town on a short flying assignment.

Megan shrugged. "West Coast. California or Hawaii, I think."

"Oh, the medical support flight to Hawaii, where they do their training in the back of the jet during the flight?" The trip came up several times on the schedule, but it wasn't as glamorous as the destination made it sound. Mitch had flown that mission before and it involved very little time actually on the ground in Hawaii. I glanced over to check on Livvy and Nathan. They were both sitting in the shade of the slide digging busily in the dirt. Megan said, "I guess so. He should be back for the supper club at Abby's this week," Megan said.

"Oh, that's right." I'd forgotten the meeting was this week.

Megan lowered her voice and leaned over. "Have you heard anything about Colonel Pershall?" We'd talked briefly about Colonel Pershall's death at the beginning of the workout, but the workout had ended that discussion.

"No, I haven't."

"I'll be glad when Henry gets back. I hate it that he's gone right now. It's . . . creepy, knowing someone out there did that to Colonel Pershall. I don't even like to think about it, but I can't help it, especially at night. Five Pines isn't that far from here."

I could sympathize. Being alone was a major part of being a military spouse and, often, the nights were the worst. "Hey, we're right around the corner, call us if you need anything. Anything. You've got our number, right?"

"Yeah, Denise made up that spouse recall roster, which I thought was clever. The guys always have a way to get in touch, but we hardly ever do."

"I know. Denise has done some great things."

"What do you think will happen to the squadron? Who do you think will be the new squadron commander?"

"I don't know. I hadn't even thought about it," I said, running my hand across my sweaty forehead and then repositioning my baseball cap.

"I talked to Henry on the phone this morning. He thinks it will be Colonel Barnes."

"Really? Why?"

"Henry says Colonel Barnes has been angling for the position and was really angry when he got the D.O. slot instead."

I sorted through squadron acronyms in my mind, and matched "D.O." with director of operations, essentially the second in command under the squadron commander. "I guess he would be next in line, but I wonder if they'll bring someone new in." The squadron had different slots, different jobs, that the pilots held. Like a pyramid, the idea was that you gradually worked your way up to the top, the squadron commander. Holding different positions was critical for promotion, but complicating the system was the fact that slots were assigned by the squadron commander and it often seemed to me that it was whim, chance, or friendship that determined how the slots were filled.

"I don't know. God, I hate to even think about what a shake-up this will cause." Megan slumped back against the bench. "The maneuvering in the squadron is driving Henry crazy. He didn't get the in-residence AQS slot he wanted and he was so upset."

Just like teachers who continued their education in the summer, the military had many schools that you could attend to enhance your promotion chances. Some were only a few weeks, but others were as long as a year and required moving to the base where they were taught. The same classes, like AQS, short for Advanced Qualifying School, were also taught by correspondence, but it looked better to take the classes "in residence."

Mitch had a chance to go next year. He was on the list to attend in residence, but he was trying to switch to the correspondence course. We didn't want to move right after Livvy's first year of school. Some guys would have pushed for the school and the move because it would be a good career move, but I was glad Mitch had a bigger picture that included how changes would impact the kids.

"Henry's so stressed right now," Megan said.

"I thought things were better under Colonel Pershall. Mitch likes working here better than anywhere else he's been stationed."

Megan shrugged. "I don't know. Henry's always stressed about something at the squadron." She glanced around, then said, "Have you heard anything about how he died?"

"Just that he was strangled."

Megan shivered and said, "Nadia heard he was strangled with a kudzu vine."

"I hadn't heard that," I said slowly. Nadia was another military spouse who taught first grade at the same school as Abby. Nadia did always seem to know everything, so she'd probably know the latest rumor. The squadron grapevine was practically wireless communication. "I don't know, Megan. We should probably wait and see what the investigators say."

Tyler shifted his arms in jerky movements as he squished his eyes together and began to cry. Megan stood up. "Naptime."

Other moms were meandering home at a much slower pace than we'd used earlier. After we'd strapped everyone back in their strollers, I walked home through the neighborhood streets, oblivious to the traditional-style brick homes set back from the road with their Palladian windows, large porches, and lush landscaping. Instead, I was thinking about what Megan said about Colonel Barnes benefiting, at least in the squadron, from Colonel Pershall's death.

I called Denise to check on her later that night while I was grating cheese for our dinner of tacos.

"How are you doing?" I asked.

"Honestly, I don't know how to answer that," Denise said. "I'm taking it hour by hour today.

I'm trying to plan a funeral service for Lewis, but I can't do much until they release . . . him."

I assured Denise I'd do anything she needed to help with the service, then said, "On a different topic, I saw Megan Fleet today and she said Henry is out of town. He's been TDY since Saturday morning. Not great news, I know, but I thought you'd be interested."

"I am. Well, there's still Carrie, and Colonel Barnes," she said and sounded a bit more like the old Denise, who'd coordinate events and dispatch problems with aplomb. She continued: "That sounds awful to throw them out there like that, but that baby-faced detective was back this morning. Follow-up questions, he said, but I don't see how he could call them that since they were exactly the same questions he'd asked me before. He was checking to see if my story had changed."

"What happened with Carrie's letters?"

"He was interested in those. He tried not to show it, but I could tell. He took them and I haven't heard anything since."

"There's my call waiting," I said. "Can you hold on?"

"No need," Denise said. "I'll call you if I find out anything new."

Mitch was on the line. "Ellie, I need you to come pick me up."

The thin whine of Livvy's voice sounded from

the living room. "Mom, Nathan took the book I was reading and won't give it back."

Distracted, I gave Nathan the "mom look" and he grudgingly handed the book to Livvy. I tilted the phone away from my mouth and said, "Get your own book." I pulled the phone back and watched Nathan stomp over to the coffee table, which was stacked high with library picture books.

"Sorry," I apologized to Mitch as I went back to grating cheese. "I'm in the middle of dinner and the kids have done nothing but argue and pick at each other all afternoon—" I broke off as his words sunk in. "You need me to pick you up?" Mitch had driven to work that morning, as he always did, and he should have been driving home about now. "Did you have car trouble?"

"No. I had an accident. I'm fine, but I need you to come get me. I'm on Scranton Road. You know the section where it dips and curves?"

I put down the cheese and grater. He had my full attention. "What happened?" That stretch of road was notorious for bad accidents. I'd seen several cars flipped upside down in the ditch.

"Don't worry. Everything's okay. My tire blew out, but I'm okay. The car needs some work, so I called a tow truck. Just come get me. And, Ellie, don't worry. I'm fine."

"You call that fine?" I asked. "That's horrible," I said, staring at the dented side panel of Mitch's small Nissan. It was already loaded on the flatbed tow truck, but I could see the path the tires had taken through the thick scrub along the side of the road. There was a gash on a pine tree where the bark had been stripped away when Mitch sideswiped it.

I spun toward him. "You could have been killed." The kids were still in the van a few feet behind us, so I didn't filter the anxiety I felt.

Mitch put his arm around my shoulders. "I wasn't. I'm okay." He stepped away and turned in a circle, holding his arms out. "Not a scratch on me. I'd have driven it home, but the air bag deployed and the front tire is basically shredded. Nothing terrible."

I gripped his hands. "Mitch, if you'd hit that tree . . ."

He silenced me by pulling me close into a hug. "That's my worrywart. Glad to see some things never change."

Of course he'd try and make light of it, but I wasn't having any of it. "This *is* something to worry about," I said into his shoulder. "Don't tell me that didn't scare you."

Mitch pulled away, his face serious. "Yes, I was scared. Terrified, actually, but that mostly came after the air bag deployed. I didn't have time to do anything except react when it happened. It's over now and you don't have to worry. I know you're prone to worry about something, even when it's over. *Especially* when it's over," he amended.

I ran my hands up and down his arms. He was right. I did have a tendency to worry too much. "No strained muscles? How's your neck and shoulders?"

"I'm okay." He caught my hands and pulled me back to the minivan, which was parked behind the tow truck. "I have those speedy pilot reflexes, that's what saved me. I'll drive. You're too shaken up. I've had time to calm down."

He was joking about his "pilot reflexes" and I had to smile, but I couldn't help but think he was right. Without his training in making quick decisions, the result could have been much worse.

Tips for Busy, Budget-Minded Moms

The Family Calendar
Post a family activities calendar in the kitchen. Find a calendar with plenty of space for each day. First, go through the whole year and note every family birthday. Next, list school holidays and business trips. Finally, list *every* family activity—dentist appointments, music lessons, social and religious activities, sports practice sessions, and vet appointments. Some people like to use different colored ink for each family member so they can tell at a glance who has activities on which days. Don't forget to add new events like field trips, business trips, plays, and recitals as they come up.

Chapter
Seven

I picked up the mail from the kitchen cabinet and went to find Mitch. We'd had dinner—the tacos had been a challenge for the kids to eat—and I knew he'd tucked the kids into bed before I made the rounds, but I hadn't seen him since then. It always took me a bit longer to get through the bedtime story, song, and prayer, because there was always something Livvy wanted to talk about. Tonight it had been why there are polar bears and "regular" bears.

Mitch wasn't playing Galaga or Pac-Man on the classic arcade game console I'd given him for his birthday a few years ago and he wasn't puttering around on the patch of land that he'd carved out in our backyard for a garden this summer. I'd stayed far away from the garden since my thumb was definitely not the green one in the family. With Mitch in charge of the garden, we'd had so many fresh veggies that I'd practically had to give away bushels of them, not to mention the six loaves of zucchini bread I had in the freezer.

I frowned and checked the garage, which looked odd with the gaping empty space where his car was usually parked. The garage door was open and when I walked onto the driveway I saw that the light was on in the storage shed. A veritable symphony of bug sounds filled the night.

I hurried through the darkness to the shed. A few more weeks and the mosquitoes and the "no-see-ums," the even smaller and more persistent gnat-like bugs, would disappear as the cooler weather arrived. It would be the best time of the year, crisp and cool and bug free. For now, we had several bug zappers around the yard and if we were going to be outside for a long time, like at the family reunion, we ringed the yard with bamboo tiki torches that burned an oil that repelled the bugs.

Mitch was hunched over something on his small workbench at the back of the shed. "Hey," I said and pulled out a step stool for a seat. He murmured an absent-minded greeting, deep in his project.

As I opened the mail, I said, "I guess I'm taking you to work tomorrow." A quick mental image of Mitch's car on the tow truck came to mind, but I pushed it away. Mitch was right. It was better not to focus on what could have happened. "You could take the minivan, but I need to get the rest of Livvy's school supplies." There was a brief mumble from Mitch, which I took as agreement. "I still have to find low odor dry-erase markers with fine tips and a specific brand of blunt scissors. I had no idea school supply lists were so specific."

I opened a bill and leaned over to set it in a stack

by my feet. The last plain white business envelope had a heavy thickness on one end that made it sag in my hand. I opened it. "Mitch, you got a squadron coin in the mail," I said as the oversized coin dropped heavily into my palm. It looked like the one Denise received with the jet engraving on one side and squadron patch with the hawk on the other.

Mitch glanced over his shoulder at it, then said, "I didn't order one. The squadron must be sending out new ones."

"Looks like your old one," I said.

There was a pause and then Mitch said, his words halting as he focused on what he was doing, "That's good . . . I've got a spare now." He set down what he was working on and stepped back, his hands braced on his hips. I'd seen that posture before, usually when he was working on something that was hard to fix. I'd seen it a lot this summer when the underground sprinkler stopped working. He spent hours digging, then fitting pipes and checking for leaks.

"What are you working on?" I trashed the empty envelopes and junk mail, then moved over to his workbench.

"Oh, not much," he said as he quickly shoved a few tools in his toolbox. "Just cleaning up. Ready?" he asked, his hand poised to switch off the overhead bulb he'd installed to give him light when he worked late out here.

"Ah—sure," I gathered up the bills and squadron coin, which I handed to him. He slipped it in his pocket. I frowned, wondering why Mitch was in such a hurry to leave. I glanced around. The shed was incredibly tidy. I knew because I'd cleaned it up before the family reunion. We'd needed a place to store all the extra chairs and ice chests. The only thing out of place now was the leaf blower that had short-circuited, and Mitch had hastily pushed it away when I walked over.

"Everything okay?" I asked.

"Sure," Mitch said easily.

"What's up with the leaf blower?" I asked as we left the shed.

"I thought I might be able to fix it, but I don't think I can." He closed the shed door, clipped on the padlock, and looped his arm around my waist.

He must be tired and ready to call it a day, I decided. "Oh, I forgot to tell you. I heard from Dan today," I said as we walked into the garage. "He's recovered and says he can start his triathlon training again in a few days. Although, he sounded pretty excited about white water rafting. Wants to know if you want to go on a trip with him to Colorado next summer."

"He's always trying some new sport," Mitch said with a shake of his head. "Next summer's too far away. I have no idea what we'll be doing next year."

"True," I said with a sigh. Mitch might be

deployed or he might be home. It was hard to make long-range plans at times.

"I'll call him back," Mitch said. "How's Felicity? Mad as ever?"

"He didn't say."

"Then she's probably still upset. She doesn't cool off quick. Hardly ever, actually."

"Well, I'm glad he's okay," I said.

"Me, too," Mitch said, looking around the garage. He'd come to a standstill.

"Are we going in?"

He refocused on me, then said, "Yes, right." He punched the button and the garage door spooled down.

"Are you okay? You're kind of preoccupied."

"No. I'm fine." We went into the kitchen. I put the bills away and curled up in the overstuffed chair with the basket of knitting supplies I'd pulled off the closet shelf earlier today. I ran my hand over the half-finished scarf. It was a sea-foam blue. It would make a perfect birthday present for Abby, if I finished it in a month, which seemed like plenty of time to knit a scarf. I loved the way the stitches lined up so neatly. Except for those on the second row. I looked closer and realized I'd dropped a stitch.

Mitch opened the refrigerator door. "I picked some more carrots today. These are fresh out of the garden."

I stopped working with the yarn and held up my

hand like a traffic cop. "No carrots. If I eat any more carrots the palms of my hands are going to turn orange." I'd intentionally fixed tacos for supper because it was something that didn't sound good with carrots. "And don't you dare thaw out a loaf of that zucchini bread. I don't want another slice of that until at least after Halloween."

There's healthy eating and then there's going way too far overboard. My idea of a snack didn't involve anything colored orange, green, or yellow, unless it was M&Ms. Or Hershey's kisses, my favorite snack, because they were small enough that I didn't feel guilty if I ate one, and—most critical of all—they were pure chocolate.

Mitch opened the freezer. "Ice cream?"

It wasn't pure chocolate, but it was pretty close.

"Do you mind if we run an errand before we pick up the kids?" Abby asked as we walked to her car. We'd just had lunch at the Peach Blossom Inn, a local bed and breakfast that served delicious Southern cuisine.

"No, I'm sure the kids are fine. The longer we stay away, the better, as far as they're concerned." It was the last day of summer vacation for Abby. She had to return to work tomorrow, so we'd planned a girl's lunch for ourselves. Our kids were bouncing and climbing at Fun Time which, until last year, had been a big box linen store. The chain declared bankruptcy, the comforters disappeared, and the huge space was converted to an indoor kids' play area with foam cushions, a ball pit, a huge climbing maze, and various inflatable bouncers. Another section catered to older kids with arcade games, a miniature golf course, bumper cars, and even a laser tag section. Despite Livvy's protests that she was too old, Livvy, Nathan, and Charlie were on the pre-K side with Anna, my favorite babysitter, watching over them. I figured it would probably be the easiest money she'd ever earned because there was so much for the kids to do.

"Great. I want to invite Carrie to the supper club." Abby turned the car in the direction of the base. "And it's obviously going to take a face-to-face encounter. I've left her a couple of messages, but she's not calling back, so I figured we could run by there on the way to get the kids."

I wanted to talk to Carrie, too, but I didn't think the supper club was the way to approach her. "Are you sure that's a good idea, to invite her to the supper club? She might feel left out since everyone else will be part of a couple. Wouldn't you feel left out in a situation like that?"

"No," Abby said, perplexed.

Of course. I'd forgotten to factor in Abby's indefatigable ability to fit into any group. She makes friends faster than I can sort and organize, and if she was invited to a supper club and everyone else showed up with their spouses, she wouldn't care.

100

She'd jump in, chat with everyone, and probably be the life of the party.

"I'm sure her isolation is a coping mechanism," Abby said. "It'll be good for her to get out. I understand she needs her time alone, but it can't be healthy for her to shut herself away in that tiny house all the time. She needs some interaction and it's my week to check on her." The squadron spouses had made an unofficial visitation chart to make sure Carrie was okay.

"I don't think our system of checking in with her is working quite like we'd hoped." She'd obviously not passed along the word that she could use help with cutting the lawn. I quickly filled Abby in on Denise's request to find other suspects. I knew I could trust Abby and since I wanted to ask Carrie where she'd been on Saturday, I figured I better give Abby some background on the letters. Even though at the storage unit I'd promised Denise that I would keep quiet about her misplaced suspicions, I hadn't made the same promise about the letters. The drive to the base went quickly because the traffic was light. As we pulled through the base's front gate, I said, "Carrie sent some vicious letters to Colonel Pershall. She's angry about Ryan's death and blames Colonel Pershall."

"But that's absurd," Abby said.

"I know. Colonel Pershall had nothing to do with it. It was an accident."

"Although," Abby had slowed down for the low

101

speed limit on base and the pace of her words matched her methodical driving, "I did hear something about how she didn't want him to go on that last deployment." Abby coasted to a stop in front of Carrie's house and turned to me. "Didn't she have a bad feeling about the deployment? Jeff told me she went to the squadron and made a big fuss about how Ryan shouldn't go because it was too dangerous."

"I didn't know that. But Colonel Pershall couldn't pull him off the deployment."

"Of course not. It was his turn," Abby said. "If Colonel Pershall had pulled Ryan off the deployment, then I'm sure every other person in the squadron would have a bad feeling, too, and want out. It wouldn't have been fair."

"And Colonel Pershall was always fair," I said sadly.

We walked up the narrow sidewalk. Carrie was allowed to continue living in base housing for up to a year. It had to be hard for her to be on base, but maybe it was the best decision for her financially. I knew Carrie was a computer engineer and did contract work out of her house for different offices on base.

I almost expected her to turn us away or not even open the door. But as soon as Abby rang the doorbell, Carrie opened the door as if she'd been watching us through the narrow window beside the front door. She whipped the door wide with such force it stirred her wispy brown bangs and she had to shake them off her face. "Well, come on in. I figure if I talk to you, you might stop calling me." The words themselves were quarrelsome, but it was hard to take her seriously when she delivered a statement like that in her breathy little girl voice. It diluted the effect.

We stepped inside and Carrie gestured to the living room couch. This floor plan was even smaller than Denise's and it only took three steps to reach the couch. Abby's house on base was the same design and even though her house was just as small, it had a completely different feel. Abby's house was cozy and warm and I always wanted to stay. Carrie's house was filled with heavy, dark wood furniture that felt too big for the small rooms and gave me a claustrophobic feeling.

From the living room, I could see into the dining room and kitchen beyond it. Stacks of paper, a phone, and several books, pens, and file folders coated the hefty dining room table a few feet away. In the kitchen, a pile of dishes waited on the counter next to several jars of craft paint and a paper plate arrayed with paintbrushes, which surprised me because I didn't realize that Carrie was into painting.

Abby and I squeezed between the weighty coffee table and the couch, then sat down. Carrie picked up a stack of papers from a leather recliner and moved them to the coffee table before she sat down in it, which dwarfed her small frame. Her feet barely brushed the floor.

Several pages of paper cascaded to the floor and I reached down to pick them up. I handed the papers back to her. She gave a tight little nod and, even though she was close enough to reach out and take them, said, "Just put them there."

Jeeze. Who did she think she was? Royalty? I tossed the papers on the coffee table and settled into the couch, amazed at how she'd changed. If I'd run into her at the store, I don't know if I would have recognized her. She wasn't the wilting, drooping, crying creature I remembered from the memorial service. Even her posture was different. She sat with her back straight. Her shoulder blades, which were pressed back, didn't touch the back of the puffy leather cushion on the chair. I hadn't seen posture that good since I watched *Sense and Sensibility*. Her face was different, too, more rigid and determined. Before, she'd been lost in her grief, her brown eyes bloodshot and teary. Now her gaze was clear and I had the feeling that even though she was the shortest person in the room, she would have looked down her nose at us if she could. Carrie tilted her head slightly and raised her eyebrows. "Well?"

Abby reached over and patted Carrie's hand. "We're just checking on you. Do you need anything? How's everything going?"

Carrie shifted her hand slightly and Abby's hand fell away. "I'm fine. Everything is just dandy," she said sarcastically.

"Okay," Abby said slowly. "Well, I'm hosting a supper club this Thursday. Jeff and I would love to have you there. Everyone misses you and it would be a great opportunity to reconnect with everyone from the squadron."

"I don't think so. I don't want more visits from the squadron, either. Pass that along, will you?" Even with the childish voice, there was no mistaking it for a question. It was an order.

There was a beat of silence and I realized Abby was stunned. She was speechless, not an easy state for her to achieve. Carrie trained her cold gaze on me and for a second I was actually frightened. I couldn't quite believe my reaction. I had a good ten inches on Carrie and my best friend was beside me. And, we were in the middle of base housing. Nothing bad could happen here. I gave myself a mental shake.

"I appreciate the offers of help, but I'll handle things," Carrie said. "I even managed to mow the grass last week on my own." Her words were weighted with meaning and Abby glanced back and forth between us, unsure of what was being communicated, but I knew Carrie was letting me know that she knew I'd seen the letter she'd sent to Colonel Pershall. "I had a little visit from a detective and an OSI agent. I understand I have you to thank for that, Ellie." Her gaze was even more frigid. "Oh I know he wasn't supposed to, but that person who came to interview me slipped up and mentioned you."

Abby leaned back a bit to stay out of Carrie's range of vision, like she'd be frozen solid if Carrie looked directly at her.

How had we gone from an invitation to a supper club to this tense situation? When Denise showed me the letters, I'd thought it was Carrie's anger and grief that led her to write those words. It seemed so unlike her. I hadn't really believed that she'd murdered Colonel Pershall, but now, seeing her arctic demeanor, I wasn't so sure. "Detective Waraday needed to know about those letters, surely you can see that," I said.

"No, I don't see that. It was a wasted trip for the detectives, a waste of their time. *Some* of us have an alibi. Besides, those letters aren't connected with his death. *I'm* not connected with his death. I didn't murder him. Don't get me wrong," she said conversationally. "I'm glad he's dead. He deserved it. It was one of those cosmic karma things. If he'd listened to me and hadn't sent Ryan on that deployment, Ryan would still be alive and so would Colonel Pershall. But he didn't listen. Ryan died and now he's dead, too. The universe has a way of evening out these things."

Her blasé attitude blew me away. I didn't have a response to that speech. On second thought, I did: time to leave. I grabbed my purse and stood. Abby bounced up like a jack-in-the-box. "We'll let you get back to work," I said.

"One good thing has come out of Colonel Pershall's death," Carrie said. "Someone really does understand how I feel. Denise."

How could she be so cold? Even if Denise now understood what it was like to lose her husband suddenly, I thought, it had to be worse to have your husband murdered. Carrie was still talking as she walked behind us. "You know, you shouldn't believe everything Denise tells you," she threw out, then picked her words more carefully. "No, I should say, what *isn't* Denise telling you?" She turned back to the dining room. "I have a great view of the neighborhood out that window and Denise keeps some . . . interesting . . . company. Every Tuesday afternoon. You should see for yourself. Two-thirty."

"Well, if this information is so important, I'm sure you shared it with the detectives," I said.

She smiled slowly. "No." She wrinkled her nose as she smiled a fake smile. "More fun this way. You tell Denise to stop sending the police my way and she doesn't have to worry about the word getting out about her little visitor."

I wasn't sure what she was talking about, and glanced back through the house to the dining room table and the large window in the kitchen beyond it. Now that I was in a different position, I could see around one of the stacks of paper on the table. A pair of binoculars stood beside her coffee cup.

Chapter Eight

That's some coping mechanism," I said as I slammed the car door.

"Okay, I was wrong on that. She's so cold and formal. And, what was all that about Denise?" Abby asked as she buckled her seat belt.

"I have no idea. Did you see the binoculars on the dining room table?" I asked and held on to the armrest as Abby accelerated away from the house. "Slow down. We're in base housing, remember?"

"Oh, right," Abby said and eased off the gas. "Sorry. She creeped me out. I wanted to get out of there."

"So what's behind her house? Has she been spying on Denise?" I asked.

"This road backs up to the section of base housing where Denise lives. There's a wooded path between the two areas, but Carrie's house is on that slight rise," Abby said as she turned a corner and I recognized Denise's street. Abby parked a few houses down from Denise's house.

Carrie would be able to see Denise's house from her window.

"Did you see the telescope?" Abby asked.

"What? No."

"It was on the back patio. I could see it through the kitchen window. I know Ryan was a big astronomy buff. Jeff said he was so excited to get that house in base housing because it was on the rise and there were fewer trees. I'm no expert, but it sure didn't look like the telescope was pointing to the sky. It was aimed in this direction."

"But what's Denise done that makes Carrie think she's got some hold over her?" I wondered aloud.

Abby raised her eyebrows in a silent question.

"No," I said, shocked. Abby had once told me that both her parents had had affairs before they divorced. She'd never mentioned it again, but I thought her history gave her a tainted, cynical perspective.

Abby made a tsk-ing sound. "It's the most obvious thing. Afternoon visits while Colonel Pershall was at work. And, he always was at work. Maybe she was lonely."

"No," I repeated, stronger than before. "There is no way she's having an affair." I badly wanted to say, "She suspected *him* of having an affair," but I'd promised not to share that bit of information, so I kept my mouth shut and thought about it. She'd certainly seen a few things that had seemed to indicate Colonel Pershall might be having an affair: the late nights, the perfume, the deception. Denise had quickly seized on an affair as the explanation and hadn't looked for other alternatives. Perhaps she had a guilty conscious? No. No way, I reiterated silently, wishing I could share my thoughts with Abby.

Abby said, "So what do we do now?"

I looked at my watch. "Today's Tuesday. It's almost two-thirty now. Let's watch and see what happens. I'd love to prove Carrie wrong." And I wanted to find out if I was being played. Either Denise hadn't told me the whole truth, which I did find hard to believe, or Carrie was making trouble for Denise. Perhaps Carrie thought I'd take her accusations straight to Detective Waraday and further complicate Denise's life.

About twenty minutes later, Abby said, "Now I understand why those cop shows always do the time-lapse thing when there's a stakeout. They're boring."

I had to agree. We'd checked the radio stations, eaten all the chocolate kisses I had in my purse, called Anna to check on the kids, and waved to the mailman.

Abby shifted in her seat and said, "Twenty minutes doesn't sound like a long time."

"Unless you're trapped in a car, watching the clock." I was surprised Abby had lasted this long. She was a "doer," always on the go. We'd had a flutter of excitement about five minutes earlier, but instead of someone going to the house, it had been Denise's sister, Nancy, leaving. She'd walked to her gray sedan, probably a rental car, and driven away.

"Did you notice how Carrie said she had an alibi?" I asked Abby.

"Yeah, she did manage to slip that in. What was up with that?" Abby asked.

"Denise doesn't have an alibi. She was home alone all Saturday afternoon, except for one trip to the knitting store, which closed early. So no one at the knitting store can say she wasn't at the golf course."

"Umm . . . since Carrie was so smug, she must be pretty sure of her alibi. I wonder what it is."

"I wish I'd asked her. Of course, since she was in her queen bee mode, I doubt she would have lowered herself enough to tell me," I said.

"She seemed to almost be enjoying herself in a self-righteous way. I know grief does strange things to people, but that was extreme. Even if she does have an alibi, she really hated Colonel Pershall and she's glad that Denise is a widow. That's twisted." Abby got an elastic band out of her purse and gathered her long hair into a ponytail.

"I know. But just because she says she has an alibi doesn't mean she's not lying. Or, maybe she convinced someone else to lie for her." I sighed, fanning myself with one of my organizing flyers.

"It all sounds so far-fetched. It's hard to believe someone would murder Colonel Pershall. I mean, this is someone we know, not someone in those bizarre news stories."

"Those bizarre news stories are about real people. And the way Carrie's changed is pretty bizarre itself," Abby said.

"She's gone from being so delicate that the whole county wanted to take care of her to, I don't know, an avenging angel–type. No, an avenging devil. Come on, let's get out of here," I said, reaching for my seat belt. "I think Carrie made the whole thing up. And if we sit here much longer, someone will probably call the security police. I think that last dog walker was staring at us."

"Wait," Abby said in almost a whisper, as if the smallest sound would give us away. "I think that car is slowing down at Denise's house."

We both leaned forward to watch. A small, beat-up blue car parked behind Denise's gargantuan SUV. A young guy got out, slammed the door, and loped quickly across the lawn to the front door. It opened and he slipped inside.

Abby and I looked at each other.

"Well," I said reluctantly, "it was a guy and he was young."

"And hot," Abby added. "Did you see those ropey-muscled arms and shoulders?"

"Abby," I scolded, "we're half a block away. We

could hardly see him." Abby had a thing for arms and shoulders.

"He was *hot*," she insisted and I knew she was right. "I may be married, but I can still appreciate a hot guy, even if I am half a block away. Do you think he's the lawn boy? I know they don't have a pool, so he can't be the pool boy."

"No! This is not Wisteria Lane. This is base housing and that's Denise we're talking about."

"Okay, whatever you say. I guess we're out of here now," Abby said.

I chewed on my lower lip for a second, thinking, then said, "Pull up in front of her house. We're going to drop in."

"What?" Abby had been reaching for the ignition. She twisted toward me. "You can't go up there now."

"Why not? She asked me to help her out. There's no reason I wouldn't stop by now and check in with her. If she doesn't answer the door, well . . . then that'll tell us something, and if she does, we might get some real answers instead of speculation."

"I don't think it's a good idea," Abby grumbled, but started the car. As she pulled to the curb in front of Denise's house, she said, "I bet you a whole bag of Hershey's kisses that she doesn't answer the door."

"You're on."

I pressed the doorbell and we waited, the only

sound the faint revving of the mailman's engine as he made his way through the neighborhood. The door opened and Denise leaned her head and one shoulder out the door. "Ellie!" she said with false brightness. "It's nice of you to come by, but now's not a good time."

"Really? I just talked to Carrie. Abby and I went over to invite her to the supper club. I thought you might want to know what she said."

Denise looked torn, but said, "How about we meet in an hour or so over at the Base Exchange? There's a new coffeehouse that I hear makes great blueberry muffins."

"I think it would be better to talk now. Carrie's insinuating some rather unpleasant things about you. Apparently, she's been watching your house and says you have a visitor every Tuesday at two-thirty," I glanced at the blue car in her driveway and her face lost its forced cheeriness.

She looked back inside uncertainly, then turned to us. Before she could say anything, we all heard another door close in the house. Denise stepped away, leaving the front door open. Abby and I took a step inside. "You owe me a bag of chocolates," I said in an undertone to Abby.

Outside, an engine revved and I glanced back in time to see the blue car peel away down the street.

"Now look what you've done," Denise said as she shoved the door closed behind me. "You might as well come on in now. He won't be back for weeks, if ever."

Not the reaction I was expecting. Abby and I exchanged glances and followed Denise into the kitchen where she was flipping two books closed and gathering up papers. "I'm sure I can guess what Carrie was insinuating, but that was a high school student who has trouble reading. I'm teaching him."

One of the books she held in her hand was titled *Reading Skills* and the other was an early reader about football. "Oh, Denise, I'm sorry."

"It's all right," she said, thawing a bit. "I hope he'll be back, eventually. He really does want to read. He ran because no one knows he can't read. He's managed to keep it a secret from his parents. They're both officers and work on base."

"How did you find out?" Abby asked, fascinated.

"We hired him at the beginning of the summer to mow our lawn." Here Abby shot me a glance and I knew she was thinking, lawn boy! Denise continued, "I left him a note when we were out of town about watering the grass for us. Lewis had fertilized the lawn and it needed to be watered consistently. Well, he didn't—couldn't—read the note and we came home to a scorched lawn. Fertilizer will do that, if you don't water it. Anyway, I was furious and about to fire him when I realized that there was more going on than him slacking off. I guessed, basically. Anyway, I convinced him to let me help him, but he won't meet me at the library. If anyone saw these books and heard his halting reading, he'd be embarrassed. So we meet here, once a week."

"Denise, what you're doing is wonderful. I'm sorry we caused him to bolt." I felt bad, too, that when she'd refused to let us in, I'd assumed the worst as well. I wondered if this was one of her projects she'd talked about, one of the things she'd found that helped her feel like she was making a difference.

She blew out a sigh. "That's okay. I'll convince him to come back. He was making enough progress that he was starting to feel encouraged. I was going to send him a message and tell him to skip our session, but I spent all morning making arrangements for Lewis's funeral. When he showed up, it was actually a relief to switch to something normal, something that had nothing to do with Lewis."

"So the funeral will be . . . ?" I asked.

"Thursday at one o'clock at the chapel," she said, her voice softer.

I nodded, understanding that she meant the service would take place at the base chapel.

"There will be a graveside service at Roseview Meadows," Denise said, naming one of the large cemeteries in North Dawkins. She paused and looked down at the books. "I really didn't know where to have him buried. We spent the last twenty years moving back and forth across the country. We haven't been back to Pennsylvania since his parents died and it's just my family down in Florida, so North Dawkins seems as good a place as any."

Would that be Mitch and me in ten or twenty years, I wondered? After skipping around the country, would any place feel like home? But then I thought of Mitch's boisterous, rambling family and my roots in Texas and knew we'd always have family to return to, unlike Denise, who seemed very alone right now.

I asked, "Anything we can do to help?" We were speaking quietly, almost reverently, as if we were in a church and couldn't make too much noise.

"Not with anything at the chapel. They're used to funerals and have them down to a routine there, it seems. If you could leave the graveside service a little early and go to the O Club to make sure everything is ready there, that would help me out."

"Of course, I can do that," I said.

Abby said, "Maybe we should go. If we're not here, your . . . student might come back."

Denise broke the somber mood and spoke in her regular tone of voice again as she said, "No, he's long gone for today. You might as well stay for a while." She moved into the living room, sat down in a chair positioned near their large front window, and picked up her knitting. "Tell me what Carrie said, besides insinuating I'm behaving like someone on a soap opera," she added, positioning a swath of blue knitted cloth so that it fell across her lap like a wave of water.

As we sat down on the couch, I said, "Those are interesting needles." I'd only used the traditional long metal knitting needles. Denise held up thick metal needles that were connected with a wire cord. "They're circular needles."

Abby leaned in for a closer look. "I've heard these are great."

"They're so much lighter and I don't have to purl as long as I'm knitting in the round. I can knit every row, which is faster for me."

"I'm working on a scarf," I said, studying the needles.

Abby did a double take and Denise stared at me as she said, "You? You knit?"

"Well, I'm certainly not in the same class as you, but I did make a baby blanket. Very basic stuff."

"That's wonderful. I'd love to see what you're working on," Denise said as she resumed knitting.

"That's good, because I'm counting on you to help me fix my mistakes. Maybe I should get some needles like those." I was amazed at how fast her needles flashed in and out of the yarn.

"So, about Carrie?" Denise asked, as she adjusted the position of the ball of yarn.

"Well, she says she has an alibi, but I didn't come right out and ask her what it was and she didn't volunteer it."

Her needles clicked out a quiet rhythm as Denise said, "I don't know about you, but I'm not putting much faith in what she says."

"Detective Waraday and the OSI agent visited her. She wasn't happy about that and she's so bitter and angry. "

Denise shrugged. "I suppose that's to be expected. Anger is one of the stages of grief, isn't it? That's what my counselor told me when my dad died. Of course, I was fifteen then, and angry about a lot of things anyway, but she told me it was natural to feel angry."

I glanced at Abby and she said, "Denise, I'm no expert, but it's not just that she was mad at Colonel Pershall and, by extension, you. She's furious in a cold, almost calculating way. I think she's a little messed up right now," Abby summarized.

I thought that was a huge understatement. "The whole thing with watching your house is slightly disturbing. I think you should be careful."

Denise stopped knitting and looked from one of us to the other. "You think she's . . . dangerous?"

"Have you seen her lately?" I asked.

"No, not since the memorial service. Like I told

you, she's not returning my calls or answering the door when I go over."

"She's completely different. No crying now, only cold fury. It's not healthy. You should be careful," I said.

"Lock your doors and all that," Abby added. The base was probably the safest neighborhood in town. Crime in base housing was practically non-existent. The frequent security police patrols and the fact that everyone pretty much knew everyone else kept break-ins and other crime down. Of course, since it was so safe, people had a tendency not to be quite as vigilant as they would have been off base. I'd been with Abby several times when she left her house unlocked when we went to the playground.

"Don't worry about me," Denise said. "I'll be fine. After all, this is the ultimate gated community."

Tips for Busy, Budget-Minded Moms

Daily calendars, which break the day down into hours, can be an invaluable tool for people with busy schedules and many appointments each day. They can also be a handy way to see if you're doing too much. Take one week and block out your days. List all your weekly activities, like work, commuting, committee meetings, exercise, shopping, picking up and dropping off kids, cleaning, volunteering, and relaxing. You might see ways to rearrange your schedule to free up more time or you might realize that you literally have more to do than hours in the day and need to reassess your activities.

Chapter Nine

"Why do I have to wait until Thursday to go to school?" Livvy said with a sigh.

"Don't worry. It'll go by quickly and then you'll be in school for years and years. Enjoy your last days of freedom."

She looked at me, her eyebrows pressed down, confused. "But I *want* to go to school."

"I know. And I'm sure you'll love it." I didn't understand why, but the first day of the school year was Thursday. I supposed Thursday and Friday would be spent mostly letting the kids adjust to their class and the new routine. Livvy and I were going through her school supplies. I handed her a box of crayons.

The first notes of "Livin' La Vida Loca" sounded from my purse. I answered, rolling my eyes, hoping Mitch had gotten a call today, too. How did he manage to change the ringtones without me noticing? I needed a belt clip so I could keep my phone on me all the time. That would show him.

As soon as I answered, Mitch said, "Funny." I could hear guffaws in the background. He must have gotten a call and immediately called me after he ended the earlier call.

"See, it's not so funny when it happens to you, is it?" I asked. I'd set his phone to play "Danger Zone" from *Top Gun*, a movie that Mitch and most other pilots couldn't stand. "Two can play at your game," I said as I heard someone shout, "Hey, Mitch, are you on that road? You know—the one that leads to the danger zone," followed by more laughter.

"Let the games begin," Mitch said rather determinedly.

"Oh, I think they already have."

"Fine. I was calling to tell you I don't need you to pick me up."

Nathan patted the refrigerator door and said, "Snack. Snack time." Livvy waved her new extra thick pencils in my face and I lost track of what Mitch was saying. When I held up a finger, meaning wait a minute, Nathan's request became a chant and Livvy waved her pencils more frantically. Why was it that when I was on the phone *everyone* wanted to talk to me? It looked like I needed to go over the phone rules again.

I grabbed the pencils before Livvy managed to put my eye out and handed them each a cheese stick, which bought me a few moments of peace, so I was able to concentrate on Mitch. He was saying, "Jeff gave me a ride to pick up my car at lunch. The tire and air bag are fixed, but I'll have to take it back in next week to get the dent fixed."

I didn't want to ask how much it would cost to fix the dent. I knew bodywork was expensive, but I was crossing my fingers that our insurance would pick up part of it. We were still paying on the new minivan and we couldn't afford a huge repair bill for Mitch's car. I was thankful that his car had only minor damage. At least we still had only one car payment.

I wanted to focus on slightly less stressful things at the moment. After dealing with Carrie, I needed to keep things simple. "Hey, do you know where the pencil sharpener is? We bought the rest of the school supplies today. I think Livvy wants to sharpen one of her pencils and try them out." When she heard my words, she nodded energetically. "Is it in the storage shed?"

"Yeah, I think I had it out there last week. Ah— I put a new lock on the shed door."

"Really?"

"Just thought it would be a good idea." His voice sounded evasive, not like his usual relaxed drawl. "I'll be home soon. I'll get it for you."

Mitch helped me out around the house, but that was going a bit far. "Thanks, but I think I can manage by myself. Why did you change the lock?"

"I figured it couldn't hurt. The Winthrops had a

break-in while they were on vacation." He told me where to find the key—he'd put it on a hidden nail on the inside of the fence—then said he had to go. He hung up so quickly I barely had time to say good-bye.

After walking up and down the fence three times, I finally found the nail with the shiny new key, hidden behind one of the posts. He wasn't kidding when he said he'd hidden it. I'd never have found it if I didn't know it was there.

I opened the shed, found the pencil sharpener on his workbench, and was on my way out when I stopped and looked back at the workbench. The leaf blower was gone. I tilted my head and walked around the small space, checking all the crevices and possible storage spots. It wasn't there.

I locked everything and went back inside, frowning. I helped Livvy sharpen a few pencils, then set her up with a tablet of paper. Nathan immediately joined her. Anything she could do, he had to try, too. I dialed Mitch's number. I was sure he'd already changed the ringtone. When he answered, I said, "Did you know the leaf blower isn't in the storage shed?"

"Yeah, I forgot to tell you about that," he said quickly. "Jeff's borrowing it."

"Really?"

"Yes. You were out shopping. I came by and picked it up this afternoon after I got the car. There's Colonel Barnes. I have to go. Bye."

I hung up the phone. Mitch and I were usually pretty honest with each other, so alarm bells were going off in my head at his evasive tone and quick escape from the conversation. It was the same tone he'd used a few years ago when he planned a surprise birthday party for me. Somehow, I didn't think a surprise party was in the works. I wanted to call Abby and ask if Jeff really did have the leaf blower, but I couldn't bring myself to do it. Too underhanded, I decided. I'd just ask Mitch about it when he got home.

The phone rang in my hand, playing "Livin' La Vida Loca" again. I had to change that ringtone. I didn't recognize the number on the display, but I did know the area code, Alabama. It had to be one of Mitch's relatives.

"Ellie, this is Dan."

"Dan! How are you?" I said, wondering why he'd call again so soon after his last call. We usually didn't hear from him for months at a time.

"Much better. Back to running and I'm doing a mountain bike race this weekend."

"That's great. I'm glad to hear it. And how's Felicity?"

"Doing good. Feisty as ever."

I took that to mean she was still upset about his training, but didn't pursue the topic. Instead, I said, "Mitch isn't here, he's still at work."

"That's okay. Just tell him thanks for the coin. It's outstanding."

"Coin?"

"Yeah, a military coin. It's got his jet on one side and a symbol on the other side, a hawk on a shield-type thing of blue, yellow, and black. Something to do with the squadron, right?"

"That's the squadron patch. I'll tell him you got the coin and that you like it," I said.

"Great. I really should get something like this going with my buddies at work. You know, take on the whole nerdy IT-guy reputation."

I had to smile at that. "Okay, Dan. Give that a try."

By the time Mitch got home, I'd almost forgotten about the missing leaf blower. Livvy and Nathan's interest in drawing had lasted ten minutes. Livvy wanted to pack and unpack her new pink kitty backpack while Nathan cried because he didn't have one. They were both tired from playing so hard in the jumpers and obstacle courses at Fun Time, but it was too late for a nap. We'd have to make it through the rest of the day somehow. I turned on some classic cartoons, which they loved more than any of the new shows. Livvy would adamantly protest that statement—she was too big for those "kiddie" shows, but she was practically immobilized when I let them watch Bugs Bunny or Daffy Duck.

With them settled, I went to cut up a honeydew melon to go with our rather unimaginative dinner of baked chicken and carrots. I'd had two carrot-free days, so I figured I could have some with supper tonight. Zucchini was still off the menu. I heard the garage door open and knew it was Mitch pulling in, which reminded me of the leaf blower. I cut the last of the melon and stowed it in the fridge, trying to decide whether I should bring up the missing leaf blower right away or wait until after dinner. After a few seconds, Mitch still hadn't walked in. I rinsed my hands, checked the timer on the stove, and then headed for the back door.

A tremendous boom, like a jet breaking the sound barrier, shook the house, rattling the china cabinet in the dining room. Nathan immediately burst into tears and Livvy looked at me with wide eyes. "What was that?" she asked.

"I don't know," I said as I hurried over and wiped Nathan's tears. He hiccupped a few times, then noticed that his cartoon was still on and he focused on it again. It was only a few seconds before Livvy, too, was enthralled in the action.

I left them in the living room and hurried back into the garage where I met Mitch. He was holding the mail in one hand and his hat in the other, looking in the back window of his car.

"What was that? A jet?" I asked. We sometimes heard jets from the base as they flew overhead and broke the sound barrier in a massive boom.

"If it was, it would have to have been directly over our house to be that loud."

"What's that in your car?" I asked, looking at a distorted piece of clear plastic through the partially rolled down window.

"I don't know," he said slowly as he placed the mail and his hat on the trunk and opened the door to the backseat. I was on the other side of the car and opened the other door.

It took me a second to recognize that the clear plastic had been a two-liter plastic soda bottle. Mitch picked it up and twisted it around. An explosion had ruptured the base of the bottle, peeling back the plastic. It looked like some sort of exotic blooming flower with jagged petals.

"Mitch, that was so loud. If you'd been in the car . . ."

"I might not have my hearing," he finished grimly.

Suddenly, I dropped down into the backseat. If Mitch's hearing was damaged, that could mean the end of his flying career. That fact seemed relatively minor when I thought of the other things that could have happened. If the explosion had happened when he'd been driving on the road, the sheer volume of the noise could have startled him so badly, he might have run off the road or crossed into oncoming traffic.

"Could this have been a joke?" I asked. Practical jokes were almost standard issue in the military. One of the classics was the command to a new airman straight out of basic training to "get two hundred feet of flight line," which is impossible. The flight line isn't an actual line, but a specific area on the airfield. I frowned, looking at the bits of plastic. This situation was too dangerous, even for the most extreme jokers in Mitch's squadron.

Mitch said, "I don't think so."

"Someone must be trying to hurt you." Even as I was saying the words, I couldn't believe they were coming out of my mouth.

"Afraid so," he said and slid into the seat beside me.

"You knew?" I asked.

"I suspected." He twisted the bottle in his fingers and the sharp edges twirled. "This pretty much confirms it."

I took the bent plastic from him, then scanned the car. Everything else in the car looked normal. "Where's the rest of it?" From the sound that shook our house, I expected to see bits of metal and—I don't know—wires. Something that looked like a bomb.

"There is nothing else. It's a dry ice bomb. Uncle Kenny made one for us when Dan and I were kids. You put dry ice in an empty soda bottle. As the ice warms, it changes into gas, carbon dioxide, I think. Anyway, pressure builds up and eventually the bottle explodes."

I handed the remnants of the bottle back to him. "I do remember seeing something about that on the Discovery Channel a while back. So that huge sound was from dry ice? That's amazing something that simple can be so dangerous. But how did it get in—" I stopped. Like Abby and so many other people on base, Mitch didn't lock his car doors when he was on the base. Just last week he'd forgotten a flash drive and I'd dropped it off for him. Because I was in a hurry, I'd simply found his car in the squadron parking lot and left the flash drive in the glove compartment. I hadn't even called him, because I knew his car would be unlocked. The base was a safe place. Well, it used to be. Lately, it seemed like it was more dangerous than the shadiest parts of Atlanta. "Your car was unlocked this afternoon?" It was more of a statement than a question.

He nodded and said, "But it was only in the parking lot for a few hours. Jeff dropped me off at the repair shop where I got my car. Then I picked up the leaf blower and went back to the base. I didn't get back until almost one-thirty and left at four-thirty. Someone had to work fast to get this in my car."

"About the leaf blower . . ." I said in a leading tone, and Mitch looked uncomfortable.

"I knew you weren't going to buy it. I don't know why I even bothered," he said a bit ruefully. "I really did take it to Jeff," he assured me.

"Why do I think there's more going on here than Jeff's yard work?"

Mitch sighed and ran his fingers through his

hair. His haircut was so short—military regulation—that it stood on end and gave him an even more frazzled appearance. "There is more to it. Jeff's taking it to a neighbor on base, an electrician. I wanted him to check it out and see if someone tampered with it."

The overhead light attached to the garage door automatically switched off, throwing a deeper shadow over Mitch's face. Despite the low light, I could still see the troubled expression in his dark eyes. "So that's why you changed the lock on the storage shed." Mitch thought someone broke into the storage shed and fixed the leaf blower so that it would shock him.

"Yeah. A lot of good that did."

"It was a bit like closing the barn door after the horse got out," I agreed, but added, "It was a good call, though. You couldn't have known for sure what was happening."

"I didn't. I thought it was odd. There are so many safety features on lawn and garden equipment now, so I thought it was unusual, but I wasn't sure it meant anything. It could have been a malfunction. I searched for recalls online, but there weren't any, so I figured it was a fluke."

I swiveled fully toward him. "But then, the accident with your car—it wasn't an accident?"

He shrugged. "Again, I can't say one hundred percent that, yes, someone tried to take out my tire. It could have been a natural failure of the tire, a blowout."

"I know you said you'd need new tires soon, but would it cause something like that?" I asked, thinking of the deflated tire and the ragged trail of bent grass that I'd seen when I picked up Mitch after the accident. Tire and vehicle maintenance were definitely Mitch's department and I only reluctantly took over those things when he deployed.

He rubbed his hand over his rumpled hair again and said, "It shouldn't have. Those tires should have been fine for another ten or fifteen thousand miles, but if the pressure was low, then that could cause the tire to flex more and overheat. If there was a weakness in the tire itself, that could have been enough . . ."

"You think someone actually let the air out of one of your tires so it would be more likely to fail?"

"I don't know," Mitch snapped, then stopped. "Sorry. I'm frustrated. Do you see the pattern?"

"Yes," I said slowly. "It's escalating. First, the leaf blower, a small incident. It might or might not have been rigged to shock you. But even if you got shocked, how bad could that be?"

"Bad," Mitch said darkly. "Electricians work with one hand for a reason. Even low voltage can be dangerous."

"Okay," I said, somewhat shaky myself. "So, counting the leaf blower and the tire blowout, that's two dangerous things that have happened to you in just a few days. Those things could have possibly been written off, but this," I said, pointing to the remains of the plastic bottle. "There's no question about this. Someone definitely wanted to hurt you. The explosion alone could have ruined your hearing, not to mention if it happened while you were driving . . ." my words trailed off because I didn't want to think about the possibility of what Mitch's reaction would have been to a thunderous explosion from the backseat.

To distract myself from those thoughts, I asked, "Where would you get dry ice around here?"

Mitch shrugged. "I'm not sure. Uncle Kenny got some for us from the ice cream store, but grocery stores sell it, too."

"So, someone saw your car in the parking lot, got some dry ice, put it in a soda bottle, and placed that bottle in your car moments before you left to drive home?"

"That's about it." Resignation and frustration laced through his tone.

I suddenly realized we'd both handled the bottle. "Mitch, fingerprints," I said.

He shrugged. "I doubt there will be any," he said, but gently placed the bottle on the seat between us.

We sat in the half-light for a few seconds, then I said, "Who would do something like this to you?"

"I don't know." His voice was quiet, puzzled.

If someone had told me a few days ago that there was a person who didn't like Mitch and was trying to hurt him, possibly even kill him, the concept would have been so absurd I would have laughed. "This whole situation is impossible. Everyone likes you," I said, almost belligerently. With his easygoing personality and subtle humor, Mitch made friends easily, and his roll-with-the-punches attitude kept him from taking anything in the squadron too personally. My quibble with him was that he was *too* relaxed and sometimes let people run over him.

"I don't think that's true," Mitch said, holding up the plastic bottle.

"Have you argued with anyone? Has anyone threatened you?" I persisted.

"No," he said dismissively. "No one's even yelled at me recently, except for Carrie Kohl."

Chapter Ten

Mitch's tone was flippant, but I wasn't about to write off anything. "Carrie Kohl yelled at you? When was this?"

"A couple of weeks ago. I saw her at Barney's, that sandwich shop right outside of the base. I was there having lunch with the guys and I remembered I'd found one of those notebook organizer things that belonged to Ryan in The Nest."

The Nest was the bar in the squadron. Most of the time it was used as a break room, but on Friday afternoons it certainly took on more of a bar-type atmosphere. The name came from the hawk on the squadron's emblem.

"It was in one of the cabinets under the bar. He probably set it down there one afternoon and forgot about it. I found it and tossed it in my car. I thought I'd drop it off at her house on my way home."

"Why didn't you bring it to the orderly room and let someone in there call her?"

Mitch shrugged. "I don't know. She seemed to be having such a bad time. I thought it might be hard for her to come to the squadron. Memories, all that. Anyway, I forgot to drop it off that afternoon, but I saw her the next day at Barney's, so I went out to the car, grabbed it, and gave it to her."

"But she wasn't happy to get it?"

"More like furious."

"Really?" I asked, surprised. Who wouldn't want to get something that had belonged to a deceased loved one? Especially a notebook that would probably have Ryan's notes and possibly even his thoughts. Some people used their daily planners as more of a diary. It could be a very valuable piece of Ryan's life.

"Once she realized what it was, she said, 'How dare you,' and threw it back at me." Mitch rubbed his chest. "Hard. I wasn't expecting that. She tagged me pretty good." His eyebrows scrunched together and he shrugged his shoulders. "I still don't get it. She was shrieking and crying at the same time, so I couldn't understand half of what she said. Something about how she was doing better and then I had to go and bring that thing to her."

I imagined Mitch was baffled by that kind of display. He probably wanted to escape in the worst way. "What happened then?"

"I picked up the notebook and told her I was sorry, that I didn't mean to upset her, that I thought she would have wanted it. There were napkins on the table and I gave some to her. By that time, she'd sat back down and was basically sobbing. There were several other women there with her. It must have been some kind of group, because they all had on red T-shirts. One of them was patting Carrie on the back and looking at me like she wanted to personally punch me in the face. She took the planner and told me it was best that I leave. I got out of there fast."

"I bet you did." There's nothing like a crying woman to send a man into full retreat mode. "Why didn't you tell me about it? If I'd known she'd acted like that, I wouldn't have been quite so shocked when I saw her letters to Colonel Pershall."

"I think that was the day that the sprinkler broke again and we had the geyser in the backyard."

"That did take over our life for a few days," I agreed.

"What's this about letters?" Mitch asked.

I ran my finger down the line of stitching on the seat of the car as I said, "Denise asked me to help her find some other suspects for the police. She feels like they're concentrating so much on her that they're not going to find the killer."

When I met his gaze, Mitch stared at me with raised eyebrows.

"I know. I know—you're not excited about this," I said. "But what could I say?"

"No is always an option," he said dryly.

"Mitch, her husband has been murdered and she's the main suspect. I figured I could help her make a list of people the police could check on."

"So who did she come up with?"

"Not many, I'm afraid. Henry Fleet, Colonel Barnes, and Carrie Kohl. And Carrie was the only one who seemed to actually have a real motive. Apparently Henry was upset about some class he didn't get to go to . . . AQS in residence?"

"Yeah," Mitch said, immediately recognizing the acronym for one of the advanced military education schools. "That can be a real career booster."

"But it turns out he was out of town last Saturday anyway, so that only leaves Colonel Barnes and Carrie. Denise said that Colonel Barnes was jealous of Colonel Pershall."

Mitch considered the idea, his head tilted

slightly to one side. "I'd say it was more of a competition. A friendly one, I thought, but I could be wrong." Mitch frowned. "Back to the letters . . ."

I told him about Carrie's letters, then looked at the ruptured plastic bottle on the car seat, then back to Mitch. "Do you think Carrie would do something like this?"

Mitch didn't answer right away. "I wouldn't think so, but . . ."

"But I wouldn't have thought she could write those letters, either."

As Deputy Collins placed the ripped plastic bottle in an evidence bag, he said, "So, we got one, too." He was a big, oversized man in his late thirties with a brown, squared crew cut, pockmarked face, and huge hands, but he handled the bottle and few plastic fragments delicately and spoke with the friendliness and courtesy of a true Southerner.

"Another one?" Mitch and I said, almost in unison.

The sheriff's office hadn't responded to our call right away. I was actually glad the deputy arrived about three hours after our call. At least the kids were in bed and I didn't have to come up with an explanation for them about the official visit.

"Yeap, this is the fifth one today."

"Really?" Mitch said, exchanging a glance with me.

Had we been wrong? Were all those things we

were worried about coincidences? Our plan had been to tell the deputy about all the weird near misses Mitch had had during the last few days, but we did that silent-married-communication thing we could do sometimes. He shook his head slightly and I knew he wanted us to keep those details to ourselves. I gave him a half-nod to let him know I agreed. If there were multiple dry ice bombs, then perhaps this wasn't a coordinated attack on Mitch. At least, that's what I thought he was trying to silently convey to me. The silent-married-communication thing didn't always work. In fact, sometimes we *completely* misread each other, but today I felt like we were on the same wavelength.

"Where were the other ones?" I asked.

"They weren't all in our jurisdiction—we cover the county, but let's see . . . it's my understanding that two went off at Taylor in base housing. One exploded in the North Dawkins Wal-Mart parking lot. It was left in a buggy and parked in the return area, and another was left in the lobby of an office park out by the interstate."

"Any sort of pattern?" Mitch asked as he waved away a gnat.

"No, sir, not that we can see right off, but I've got all your information and we'll contact you if anything comes to light. Most likely, it was kids. I will be glad when school starts again."

I shifted my shoulder blades to unstick them

from the fabric of my shirt. "You think they were all pranks?"

"Can't say at this point, ma'am, but school does start next week and there's always some juvenile mischief during the last days of summer. We'll coordinate with Taylor's security police and the North Dawkins Police Department." His face was ruddy from the heat and I knew he was ready to leave, but I asked, "Aren't you going to fingerprint the car?"

He smiled ruefully. "We're a small force, ma'am, and don't have the manpower or the money to fingerprint everything. Now, if this had been a carjacking or a robbery, well, that would be different."

"I see."

As the deputy drove away, dusk was deepening, but it hadn't cooled off yet. I pushed my bangs off my forehead as I said, "He might have taken fingerprints if we'd told him about the leaf blower and the tire blowout."

"I don't even have the leaf blower here right now and I handled it so much that I doubt there would be any other prints left on it besides mine. Same thing with my car. We've already touched both handles on the back doors on the car. We've probably smudged anything that was there, if there was anything to begin with."

"And the tire is gone, too, isn't it?" I asked, disheartened.

Mitch nodded. "I called the repair shop to see if they still had it, but it was picked up for recycling yesterday."

"Were we wrong? Maybe you've had a streak of bad luck."

"It's possible," Mitch said, but there wasn't much conviction in his voice.

The next morning when the alarm went off, I felt as if I'd pulled an all-nighter. Too bad I'd spent the whole time punching my pillow and doing clock checks every thirty minutes while Mitch twitched beside me deep in REM. Needless to say, I was not in the best of moods that morning and had practically growled at Mitch when he kissed me good morning. I felt slightly better by the time I'd had a shower and applied a little makeup. Mitch was ready to go by that time and leaned around the bathroom door frame, his keys and hat in his hands. "Safe to come in now? Feeling more human?"

"Marginally."

"You might think about coffee this morning. You look like you could use a cup."

"Thanks. Just the words of encouragement I need to hear today," I said as I applied a coat of mascara.

"Hey, I didn't mean it that way," Mitch said, backpedaling.

"I know, but I couldn't sleep last night. What are

we going to do?" I asked, looking at his reflection in the mirror.

"We're going to go about our day like we normally would. I'm going to go fly and you and the kids should do what you'd usually do. As far as we know, today's an ordinary day. You and the kids should be fine."

He meant that so far the attacks, if they were attacks, had been targeted at him. I rarely used the leaf blower and both the tire blowout and the dry ice bomb had involved his car, not mine. "That's not really a comfort," I said as I screwed the mascara brush into the tube and tossed it in a drawer. "Be sure to lock your car doors today."

"Will do," he said and gave me a quick kiss.

As he walked out of our bedroom, I noticed his squadron coin was on the dresser. I picked it up and ran quietly through the house. By some miracle, the kids were still asleep. Usually by this time Livvy had already dressed herself and was ready to "help" me fix breakfast. I heard a noise from down the hall, soft singing, and realized she was awake, but playing in her room.

I caught up to him in the garage, which was about fifteen degrees warmer than our house and sticky with humidity. "You forgot your coin," I said.

He glanced at it and frowned as he patted his pockets. "I've already got mine on me. Never leave home without it," he said as he fished it out of one of his flight suit pockets. He compared the two and handed the one I'd been holding back to me. "That's not the squadron coin. See the black on this side?" he said, pointing to a small area on the side with the hawk.

"But Denise has one exactly like it with the black area on the side with the hawk. I saw it when I went to her house. Are you sure they didn't update the coin and mail a new one to everyone?"

"No. The squadron doesn't mail coins."

"Well, someone mailed one to us and one to Denise."

My fingers closed around the coin and I gripped Mitch's arm. "And Dan got one in the mail, too."

Despite the heat of the garage, a coldness settled on me and I felt the hairs on the back of my neck stand up as I ran though the events of the last few days. "You've got to call him."

"Ellie—"

"Right now," I insisted. "Why didn't I connect it before? Don't you see? Three people have received these coins in the mail—Colonel Pershall, you, and Dan. Colonel Pershall's dead, someone took a shot at Dan, but his heat exhaustion probably saved him, and now you've had all these weird things happen to you." Mitch paused with his car door halfway open as I said, "Dan called yesterday to thank you for sending him a coin. I forgot to tell you about it. The dry ice explosion kind of dominated my thoughts last night. You didn't send it to him?"

"No. Are you sure it looked like this with the black on one side?" Mitch asked as he took the coin back for a closer look.

"I haven't seen it, but he described it and I'm pretty sure he mentioned three colors, yellow, blue, and black. I know Denise's coin looked exactly like this."

Mitch checked his watch and said, "I can't cancel now. I have to go." He returned the coin to me.

We both heard a rifle shot in the distance. Our gaze locked. "Starting early today, aren't they?" I said, trying to play it cool since the sound was obviously far away from us.

"Yep, it was from the wildlife area," Mitch confirmed, but grooves etched into his forehead as he frowned.

"Okay, you go on. I'll call Dan and ask him to take a picture of his coin and e-mail it to us. Then, if they're all the same," I took a deep breath and said, "I'll call Detective Waraday."

I was still thinking about the coins during the morning stroller brigade workout. I'd called Dan right after Mitch left this morning. I'd forgotten about the time change and I hoped that Dan had been awake enough to remember he'd had a conversation with me. If he thought my request was slightly odd, he hadn't said anything.

We crested the rise in the new area of the subdivision and paused for a biceps workout with elastic bands. We were slightly past the point where Dan had collapsed. I counted through the reps and tried not to think about what a scary sight it had been to see Dan whisked away in an ambulance. Tina counted down to the last repetition and we switched to working our triceps. Colonel Pershall, Mitch, and Dan. Why them? Why that combination? What did they all have in common?

Nothing.

Mitch and Colonel Pershall were in the military, but Dan wasn't. Dan and Mitch were related, but Colonel Pershall didn't even know Dan. They weren't even acquaintances. Mitch and Colonel Pershall were pilots. Dan worked in Internet technology. Besides the fact that they were all male, I couldn't find any common denominators. Mitch seemed to be the only link between the two.

I twisted the bands in my hands, thinking about those names, and suddenly had a thought. What if it was like one of Livvy's grouping problems—which one doesn't fit?

"Ellie? The bands?"

"Oh, here you go," I said and handed the bands to Tina, lost in thought.

"Are you all right?" she asked.

"Um . . . yeah. Just thinking. I have to make a phone call. I'll catch up with you at the next station," I said.

"Okay, ladies, let's enjoy the next flat section,"

Tina said and headed back to the head of the pack. The strollers streamed by me as I pulled out my phone and dialed Mitch's number.

He sounded distracted when he answered, so I said, "Are you busy right now?"

"The bread truck is here. We're about to step. Like the ringtone, by the way. What's going on?"

So he was going to play it cool now and pretend that he didn't care if I changed his phone, but I knew he couldn't be happy that "Feelings" announced he had a call.

I'd completely forgotten about his flight. The bread truck was a boxy truck that took them out to the plane. Now was probably not the best time to talk about my suspicions, but I wanted to bounce them off him and if I was right . . . well, he needed to know. I heard a shout in the background and said, "I was thinking about Dan and the coins, trying to figure out some connection between you, Colonel Pershall, and Dan, but I couldn't come up with anything."

"Yeah, me either," Mitch said.

"But what if we switch it around? What if one of you guys doesn't belong in the equation?" I ran my hand back and forth across the stroller handle.

I paused, waiting to see what he'd say.

"Probably Dan. I mean, he's my cousin and all, but I worked with Colonel Pershall, saw him every day, lived in the same city, and worked in the same place."

"Exactly," I said, glad that he'd drawn the same conclusion as I had. "What if one of the incidents was a case of mistaken identity? What if someone mistook Dan for you?"

There was silence on the line, but I knew I hadn't lost the connection. Finally, he said, "You think someone thought they were shooting at *me*?"

"As much as I'd like to say no, I think it all fits together. You jog nearly every day. You and Dan are the same height and build and both have short, dark brown hair. Even your mom thought she'd seen you—not Dan—leaving for your jog the afternoon of the family reunion. And, to top everything off, we were all wearing the same T-shirts, so there wouldn't have been any difference in the clothes, either."

"You really shouldn't sound so excited at the thought that someone was taking potshots at me."

"Mitch! I'm not excited. Well, okay, maybe a little bit, but it's only because it's a step toward figuring out what's going on." My voice sobered as I said, "You know the thought of someone trying to hurt you scares me to death." Nathan kicked his feet, impatient to get moving, which caused the stroller to move backward and forward. I released the brake and pushed with one hand.

"I know, but I'm fine right now and I intend to stay that way. We need to see that coin Dan got in the mail before we make any more assumptions. His coin might be completely different."

More noise from his end indicated he had to go. I said, "Call me when you land, okay? And fly safe."

"Always do," he said.

We said good-bye and I put the phone back in the basket of the stroller. I caught up with the group, but my thoughts were centered on Mitch and why someone would want to harm him and Colonel Pershall. I still couldn't work out that one.

Megan Fleet was trailing along, barely keeping up with the group. I picked up my pace and caught up with her, thinking it would be nice to have another friend in the neighborhood. School was starting and Abby and Nadia would be extra busy. I'd see less of them and I tended to get wrapped up in my own activities. Maybe it was time to make an effort to get to know Megan a little better. "How are you doing?" I asked, glad to see she returned for another stroller workout.

"Sore, but I keep telling myself it'll be worth it. I've got to get back into my size fours."

"Size four is long gone for me," I said with a laugh. "I just want to stay the size I am right now and not go up."

"Hey, did you see that?" Megan stopped and pointed to one of the completed but still vacant houses. A FOR SALE sign stood in a yard of dirt along with a few stubby plants. "That house with the red brick and the black shutters—I thought I saw a face in the window."

"Probably just a contractor or work crew."

"I don't know . . . we looked at that house. It's finished. It's probably just kids," she said with a shrug. "Last week, I saw some teenagers I didn't recognize in one of the empty houses. As soon as they spotted me, they cleared out." She glanced back at the house. "I always check out that house because we almost bought it. You know how it is when you buy a house. You're always comparing, trying to figure out if you got the best deal. I really hope the value holds in this neighborhood. I think we picked a bad time to buy."

"Why's that? Magnolia Estates is a good neighborhood and property values have gone up. We didn't buy, we're renting, but that's what the neighbors say," I said as Nathan's movements caused the stroller to bob back and forth again. Livvy was deep in a picture book and didn't care if we were moving or not.

"I wish we'd rented," Megan said dismally as we started walking again. "It looks like we're moving in the spring. Henry's tried to get a job at the wing. He was so sure he would get a PCA, but he got a PCS."

"Let's see, PCA," I managed to say between huffs as we took the next hill. I scrolled through my mental list of acronyms and translated the military talk. "That means Permanent Change of Assignment, right? So he thought he'd get another assignment here at Taylor at Wing Headquarters?" PCS stood for Permanent Change of Station, a move to a new base. So much for a new friendship. Oh well, if nothing else, the military had taught me to make the most of the time I had with people. Then there was always e-mail after the move.

"Yes. If we're lucky, we'll be able to break even on our house. If not . . ." Her voice trialed off and I smiled sympathetically. Buying a house when you're a military family is always a gamble. Will the market hold? Will property values go up enough in the short time you're in the house to make it worthwhile? If values drop, then renting looks more like a wise investment instead of throwing money away. Megan looked so depressed that I asked where they were going. Sometimes the new location is enough to cheer you up.

"It's the UAV squadron in the desert."

"Oh, too bad," I said as the road curved and we reached my favorite turn, which shifted the intense sunlight from our faces to our shoulders. Usually the words "the desert" referred to the Middle Eastern deserts, but this time Megan was talking about being reassigned to a base in the desert of the United States, specifically, Nevada. "How's Henry taking the assignment?" UAV,

Unmanned Aerial Vehicles, were touted as the future of the air force. They were control aircraft that gathered intelligence, even deployed missiles, and dropped psy op leaflets. Pilots flew them from remote locations on the ground through remote control and hated the assignments because it took them out of the cockpit. They wanted to fly a "real" plane. For years, a UAV assignment was considered the kiss of death to an aviator's career. I'd heard the military was shifting to special training courses that would allow nonpilots to train and then fly the drones, but pilots were still being assigned to fly the UAVs.

I glanced at her and now that the sun wasn't glaring in my eyes, I could see her better. Her mouth quirked down. "There's not much he can do at this point."

"Ab time," Tina announced and soon we were too out of breath to carry on the conversation.

When I returned from the stroller brigade workout later that morning, I was drenched in sweat and still stumped as to why someone would target both Colonel Pershall and Mitch. I fought off my worries and focused on keeping things as normal as I could for the kids. I slid a book on tape into the player and left Livvy with instructions to turn the pages when the chime sounded.

I managed to shower in record time and changed into my organizing work clothes—jeans, a short-sleeved navy shirt, and tennis shoes.

Organizing was dirty work. For initial appointments with potential organizing clients, I dressed in business casual, but once I switched to doing the actual work, helping people sift and sort through the accumulations of their lives, well, that required clothes that weren't dry clean only.

I checked the computer, but there wasn't an e-mail from Dan. I debated calling him again, but didn't, deciding I should give him until at least after lunch before I began pestering him.

The doorbell rang and Livvy jumped up and ran for the door, announcing, "Mom, Anna's here." Nathan chugged along in her wake, repeating, "An! An! An!" Obviously, they were heartbroken I was leaving them this morning. I gave the kids kisses and told Anna where I'd be.

"Got it, Mrs. Ellie," Anna said, addressing me in the traditionally Southern way, adding the title of Mrs. to my first name. With her soft accent, it sounded like "Miz" Ellie. She dropped a tote bag full of craft items on the table. "We'll have a good time." She turned to the kids and said, "Do y'all want to make sock puppets?" I left them practically jumping up and down with excitement.

I don't think they even noticed when I left the house. I'd been waiting for Nathan to go through the clingy-don't-leave-me stage, but I was beginning to think he'd skipped it altogether. Somehow my expectations about what my kids were going to do or how they were going to develop were always slightly off. Scratch that. If I was honest with myself, I was usually totally off base and they completely surprised me.

My organizing client, Stephanie, lived in a subdivision down the road from ours, but that was about the only similarity between the two neighborhoods. Regal Oaks dwarfed our neighborhood in size since a golf course was part of it and the houses were more like mini-mansions than the more modest homes in Magnolia Estates. The lawns were expansive, cut through with circular drives that bisected wrought-iron fences.

I spent the short drive to her house thinking about the coins. I didn't like the ideas that were popping into my head. I resolutely pushed those dark thoughts away. There was nothing I could do about it now and Mitch was right, worrying wasn't going to change anything.

I sent up a quick prayer for protection for him and our family, then I checked my phone as I pulled up in front of Stephanie's house. No messages or missed calls, which was good. I never worried about Mitch when he was flying. It was his job, so routine that I rarely even thought about it, but today I couldn't help counting the hours. I knew he was probably safer in the air than on the ground, but I would feel better when his flight was over. Five more hours until he was down.

Stephanie looked surprised to see me when she

opened the door. She raised her carefully sculpted eyebrows. "Ellie?"

"Hi. It's Wednesday. Eleven o'clock." She looked perplexed, so I added, "Our usual time?"

"Oh, that's right. I meant to call and cancel. I'm hosting a meeting this morning, but I'm sure you can carry on without me," she said, throwing the door open. "This is a perfect example of why I need you."

In the few years that I'd been a professional organizer, I'd found my clients fell into two categories, the reluctants and the affluents. Reluctant clients were embarrassed. They really wished they didn't need a professional organizer. They felt they shouldn't have let their lives get so disorganized. Affluents were at the opposite end of the spectrum. They were accustomed to hiring help for everything. They freely admitted their need for help without the least bit of guilt.

Stephanie definitely fell into the affluent category. She'd originally hired me at the beginning of the summer to organize her garage and pool house. When that project was finished, she decided she wanted to clean out the loft area at the top of her curved staircase. Designed with bookshelves across one wall, the area made a perfect reading nook. Stephanie's interior designer had placed two leather club chairs, a low table, and reading lamps in front of the bookshelves. In the year that Stephanie and her husband, an electric company executive, had lived here, the art objects and leather-bound books had been rearranged to make room for growing stacks of papers. Everything including bills, homework papers, bank statements, and school lunch menus had mushroomed from the lowest shelves and now teetered waist high. Stephanie had said, "I've decided I must do something about that mess of paperwork upstairs. I'd like to tackle that next."

Like the private school her children attended and the Lexus she drove, I had a feeling Stephanie considered me a status symbol. I'd heard her on the phone. "Darling, I can't talk right now. I have my professional organizer here." She did very little of the organizing. She flitted in and out of the room and made it quite clear that answering questions would be the extent of her involvement, which probably should have bothered me more than it did, but I figured it was one of the easiest organizing jobs I'd handled. She wasn't *that* unorganized. A few weekends and she could have sorted out her pool house and garage herself. Ditto for the paperwork in her loft. But if she wanted to pay me to do it, I'd certainly show up each Wednesday, do the work, and cash her checks.

"You go on," she said, nodding at the sweeping staircase. "I'll pop up to check on you. I have to finish the food and then change out of this old thing. "This old thing" was a designer hoodie, sweatpants, and white shirt. The T-shirt alone probably cost more than my whole outfit.

I went upstairs, passing vanilla-scented candles ringing an arrangement of fresh calla lilies on a marble-topped table in the entryway. Stephanie went in the dining room and began removing petit fours from a pink bakery box and putting them on a tray. I dropped my Kate Spade tote onto one of the club chairs. As far as handbags went, I could probably go toe to toe with Stephanie, if it came to a competition. I had a weakness for designer bags and I spent more of my earnings from my organizing jobs at online auction sites than I should. The tote was big enough to hold all my organizing paraphernalia. I pulled out my markers, sticky notes, garbage bags, and file folders, then I rotated my shoulders and got to work, picking up where I'd left off last week.

Stephanie trotted upstairs later to look over some papers I'd set aside for her. She'd changed into a pair of black pants and a sleeveless turquoise sweater with a red circular pin clipped on the collar. The clothes were casual, but I knew they hadn't come from the discount rack. She glanced through the papers and answered my questions. When the doorbell rang, she said, "Carry on. If you finish before we do, let yourself out through the kitchen."

The message was clear. Don't disturb us and don't be seen. The women began to arrive. The voices swelled and I could hear them exclaiming over the food. The voices moved to the living room as I sorted homework papers from utility bills. I whittled fives stacks of paper down to the essentials, clearing several shelves for Stephanie. My time was almost up. I labeled what I'd done, then began packing up supplies. I'd hoped the meeting would disband before I had to leave, but it looked like I'd have to try to sneak out. I hadn't been paying that much attention to the ebb and flow of voices. I'd assumed the meeting was for one of Stephanie's many charitable causes, but then I heard a voice I recognized, a breathy, child-like voice. I paused in the middle of my sorting as Carrie Kohl's voice floated up to the loft.

Tips for Busy, Budget-Minded Moms

Decluttering Your Schedule
- If you don't have enough time blocks for all your weekly activities, you're going to feel overwhelmed. Just like you have to declutter your home, sometimes you have to declutter your schedule. Approach the task as if you were thinning your closet. Purge your schedule, keeping the things you really need to do and the activities you enjoy.
- Look for ways to cut back or reduce hours spent on certain activities. Perhaps instead of volunteering every week at your kids'

school, you could volunteer for one-time special projects, like the book fair or field trips.

- Work schedules are often unmovable, but if you see an opportunity, ask if you can telecommute, even one day or one after-noon a week.
- Assess your kids' schedules as well because everything they do, you do. For your sanity, you might need to limit after-school activities. We all want our kids to be well rounded and have plenty of opportuni-ties. You can still let your kids try activities and keep your schedule from getting too packed. Look for short-term classes at com-munity colleges or parks and recreation cen-ters. These classes usually last a few weeks and will let your kids try activities. If they find something they like, you can look for a long-term class and work it into your schedule. If they hate the activity, you're not locked into a contract for a year. Some schools have after-school activities and clubs that run for a few weeks.

Chapter
Eleven

Carrie's wispy voice was unmistakable as she said, "I don't think we're doing enough."

This statement was met with a short silence and then a few protests. I thought it was Stephanie who said, "I understand your frustration but, overall, we're making progress. The photo in the newspaper—"

Carrie interrupted Stephanie. "I know the signs and marches are drawing attention, but we need to do more. There are people dying and we're sitting here in our comfy world, ignoring it. I think we should do something that will wake people up."

I walked over to the handrail at the edge of the loft and looked down at the group of women gathered in Stephanie's living room. The foreshortened view was an odd one, but I picked out Carrie right away. She stood beside several posters that were propped up along one wall. I shifted and managed to read a few of the posters upside down. "Peace Now" and "Bring Them Home" seemed to be the main theme. I squinted and tilted my head to read one of the more wordy ones, WE'RE NOT THE WORLD'S POLICE.

Another woman who had short gray hair and glasses said, "Carrie's right. We need something dramatic. A group of people with signs isn't enough to get the attention we need. Think about PETA, throwing red paint on people wearing fur, and Green—"

Stephanie's voice cut through the rising murmurs of the group and I was surprised at her unrelenting tone. "We're here to raise awareness, not to participate in exploits that will get our members arrested. Joyce, you know radical publicity stunts would do very little to persuade people to join our side, especially if they believe we're extremists. Our role in North Dawkins is to raise awareness and create an atmosphere where we can dialogue with people about military intervention. This is a conservative area and if we're thought of as fanatics we'll lose any chance we have to persuade people."

Carrie jumped in when Stephanie took a breath. "But how are we going to dialogue with people when no one knows we're here? We need something to put us on the map. Joyce and I have a plan to raise our profile. In fact, we did a little test run that was quite successful."

Stephanie cut in quickly, "Any activity has to go through the Peace Now Activities Committee. *And* it must follow our guidelines of nonviolence." Carrie opened her mouth to say more, but Stephanie swept on, saying, "With that in mind, let me remind you that our march last Saturday at Taylor Air Force Base was a success. We had a good turnout and even made the *North Dawkins Standard*."

"Sure we made the paper," Carrie said as she tossed her head to get her hair out of her eyes, "but how many people who work at the base saw us? We should have our march during the week. The base is almost deserted on weekends, so we still didn't have an impact on the base population."

Joyce chimed in. "Carrie's made an excellent point. On the newspaper issue, what we need is coverage in the Atlanta newspapers, not our local rag. That's where we should aim."

Carrie nodded her head emphatically.

Stephanie held up her hands. "Joyce. Carrie. Please, no more interruptions. Our strategy is not up for discussion. It's already laid out. We're focusing on our local area. Regional and national expansion will come in time, but we're building our base here in North Dawkins."

A few notes of music sounded from my cell phone and I lunged for it, cutting off "Maniac" as quickly as I could. A few curious faces had turned up at the noise, including Carrie's. I had a text message from Dan. He'd also sent me photos. I squinted at the pictures, but they were too small to see any details. The side of the coin with the replica of the patch had the same black area as Denise's coin. On the small screen of my phone, the black area was a blob and only grew fuzzier as I zoomed in on it. I sent the photos to my e-mail account at home and quickly packed my supplies. By the time I'd finished cleaning up and had left Stephanie a note about what I'd done this week, the noise level downstairs had risen. It sounded like the meeting was breaking up. I went down the stairs and slipped into the short passageway through the butler's pantry toward the kitchen.

"I told you she wouldn't get it." The words weren't whispered, but they were quietly spoken and I stopped short, instinctively realizing the people in the kitchen didn't want to be overheard. I backed up a step as Carrie's breathy voice continued, "She can't see past the idiotic guidelines." Heels clicked on the hardwood floor behind me and I knew that if I tried to backtrack and leave through the front door, I'd run into more of the women from Stephanie's meeting.

You wouldn't think it would be a big deal if my path crossed with one of the committee women, but only two weeks ago I'd heard Stephanie yelling at the landscapers because they'd interrupted a pool party she was hosting. She didn't want "the help" to be seen. I'd rather not lose a client, if I could help it, so I stayed put in the shadowy passageway. Maybe the women would clear out quickly.

I could still hear the women in the kitchen. "True. Well, we had to give it a try." The speaker took a few steps into my line of vision as she set her coffee cup down in the sink. I recognized the gray-haired woman with the glasses, Joyce, who'd been nodding in agreement with Carrie during the meeting. "Stephanie would have been a valuable ally since she's got so many connections in North Dawkins. It's a shame she's so close minded."

"We don't need her." Carrie's voice dropped even more. "I tried out my idea yesterday. So easy. I got everything I needed at Publix and no one suspected a thing. And, there's no way to connect us to it. Tomorrow we can set off a few—"

She broke off as more people entered the kitchen. The words "set off a few" seemed to ring in my ears. There were only a few things you "set off." Firecrackers and explosives being the two that came to my mind first. There was some chatter and clanking of plates and coffee cups, then all the women left the kitchen together. Once the room was empty, I waited a few beats, then shot through it like a mouse scurrying along a baseboard. I navigated through the garage and hurried to my minivan, which was parked on the street.

A wall of heat hit me as I climbed in the minivan. It felt like I could bake bread in there. I started the engine, cranked the A/C, and rolled the windows down a few inches to let some of the heat escape. I sat in the minivan chewing on my lip, considering what I should do. My stomach growled and I realized it was after one o'clock and I hadn't eaten, so I dug a few Hershey's kisses out of my tote and peeled back the foil. I always thought better when chocolate was part of the process.

It had sounded like Carrie and Joyce were planning to set off some explosions. A good citizen would report that to the police, but I was reluctant to call them right this moment. I chomped more melting chocolate. For one thing, I had about ten minutes before I needed to be back at home to relieve Anna, and I knew that it could take forever to get my information to the police and answer all the questions they'd have for me. The other factor that held me back was that I'd overheard snippets of conversation. What if I was wrong? And, I needed to look at the photos Dan had sent me. I might as well wait and see if my hunch about the coins was right. If I was right, I'd have to call Detective Waraday anyway and I could tell him about Carrie then.

As I watched the women drift toward their cars, I spotted Carrie and Joyce walking down the driveway. Carrie waved to her, called out, "See you tomorrow," and then drove away in a blue Accord. The older woman went to a beige minivan and drove in the opposite direction. At least it didn't sound like they were planning to "set off" anything right away.

After I'd paid Anna and settled the kids in their rooms for a "rest time"—they were way too grown-up to have a naptime—I looked at the pictures from Dan. They were excellent and on my computer I could see every detail. I compared the photos to the coin we'd received in the mail. The coins were exactly the same. Each one had an etching of the refueling jet on one side and a replica of the squadron patch on the opposite side with the hawk on the shield of yellow and blue. And each coin had a small black area on the blue section. I zoomed in and studied the black blob on the photograph, then got up and pulled a magnifying glass out of Nathan's bug-catcher kit. Even though the magnifying glass was rimmed in bright green plastic, it worked just fine and magnified the small daub of paint. It was a skull and crossbones.

Most people want to look younger than they are, but I suspect for those people who do actually look younger than their real age, it can be a real pain, especially when you're the head of the criminal investigation unit of the Dawkins County Sheriff's Office. Even though it had been over a year since I'd seen Detective Waraday, he still looked like he'd just received his high school diploma and tossed his cap in the air about an hour ago.

The kids were in their rooms so the house was fairly quiet and I found myself nervously tidying up construction paper and crayons from the kitchen island while he clicked through the pictures from Dan and compared them to the coin on the table. I hadn't had any lunch and a headache was beginning to gnaw at my temples. My stomach let out an audible growl and I decided it wouldn't be rude to eat in front of Detective Waraday if I offered him a sandwich, too.

I pulled out bread and sliced turkey. He turned down the sandwich, but accepted a glass of iced tea. It sat on the other end of the island, water beads gathering on the glass, as he focused on the computer. I poured myself another tall glass of iced tea and sat down to eat my sandwich.

When I'd called him fifteen minutes ago, I'd said my name and then to refresh his memory, I'd said, "You interviewed me when you were investigating the Jodi Lockworth case."

"I remember you, Mrs. Avery," he'd said and even with his Southern accent, the words had been curt. The fact that I knew about a slipup on his part during the earlier investigation probably didn't help endear me to him. I got the message that he didn't want to be reminded of that case, so I got right to the point and told him what I'd found and that it might be linked to Colonel Pershall's death. I'd expected tons of questions, but he'd only said, "I'm in the area. I'll be there in ten minutes."

Now he looked up and said, "I'll need a copy of these photographs."

"I can forward them to you," I said. He stepped

back. I dusted the crumbs from my fingers, feeling better since I'd had something to eat. I moved over to the chair and typed in his e-mail address as he gave it to me. He used a pencil from my desk to edge the coin into an evidence bag, then sat down at the island and pulled out a small note-book. "Now, tell me about the coins."

He stopped me several times to ask questions and clarify points. Finally, he said, "So we have three identical coins, sent to three separate people, each of whom has had some sort of accident in the past few days," he summarized. I'd told him about Mitch's accidents earlier.

I nodded, then added, "One of them fatal."

He didn't say anything, but stared at the photo of the coin on the computer monitor. "Where do you get these coins?"

"The squadron hands them out when someone in-processes, but you can buy them over the Internet. One of Mitch's old commanders had a specific coin made to hand out at his retirement ceremony."

"Where's the leaf blower?" he asked.

"One of Mitch's friends has it. He's having an electrician look it over." I wiped my hand over the counter, collecting a few stray crumbs.

"And I suppose the tire is in a pile at a service station somewhere, or has it already been scrapped to make a playground?"

"I'm afraid so," I said as I dropped the crumbs

in the sink. "We didn't realize anything was wrong until the dry ice explosion. You do have that, or what's left of it. A deputy came and took our statements after the explosion. We didn't make the connection about the coins until I saw Mitch's original squadron coin this morning and realized it was different from the one we'd received in the mail."

He looked up from his notebook. "Anything else?"

"Well, yes. Today I overheard a conversation." I repeated what Carrie had said. I also relayed what Mitch had told me about Carrie's unexpected reaction when he returned Ryan's daily planner.

When I got to the part about Carrie, his pen paused and without raising his head, he looked at me. "You think Carrie Kohl is behind the plastic bottle explosions and the coins? You think the two things are connected, that Carrie Kohl has some sort of vendetta against the squadron?"

"I don't know. It's possible. I'm just telling you what I know."

He dropped his gaze back to his notebook and, even though it was miniscule, I saw a slight shake of his head. He finished writing, then put the pen and notebook away with a finality that indicated he thought my information was less than important. "Mrs. Avery. I understand Mrs. Pershall is your friend, but some interesting evidence has come to our attention in that case."

So they'd uncovered Denise's divorce preparations.

Waraday continued, "Our investigation is focused exactly where it should be and trying to distract us with these minor incidents doesn't help Mrs. Pershall."

A flare of anger raced through me. My heart began to pound. "I'm not saying they are related, but shouldn't you investigate to find out?"

"Oh, we will, Mrs. Avery, but don't set your hopes on this. The most obvious answer is usually the right one." He took a sip of his tea and looked up, surprised. "This is excellent. Most people don't put in enough sugar."

"I grew up in Texas and my husband's from Alabama. We may have lived all over the U.S., but we know how to make iced tea." Still irritated with him, my voice was sharp.

He ignored the tone and drained the glass in a few gulps. "Yes, you do." He set it down with a click and stood. "We'll follow up on this information." He didn't say it, but his attitude clearly indicated not to expect any big changes.

His phone buzzed and he checked it. His whole demeanor shifted into a more serious mode. "Thank you for your time, Mrs. Avery," he said as he walked to the door. "We'll be in touch."

I watched him drive away, surprised that he turned right at the end of our street into the new section of the neighborhood, instead of left, which would have taken him out of Magnolia Estates. I frowned at the large pond at the end of our street. A few new homes broke the monotony of trees on the far side of the pond. I saw his unmarked car flit past the openings in the trees as he drove up the street's steep incline. The car was visible for a few seconds through a break in the pines at the top of the hill, then the solid barrier of trees blocked him from view. The way he'd left so quickly indicated he had some place he needed to be, but why would that be in the nearly deserted new section of our neighborhood?

I heard a soft scraping sound behind me and turned to see Rex slinking into the kitchen with my precious blue scarf dangling from his mouth. A long string of blue ran from it back to the basket in the living room where I'd been stashing the project when I wasn't working on it.

"Rex!" I yelled. He dropped it immediately and made for his kennel, his head low.

I raced over and carefully picked up the scarf, like it was an accident victim. I felt like I should call for an ambulance. All those hours of work and now it was full of holes and dog slobber.

I picked up the phone and dialed Denise's number. When she answered, I said, "I have a knitting emergency."

"Bring it over," she replied without hesitation.

The garage door rattled up at the usual time that afternoon and I breathed a sigh of relief. Mitch had called me when he landed to let me know his flight was over and that he was heading home.

He opened the door and there was the usual chaos for a few minutes with Rex trotting down the hall, barking, and Livvy and Nathan shouting, "Dad's home!" When everything had calmed down and I shooed the kids outside to play in the sandbox, I turned and saw Mitch checking out the coin photographs on the computer.

"They're the same," he said flatly as he clicked the mouse.

"I know. I called Waraday. He took ours. I told him about Denise's, but no one's been by her house to pick hers up. I had a knitting disaster. Basically, Rex ate my scarf, so I went over to Denise's after naptime and she helped me salvage what I could."

I'd calmed down enough that I could talk about it without clenching my fists and I thought I was being very reasonable, but then Mitch, his face deadly serious, said, "And were you able to save it?"

I punched his arm and said, "Okay, I know it's only knitting, but I worked hard on that scarf and to see it strung out across the living room carpet was upsetting, but, yes, Denise was able to help me fix it."

"Well, thank goodness."

I ignored his mock seriousness and continued, "I was going to call her anyway and let her know about the coins. I'd want to know if the police were on the way to my house, but it doesn't look like Waraday's taking the coin thing too seriously. No one came by to look at her coin while I was there. Although, Waraday did want to know where the tire and the leaf blower were, so maybe he'll follow up with that."

Mitch poured himself a glass of iced tea and said, "I've got the leaf blower in the car."

"And? Did Jeff's friend find anything?"

"It was rigged so that it would deliver a shock when it was turned on." The words came out reluctantly.

I sat down on the nearest bar stool, feeling a little lightheaded. "Someone really is out to get you," I said in amazement. "You're the only one who uses it."

Mitch swallowed some tea and nodded. "I know."

I ran my hands over my forehead and said, "Do you think Carrie would have done something like that?" I relayed what I'd overheard at Stephanie's house and said, "Somehow I can see Carrie setting off those plastic bottle bombs—she's so angry. I think she'd like to see the destruction, but I have a hard time picturing her breaking into the shed and rewiring the leaf blower. Would she even know how to do that? I know I wouldn't."

"She's a computer engineer, right?" Mitch asked and I nodded. He shook his glass and the ice cubes rattled. "Well, if she's got a degree in engineering, she knows something about wiring and it probably wouldn't be too hard to apply what she knows about computers to a leaf blower. They're not that complex. Certainly not as complex as a computer."

Mitch drained the last of the iced tea, rinsed his glass, and put it in the dishwasher, all his movements mechanical, his concentration focused inward.

"Are you okay?" I asked. Mitch wasn't usually so intensely focused and preoccupied. He was all about going with the flow and relaxing. "Things will work out" was usually his motto, but right now he looked edgy and tense.

He shoved the dishwasher door closed and turned to me. "I don't like being backed into a corner."

"I know. What are we going to do?"

He sighed in frustration and came around the island. "Nothing," he said. I wrapped my arms around him and nestled my head into his shoulder as he said, "There's nothing we can do, except wait."

Chapter
Twelve

S tay home?" he said in a tone that indicated my idea was as ridiculous as if I'd suggested he should fly his refueling jet to the moon. "Why would I do that?"

"Because someone's trying to hurt you." I didn't add, "Duh!" to the end of the sentence, but I wanted to. Early morning sunlight pressed through the plantation blinds, throwing long shadows across the ceiling. I'd been awake for about half an hour, watching the room gradually lighten and thinking about everything that had happened.

Mitch turned off the alarm and said, "Ellie, I can't cower here at home. I have to go to work."

"Why? Why can't you stay home? You've got leave. You could take a few days."

"I haven't put in for it and I can't stay here indefinitely. We don't know how long this is going to last. It could go on for weeks and I have to go to work. You know, make money and all that." He said it rather flippantly, but I knew he had a point. It was his income that paid most of our bills and even though he did have plenty of leave days racked up, they wouldn't last forever.

"Besides," he said in a more serious tone as he clicked on the lamp, "if we're right and whoever's doing this is connected to the squadron and I suddenly don't show up for days and days, it'll tip them off that we've figured out that I'm a target."

I rubbed my eyes. "But how can you be on your guard every minute? You can't."

"No, I can't, but there's no guarantee that I'm safer here, either. In fact, nothing's actually happened to me at work." His words slowed down and he said thoughtfully, "Which is interesting because it means that the person doing these things doesn't want to attack me directly. At the squadron, surrounded with people all day, is probably one of the safest places for me to be."

"I don't quite agree with that logic. It sounds good, but it doesn't feel right," I said as I punched the pillow into place under my head. I had ten more minutes before I had to start my day.

"I know." He kissed me and said, "I promise you, I'll be careful. I'll take a different route to work and check out my car. I'll put those threat avoidance training classes I've taken into action. Today's a half-day anyway."

"Why?"

"Colonel Pershall's funeral is this afternoon," he said as he pulled his "blues" uniform, the service dress uniform of dark blue pants and light blue shirt, out of the closet and set up the ironing board. Mitch always did his own ironing. Apparently, my ironing skills weren't quite up to military standards.

"Right. I'd forgotten with all the first-day-of-school excitement," I said, watching him take the plastic dry cleaning cover off the dark dress coat with his silver wings and lines of ribbons. Mitch only wore the coat for special occasions, like promotions and funerals.

Despite my lingering doubts about the safety of it, Mitch had gone on to work, but I'd seen him do a careful walk-around of his car. He even checked the undercarriage before he started it. That image of him shifting around on the garage floor told me he was taking this whole situation as seriously as I was. I just hoped he was right about being safe at work.

Livvy marched down the hall ahead of Nathan and me, leading the way to her classroom. There had been a moment in the school parking lot when she first climbed out of the minivan when a look of nervousness crossed her face. Cars had over-flowed the parking lot and late arrivals were parking up and down the neighborhood street in front of the school. Masses of parents with chil-dren in tow were flowing into the building. Once we were inside, Livvy regained her composure and confidently said, "It's down here, Mom." The memories from last week's Meet Your Teacher Night had obviously kicked in and she followed the blue floor tiles to the kindergarten wing. I held Nathan's hand and his short legs pumped double time to keep up with the pace. Fresh paint mingled with the unmistakable smell of pancakes coming from the cafeteria.

We entered Mrs. Ames's kindergarten classroom where kids and parents were milling around. Mrs. Ames had told us on Meet Your Teacher Night that she'd been teaching for thirty-two years and loved kindergarteners. She had the figure of Mrs.

Claus and wiry brown hair threaded through with gray. I captured several pictures of Livvy beside her desk before Mrs. Ames announced, "Students, please line up to get your name tags." The kids scurried into a wobbly line.

Nathan pulled on my hand and whispered loudly, "Where's my sticker?"

I swung him up on my hip and said, "Those are name tags for the kids in the class."

His lower lip protruded. "But I want a sticker, too."

Mrs. Ames and her assistant quickly sorted out the name tags. Then Mrs. Ames said, "Parents, thank you so much for coming in today. We're very happy you're here and we're so glad to have such a supportive group of parents. We have a lot of learning to do today and it's time for us to get started. Students, please sit criss-cross applesauce on the carpet. We're going to start the day with a story." She showed them the book, *The Kissing Hand*, and they moved to the carpet. Livvy didn't even wave. She was focused on getting a seat close to the rocking chair. Mrs. Ames's assistant began shooing the parents to the classroom door.

I edged to the door and Nathan said, "I want to hear the story."

"We have to go," I whispered as one of the kindergarten students started to cry. Mrs. Ames's assistant moved to the red-faced little boy and I edged to the door, watching to see if the tears would infect Livvy, but she was fine.

"Why does Livvy get to stay?" Nathan whined. "I want to stay, too."

"We have to go," I said quietly again and Nathan broke into a wail. "I want Livvy!" Fortunately, he wasn't making quite as much noise as the boy in Livvy's class, so I scooted out the door and hurried down the hall with Nathan's howl trailing over my shoulder.

I tried to explain that Livvy had to go to class by herself and that Nathan and I would have time together, but two-year-olds don't want explanations and reasoning, they want what they want and they want it *now*. We made it to the car and Nathan shifted from all-out tears to a hiccupy, sniffy cry. I really hadn't seen this coming. I guess I should have. Livvy and Nathan spent all their time together except for a few play dates Livvy had with other kids this summer. They'd been nonstop companions. With his major cries subsiding, I felt my throat tighten as the full impact of the day hit me.

Everything would be different now. It was a new stage for our family. Since this school had all-day kindergarten, Livvy would be there seven hours, the majority of her day. Things were going to shift in her life and mine, too. I blinked away the sheen of tears that threatened to blur my vision. I wouldn't know *everything* that was going on in her life now. She'd have new experiences that I wouldn't be a part of and if she had problems, I wouldn't be able to fix them for her. I knew it was a good thing she was going to kindergarten, but I couldn't help feeling a bit sad about the transition.

I sighed as I pulled into the garage, thinking what a morose pair Nathan and I made. I made us a snack of animal crackers and apple juice and read Nathan his favorite book about trucks. Rex seemed to sense our mood. He curled up and draped his head across my feet. Despite the heat of the day, I liked the weight of Rex's furry jaw on my toes and Nathan's sweaty body snuggled in my lap. Nathan's tears dried up and by the end of the book he was making vrooming noises as we turned the pages. We closed the book and I kissed the top of his head. "See, this isn't too bad, is it?"

And it wasn't. It would be good for me to have more one-on-one time with Nathan, something he'd never had, and kindergarten would be good for Livvy. She'd make new friends and learn all those important things that you need to know for school, like how to wait in line and sit crisscross applesauce.

Nathan and I spent the morning together building with his blocks. I only called to check on Mitch once. Anna arrived at noon to stay with Nathan while I went to the funeral. Since Anna was home-schooled, her mom allowed her to babysit during the day if she was caught up on her work, so she could save money for college. I figured I'd already contributed enough to her college fund to cover at least one semester. Nathan had bounced back from his crying jag and was delighted to learn he'd have Anna all to himself for several hours.

Once through the gate and on the base, I turned into base housing. Denise had called and asked if I'd pick up a picture of Colonel Pershall from her house. She wanted to display it at the chapel. "I walked off and left it on the coffee table," she'd said distractedly. "There's a huge blowup of Lewis's official photo by the casket, but I wanted a picture of him out of his uniform, in casual clothes, to put beside the condolence book. I wanted to take it to the reception at the O Club, too."

I told her not to worry. I'd pick it up and bring it to the chapel and make sure it was transferred to the reception.

"Thanks, Ellie. That's one less thing I have to remember and, at this point, I need all the help I can get. Please keep an eye on it for me. That's the only recent photo I've got of him. We kept saying we were going to have a new portrait taken, but never got around to it." She'd given me instructions on where to find a key hidden in the carport since she and her sister were already at the chapel.

I wondered how Livvy was doing. Was she

having fun? Had she made a friend to play with at recess or was she spending it by herself? Seven hours seemed like a long time. As I walked into the carport, I brushed down the skirt of my sleeveless black dress when the breeze caught it. It was a warm, blustery day and I had to tuck my hair behind my ears to keep it out of my eyes as the wind tossed it into my face. My heels clicked across the concrete of the carport and I adjusted my stride to cover a smaller area. It felt like forever since I'd worn heels, but it had been only a few years since I'd dressed up Monday through Friday when I'd worked in a public relations firm. Wearing the mom uniform of casual clothes like jeans and T-shirts had spoiled me.

I found the key nestled between two empty flowerpots on the third shelf of a shelving unit in the carport, just where Denise had said it would be. I unlocked the kitchen door and left it propped open with the key in the lock. This would only take a second. I went through the kitchen into the living room and picked up the picture, a framed eight by ten, from the coffee table. Colonel Pershall was smiling widely as he leaned against his sporty red car on a bright fall day with one arm looped around Denise's shoulders. I stared at it for a moment, then I heard a faint sound from inside the house. I tilted my head. It hadn't been the creak or groan of the house settling, but something different, something that would have been a normal sound and wouldn't have even registered, except that no one was supposed to be in the house. I didn't think Denise had any pets. Maybe she had a cat that I hadn't seen on my occasional visits to her house. A very shy cat?

I heard it again and this time I identified it—a drawer closing. Definitely not a cat. I gripped the photo to my chest and turned toward the sound, which had come from the back of the house. I could see the short hallway that led to the bedrooms. A shadow moved across the doorway of the room Denise used as a home office.

I guess I hadn't made much noise when I came inside. I hadn't intentionally been trying to be quiet, but I was now. I took a slow step back, relieved that no floorboards creaked. A deep voice muttered a curse as another drawer closed and yet another was yanked open.

Two cautious steps brought me to the kitchen. I didn't know who was in the house and I didn't want to find out. I'd heard about thieves that targeted homes during funerals since the day and time when no one would be home were listed so conveniently in the paper. I didn't know if that was happening here or if it was something connected with Colonel Pershall's murder, but I wasn't going to wait around to find out. First order of business was to get out of the house.

"Ah, finally," the words were spoken in a sigh of relief in what I could clearly hear was a masculine voice. I scooted into the kitchen and felt a draft of air whoosh past me. The back door, only half-open, wavered in the gust, then slammed shut.

I froze and all sounds from the back of the house stopped. I darted across the kitchen, not caring if I made a noise. I just wanted out. I twisted the door-knob, wrenched the door back, and was on the step leading to the carport when I heard a puzzled voice behind me. "Mrs. Avery?"

It was the "Mrs. Avery" that stopped me. I didn't think thieves or bad guys were that polite. I twisted around as I backed away, then came to a standstill. I recognized the shaved head, dark eyebrows, and small dark eyes. "Colonel Barnes?" Despite his size and intimidating appearance, I wasn't afraid. When you see a familiar face instead of the expected ski-masked or hooded figure, it's almost a relief. And he looked embarrassed, not threatening or angry. "What are you doing here?" I asked, then realized that no matter how comfortable it felt to see someone I knew instead of a stranger, the best choice was still to leave.

I backed up a few more steps and was clear of the carport. I'd parked in the driveway, but hadn't driven inside it, so now I was even with the hood of the minivan. I pulled my keys out of my pocket as he lifted a sheaf of pages and said, "I needed to pick up some paperwork and didn't want to disturb Denise today."

My heart was still thumping, but it had slowed down a notch. His explanation sounded reasonable. Except . . . why would he be cursing and slamming drawers? Maybe he had a temper and exploded when the smallest thing went wrong?

I clicked the remote unlock feature on my keychain and opened the driver's side door. "How did you get in? The door was locked when I got here."

"Same as you, I imagine," Colonel Barnes said over his shoulder as he pulled the kitchen door closed and twisted the key that I'd left in the lock. "I used the key." He pulled it out, walked to the shelves, and replaced it between the flowerpots where I'd found it.

"But it was between the flowerpots when I got here."

"Why are you here?" he countered, stepping out of the shadow of the carport into the sunlight. He paused at the edge of the carport, squinting in the light as he untucked his hat from his belt and put it on.

I held up the framed photo. "Denise asked me to pick this up."

The wind buffeted the car door against me and I thought I saw a look of relief cross his face, but it was hard to tell since the wind flipped my hair over my eyes. I pushed it back as he said, "I unlocked the door, then put the key back. I didn't want to walk off with it. I did that last Christmas when Lewis and Denise were out of town. Bonnie was mighty upset with me the next day when she came by to bring in the mail for them." He pointed to the door with the papers. "It has a night latch that locks when you close it."

"Oh. I didn't know that," I said. "Well, I'd better go."

I climbed in the minivan and backed out of the driveway, wondering where Colonel Barnes's car was. There wasn't one on the street. I drove slowly past him, then watched him in my rearview mirror. Since the speed limit in base housing is fifteen miles an hour, he was walking almost as fast as I was moving. About three houses down the street, he turned up a driveway and went inside a house. Of course, he lived here—that's why his car wasn't out front.

It's a good thing the speed limit was so low because I was thinking furiously and barely moving as a result. Should I call Denise and tell her Colonel Barnes was rifling though the office in her house? Surely now was not a good time. I decided to wait until after the funeral was over, then mention it to Denise.

To get to the base chapel, I took a different route through base housing, one that took me past Carrie's house, and I couldn't help but stare at it as I went by. There was nothing out of the ordinary about it. It looked exactly like the other houses, a small ranch house with an attached carport.

The car parked at the curb on the far end of the

street caught my eye because it was a small Nissan, the same model as Mitch's car. Then I did a double take as I passed it.

It *was* Mitch's car. I could tell because he was in it. What was he doing?

I made a lumbering U-turn at the end of the street and parked behind him. I marched up to the idling car and stopped at the passenger door. The automatic door locks clicked to unlock the car. I yanked the door opened and leaned down. Mitch's face was a mixture of guilt and irritation. "This is careful?" I demanded. "Sitting on a deserted residential street in the middle of the day? Alone?"

The irritation won out as he said, "If you're going to yell at me, at least get in the car. You'll draw less attention that way."

I didn't move. "Why?"

He lowered his voice as if that would motivate me to do the same. "Because if someone is yelling in the street it might tip off Carrie that someone is watching her house."

"You're watching Carrie's house?" I asked more quietly, not because I was worried about drawing attention, but because I wasn't sure I'd understood Mitch.

"Yes. Now, would you get in the car?"

I didn't move. I didn't like his peremptory tone.

He leaned closer and added, "Ellie, please." His voice was more pleading and less bossy, so I slowly slid in the seat and closed the door.

"What's going on here? Working out of your car today?" I asked archly. It looked like he'd been there for a while. An open laptop was propped up against the steering wheel, his cell phone sat on a stack of papers on the dashboard, and a half-empty bottle of Dr. Pepper rested in the cup holder. He reached in the back and dragged his soft-sided lunch box into the front seat. I'd insisted on packing his lunch this morning. I'd figured with all the strange things going on, it was better for Mitch to eat something that I'd prepared rather than something he bought. You know, just in case.

"Yes. CBTs," he said as he took out the turkey sandwich I'd made for him. CBT was short for Computer Based Training. Mitch had several training lessons he had to complete using the computer. Sometimes he did the computer training at work in the squadron. Other times, he brought the laptop home or took it on a trip to complete the training. "Had lunch yet?" he asked.

I took a sandwich half and said, "No, I haven't. And no cracks about how cranky I get when I haven't eaten. This has nothing to do with me and everything to do with you."

He'd been poised to say something, but changed his mind. We ate in silence for a few minutes as he tapped a few keys on the laptop. I said, "So. Technically, you're working?"

"There's no technically about it. I am."

"Mitch," I said with a sigh. "You do realize how vulnerable you are here?"

He looked at me for a moment, then said, "This is why I didn't tell you. I know how you worry. No, wait, before you say anything else, hear me out." His gaze held mine.

"There have been plenty of opportunities for someone to hurt me. I've gone jogging for the last three nights. That's the ideal time. That's when I'd do it, if I were trying to take me out. I'm alone and I've been jogging through the new part of the development. It's mostly deserted out there. But nothing has happened to me. This street is a whole lot safer than that situation. It's the middle of the day in a residential neighborhood, a neighborhood that's on base."

"Granted, it's probably the safest neighborhood in all of North Dawkins, but I don't like it. You're still sitting here alone. Bad things happen on base, too."

"I know," he said, his voice somber. "I'm only doing this because the police haven't done anything with Denise's coin. No one's even been by to pick it up."

"How do you know that?" I asked and realized I was pointing my half-eaten sandwich at him accusingly. I retracted my hand and took a bite of the sandwich.

"I called and asked her this morning. They're not taking it seriously."

"So you decided to take things into your own hands and come out here and watch Carrie's house?"

"Yes, I did," he said calmly, and when I would have said more, he added, "And, don't tell me you wouldn't do the same thing, if the situation were reversed. I know you and you would do the same thing. In fact, you *have* done the same thing."

I swallowed my words. He was right. I had done quite a bit of sleuthing on my own and I'd usually tried to keep Mitch in the dark about it because I knew he wouldn't want me to do it and he'd worry about me.

He continued, "I think you're right, that something is going on with Carrie. She may have sent the coins, but if the police aren't going to pursue it, then the only way we're going to find out what's going on is to check up on her ourselves." Mitch held out a bag of Sun Chips. "Truce?"

"Okay," I said reluctantly as I took one out of the bag. I was usually the one arguing for action with Mitch lobbying to let the officials handle things. I wasn't sure I liked my new position, but I didn't want Mitch to get hurt. On the other hand, I'd never been one to wait around for someone else to do things. "With one condition—keep me in the loop. I want to know what you're doing."

"Deal," he said with only the tiniest hesitation as he carefully selected a chip.

"Have you seen anything?" I asked.

"Nothing more interesting than kids going to school and dog walkers. This really has got to be one of the most boring neighborhoods," he said with a sigh. "So why are you here?"

I told him about the picture and said, "Colonel Barnes was there when I got there."

"In the house?"

"Yes." I reached for another chip. "He said he was picking up some paperwork and didn't want to bother Denise today. Apparently, he and Bonnie checked the mail for the Pershalls when they were out of town so he knew where the key was. Do you think that's a little odd?"

"Yeah, especially if she didn't know he was coming over at all. I wouldn't want someone inside our house if we weren't home."

"That's what I thought. I'll tell Denise about it today after the funeral. Megan, Henry's wife— you remember her from the last squadron cookout, don't you? Medium height, really fair with whitish blond hair and the new baby? She's joined the stroller brigade. She told me that Henry thinks Colonel Barnes will be the next squadron commander."

Mitch shrugged one shoulder. "Could be, but it's hard to predict stuff like that. He might get it, sure, but it's not like it's a foregone conclusion that the D.O. will step into the commander slot. I think that's a decision the higher-ups at the command level make."

"Denise said there was some sort of rivalry between those two. And remember, he was one of the people she thought might have something against Colonel Pershall," I said, dusting the crumbs from my fingertips.

Mitch stared down the street, thoughtfully. "I know Colonel Barnes is ambitious. He'd love to be squadron commander because it would help him get promoted to general—he even jokes about it, saying things like, 'When I'm a general you won't get away with things like that.' He's always laughing, but people don't joke about things like that unless it's something they've thought about."

Mitch didn't talk about becoming a general someday. In fact, it was usually the opposite. "That's true, you never joke—or even talk—about being a general," I said.

Mitch was still staring at Carrie's house, but when my words registered he said, "That's because it's not going to happen. There's too much politics involved for me to even get to that level." He went back to studying the street. "But would Colonel Barnes kill Colonel Pershall? I don't know. They go way back—roommates at the Academy, I think."

"I guess the obvious thing would be to find out what he was doing last weekend, if he was even in town." I pushed my bangs off my forehead. Even with the windows down and the blustery day, the temperature inside the car was uncomfortable. I pulled a piece of paper, a flyer that someone had left on the car advertising tax preparation, out of the pocket on the door and began fanning my face.

"Shouldn't be too hard. I can check the schedule." Mitch reached for the ignition. "Want me to turn the air conditioner on?"

"No, that's okay," I said as a breeze swept through the open windows. "If Colonel Barnes murdered Colonel Pershall, why would he target you, too?"

"I have no idea," Mitch said as he crumpled the chip bag, frustration obvious in his tone. "It's not like I'm in competition with him for the commander slot. I'm way down the rung from him on that ladder. Maybe it's not me, specifically. Maybe he's got some sort of grudge against military personnel in general. Maybe it's a random thing. Or, what if we're wrong and Carrie didn't place the dry ice bombs? Maybe Colonel Barnes did."

"I don't know," I said, fanning slower as I worked out my thoughts. "The dry ice bombs could have been random, but the other things were pretty specifically aimed at you. And he lives on base. If he wanted to target military folks, he's got plenty right in his backyard—literally. Why would he go all the way out to our house and sabotage the leaf blower and possibly your tire? Have you had a run-in with him? Made him mad?"

"Not that I know of. We haven't even flown together for, man, I don't know how long.

Months, probably. I do see him in the squadron, but that's usually passing in the halls or maybe at a commander's call."

"There's got to be something," I said. My fanning created a tiny breeze, lifting strands of my hair up and floating them around my face.

"Well, I don't know what it could be, but I'll look at his schedule for last weekend."

I checked the time. "I should go. The funeral starts soon."

"I know," Mitch said and shut down the laptop.

"Are you going to stay here?" I asked, eyeing his blue coat hanging in the back. I didn't think attendance at the funeral was mandatory, but I doubted Mitch would want to miss it.

"No. Gary Donahue—" he broke off.

I took my hand off the door handle. There was movement on Carrie's porch. She was walking carefully down the steps. "Doesn't look like she's going to the funeral," I said. She wore a red T-shirt, jeans, and a baseball cap and was carrying several pieces of poster board. She deposited those in the backseat of her car, then returned to the house.

Mitch dialed a number on his cell phone. "Gary. Mitch here. It looks like that little project I mentioned—well, I might need you to meet me."

I could hear Gary's response clearly in the confined space of the car. "Let me know the place and I'll be there. Today's my day off."

Gary Donahue was a friend from church. He was a police officer in North Dawkins and a part-time reservist in the air force, which meant he worked one weekend a month. They hung up and I asked, "Gary's backing you up on your surveillance?"

Mitch nodded. "I can't stay here all day. I do have to show up at the squadron. I called him this morning and talked to him after Denise said no one had picked up her coin. Gary says there's something going on in Dawkins County that's tying up most of the law enforcement personnel. He couldn't give me any details, but he said that's probably one reason nothing's been done. I told him if no one else was going to check up on Carrie, then I would, and he offered to relieve me during the funeral. Said I was only taking him away from mowing the yard."

There was a short silence, then Mitch said in a deliberately casual voice, "By the way, I heard some interesting news about the investigation. The toxicology report said Colonel Pershall had a drug in his system—I've forgotten the name—but it was similar to those date rape drugs. The killer probably used it to get an advantage over Colonel Pershall because he was such a big guy."

I frowned. "I don't suppose Gary is your source on this?"

He switched his gaze from the house to my face and gave me a significant look, then refocused on Carrie's house.

"Okay," I said, taking his silence as a yes. "Why would Gary give you that kind of info?"

"Oh, come on, Ellie. You've twisted a few arms in the past, too, so you could find out what was happening on the inside of an investigation. The info won't go farther than me."

He was right. I'd convinced a few well-connected friends to share tidbits of info with me in the past, but I couldn't help teasing him a little. "You told *me*, though. Maybe you're not so discreet after all."

Even though he kept his face in profile, I could see a hint of a smile as he said, "You're my wife. Telling something to me is like telling you. I don't want you accusing me of holding out on you. I figure the more we know, the better. And," he swiveled his head slightly, "I know I can trust you implicitly."

"True. I am the soul of discretion." I smiled back at him, then turned serious. "I wonder how the murderer got Colonel Pershall to take the drug?"

"Traces of it were found in one glass at the golf course restaurant. Five Pines was celebrating its anniversary by serving mint juleps to members and guests all weekend. Colonel Pershall's golfing buddy says free mint juleps were delivered to their table, but he didn't notice the server. Couldn't even say if it was a man or a woman. They found a black shirt with the Five Pines logo in a trash can near the restaurant."

"So that's what the waiters wear at the restaurant? Black shirts?" I asked, switching the fan to my other hand. "Did you and Jeff go to the restaurant when you played there?"

"We did. It was crazy. Yeah, everyone who works there wears the same thing, black polo shirt, black baseball cap, and khaki pants."

"So someone could blend in pretty easily if they were in the company uniform?" I said thoughtfully. "And you said it was busy?"

Mitch nodded. "We won't go there again. It was packed—Saturday afternoon and all." Mitch shifted a bit and said, "If someone was dressed like an employee, it wouldn't be hard to slip in the restaurant, add something to a drink, and deliver it to their table. It's the kind of place where one person takes your order, but a different person brings your food."

"Who was his golfing buddy?"

Mitch shrugged as he slipped the laptop into its case. "Don't know."

I made a mental note to ask Denise if she knew who Colonel Pershall had been golfing with that day, then said, "Really? You mean our very own Deep Throat wouldn't tell you more?"

"Isn't that enough?" Mitch's gaze sharpened. Carrie emerged from the house with a backpack slung over her shoulder. She locked the front door, let the screen bang shut behind her, and trotted quickly to her car.

Tips for Busy, Budget-Minded Moms

Whenever you can, consolidate tasks to make more time in your schedule.

- Don't run errands every day. Save the errands and do as much as you can at one time.
- Fold laundry while watching your favorite television show.
- Bring work/tasks with you to children's activities. You can get a lot done while waiting in the carpool line or at swim practice.
- Add a little relaxation to your commute by listening to books on tape.

Chapter Thirteen

"What will you do now?" I asked.

"Follow her," he said, fastening his seat belt. "I'll call Gary when she stops and have him keep an eye on her."

I didn't want to leave Mitch, but I had to get to the funeral. I still had the photo of Colonel Pershall in my van and I'd promised Denise I'd get it to the chapel, so I really should get there early to get it in place before the mourners arrived.

Mitch saw me hesitating and said, "Trust me?"

I'd trusted Mitch for years. We'd spent a lot of our marriage apart with him jaunting off to different parts of the world and I'd decided early on that I had to trust him. I knew some wives who constantly checked up on their husbands when they were away and always suspected trouble, but I'd vowed not to do that. Mitch *was* trustworthy. "You know, that's one thing I've never worried about. Now's not the time to start," I said as Carrie's car rolled out of the driveway.

"I'll be at the funeral. I may be late, but I'll be there," Mitch said.

"I'll save you a spot at the back."

I pulled on the handle, but he put a hand on my arm and said, "Wait until we see which way she goes."

Carrie backed into the street, her car pointed in our direction.

"Down," Mitch said, but I was already scrunched over.

The car surged by us and we cautiously popped our heads back up. "Okay, she's turned," Mitch said and then gave me a rather lingering kiss.

"You're going to lose her," I said, a bit breathless.

"Nope. Base speed limits, remember? Plenty of time." He smiled as I stepped out of the car, then he spun the wheel into a U-turn and was off.

I hurried to the van and executed my own U-turn, or I tried. A car parked on the opposite side of the street forced me to make a three-point turn. A minivan isn't the ideal choice for shadowing another car. Good thing Mitch was doing the tailing. When I finally got to the corner, I could see Carrie's blue Accord at the four-way stop at the edge of base housing. Mitch was hanging back with another car between him and Carrie.

Carrie turned right at the next street. It ran the length of the base and would end at the front gate. I watched Mitch let another car slide between him and Carrie before making the turn.

I signaled for my turn—the base cops are sticklers for obeying traffic rules—and turned into the chapel parking lot past the sign that listed the service times for Protestant and Catholic services. I knew there were also services for other faiths, including Jewish and Muslim, but they worshiped in other chapel buildings down the street. Like most of the other buildings on base, the chapel was built with red brick and if you didn't notice the small steeple almost hidden among the magnolia trees and the high stained-glass windows that lined the building, you wouldn't realize it was used for religious services.

I paused in the entryway to get my bearings. Mitch and I attended a church off base that was closer to our house, so I'd never been inside the chapel. A long hall ran off to the right with offices and classrooms. Directly in front of me, double doors opened into the sanctuary, which was lined with two rows of blue upholstered pews. I could see the dark wood of the casket through the double doors, positioned in front of the raised lectern. The casket was closed and the large official portrait of Colonel Pershall, stiff and unsmiling in his uniform, stood beside it on an easel. Several flower arrangements ranged alongside the casket.

I could see why Denise wanted to display the other photo. It showed that there had been more to Colonel Pershall than just a military man. I spotted the condolence book on a small table near the double doors and set the photo near it. People began to arrive, sign the book, and linger in the entryway. I saw Denise in a dark blue suit with a corsage pinned on her lapel and went over to tell her I'd brought the photo. She nodded and said thank you. I gave her a hug and stepped back so that other people could talk to her. She greeted everyone by name and accepted their sympathy. I wondered how she did it—how she remained so composed. The chaplain, a captain, moved through the crowd and directed everyone to the sanctuary. I spotted Jeff, Abby's husband, in his blues and looked around for Abby, but then remembered it was the first day of school and she'd decided that she couldn't take off on such an important day.

Colonel Barnes extended his bent elbow to me and said, "Mrs. Avery?"

I realized he was an usher. "Oh, yes. Thank you. Somewhere in the back. I need to save a place for

Mitch," I said as I put my hand on his arm. It felt weird to walk into the sanctuary with him, considering that Mitch and I had been discussing him as a possible suspect. We walked sedately down the aisle. "It's hard to believe this is happening, isn't it? It seems almost surreal," I said, partially to cover the awkward silence between us.

"That's a good way to describe it. One minute he's standing there cleaning his irons, gloating over his score, and the next, he's gone."

I paused at the end of the row. "You were there? At the golf course?"

"Of course. We played every weekend we could."

"Did you eat lunch with him, too?" I asked as we reached the section where people were being seated.

He nodded. "We always stopped for a bite to eat after." He pulled his arm away and gestured at the pew. I took a seat. Now was not the time to ask questions, but . . . he was there *at the golf course.*

I watched him walk back to the entryway. With his shaved head and big build, he was easy to pick out as he escorted other people to their seats. I watched his shiny head as he trooped up and down the aisle.

The music, which had been a prerecorded soft murmur, faded and an organist took her place at the front of the chapel. The last of the mourners were seated and I looked for Mitch, but didn't see him. I shifted toward the front again and looked around at the mix of people who'd arrived for the service. Military members in their dark blue uniforms sat beside people in business suits. I'd seen several laminated name tags dangling from lanyards around the necks of many people in civilian clothes—probably civil service employees who worked at the base. I also recognized Detective Waraday seated on the other side of the chapel next to a slender woman with short, straight brown hair and a boxy navy pantsuit. Since both of them were scanning the crowd with single-minded determination, I assumed she was the OSI officer that Denise had mentioned. The organist launched into a hymn that I didn't recognize as Denise and her sister were escorted to the front row.

Mitch slid into the pew beside me just as the chaplain began to speak. I raised my eyebrows and he whispered, "She went to that barbeque place across the street from the front gate. Looked like she was meeting a group of women there, all in red T-shirts like hers."

"Is Gary there now?"

Mitch nodded.

"Colonel Barnes was at the golf course with Colonel Pershall on Saturday," I whispered.

Mitch reared back a few inches. "How'd you find that out?"

"He's an usher. He mentioned it when he seated me."

Mitch rolled his eyes and muttered, "Only you."

We fell silent and switched our attention to the service. Well, I tried to concentrate on the chaplain's words, but my thoughts kept drifting, first to Colonel Barnes and then to Carrie. Whatever she was up to, I had a feeling it wasn't good.

Denise had told me she wanted to keep the service simple and, except for the protocol involved because the base commander was in attendance, she seemed to get her wish. The chaplain spoke, then there were a few eulogies including one with a funny story from Colonel Barnes. He described how Colonel Pershall had tried to smuggle three watches, a compass, and a Swiss army knife into their survival training course at the Academy.

I saw Megan sitting alone a few rows in front of us. Henry must still be out of town. Would Colonel Barnes really benefit from Colonel Pershall's death, like Megan had thought? An extra long pause drew my attention back to the front. Colonel Barnes seemed genuinely choked up as he folded his small paper. "I had more." He shrugged and put the paper in his pocket. "I think this will suffice—nothing will be the same without Lewis." He swallowed hard. "He will be missed."

I felt my throat prickle. I straightened my shoulders and stared at a blue piece of glass in the stained-glass window. Colonel Pershall would be missed. He'd been a good man. Mitch took my hand and I noticed his eyes were extra glossy. I was sure there wouldn't be any tears from the guys—military men could rival the British with their stiff upper lip routine, but I knew he was incredibly sad about Colonel Pershall's death.

I noticed that Denise was still dry eyed and composed. The chaplain closed the service in prayer. Colonel Barnes was one of the pallbearers. The group lifted the casket and followed the chaplain down the aisle. Colonel Barnes marched stiffly by, his face now shuttered and all emotions in check. The ushers dismissed us by rows and Mitch and I stood up. "I'd never been to a military funeral before. It wasn't that different from a civilian funeral."

"The graveside service will be. That's where they'll play 'Taps' and present the flag," Mitch said, then asked, "Want to ride with me to the graveside service?"

"I can't. I told Denise I'd leave the graveside service early and check on the reception." Mitch nodded and went to talk to Jeff as I picked up the photo of Colonel Pershall and joined the crowd that was slowly moving toward their cars. Because of where I'd parked, I was waved into the line of traffic fairly close to the hearse and the limousine carrying Denise and her sister. The graveside service would be off base, so I turned on the minivan's headlights.

At the front gate, the security police had stopped the cross traffic for the funeral procession. As I entered the intersection, red taillights flared and I hit my brakes. A large piece of white paper plastered itself to my windshield.

I had a quick impression of bold red strokes of paint spelling out the words PEACE NOW before the wind whipped at the edges of the sign. It flapped against the glass for a second, then the wind pulled it away and sent it spiraling across the intersection.

Several red-shirted women stood at the side of the road in front of the barbeque restaurant, holding signs. The wind ripped another one of the flimsy poster board signs out of their hands and sent the paper cartwheeling across the street. The caravan of cars began moving again and as I drove by the women, I spotted both Carrie in her baseball cap and Stephanie. They were enthusiastically chanting, but I couldn't hear them because my windows were up.

Well, it looked like the Peace Now Committee had changed their march to a weekday as Carrie suggested. Although, to me, it didn't look like much of a march. They weren't going anywhere, just standing on the curb, and I doubted they'd be able to get on base with their signs and chants.

The cemetery wasn't far. This part of Georgia was dotted with small cemeteries and family plots, but Roseview Meadows was a large modern cemetery with all the headstones set flat in the sculpted, rolling hills. I parked on the winding gravel road and joined the group gathering around the lines of chairs. This was a smaller group than had been at the church. Many people had probably returned to work, but it seemed most of the squadron was here. I saw Mitch and we moved toward each other through the crowd. "Did you see the protest march?" I asked.

He nodded. "Kind of pathetic, if you ask me. How many people were out there? Ten, maybe fifteen." We found a seat at the back and Mitch continued, "But, hey, if that's what they want to do, it's their right."

"Do you think they're accomplishing anything?"

"I think they *feel* like they're doing something. Will anything change on base? No."

The blustery wind had wiped the humidity out of the air, but it was still in the mid-nineties. When the graveside service began, I forgot about the heat. This service was shorter and I again had to blink back tears as I watched the iconic image of the folded flag being presented to Denise. I knew there were so many funerals for veterans that the military was having a hard time providing buglers for every service and sometimes a recorded version of "Taps" had to be played, but today there was a bugler and as he played the somber notes I had to find a tissue. As soon as he finished, I squeezed Mitch's hand and slipped out to leave for the O Club.

I was almost back to the line of cars parked on the winding gravel road when Colonel Barnes passed me, walking toward the graveside service. He didn't say anything, just nodded and walked briskly across the grass. Why was he late? Shouldn't he have been in the first group of people to arrive, since he was a pallbearer? A small black car plodded by, carefully moving between the twin lines of parked cars.

A flash of red caught my eye and I saw three women in familiar red T-shirts at the very end of the road where the last cars were parked. It looked as if they'd just arrived, because one of the doors on the car they stood beside was still open, along with the trunk. I recognized Carrie's red baseball cap, but didn't know the woman beside her who was adjusting her fanny pack. Then I spotted Joyce removing some of the now familiar poster board signs from the trunk.

"Not here," I said with a groan and reversed my course back to the graveside. I was so angry I wanted to punch something, but I channeled all that fury into striding quickly across the grass. The service seemed to be wrapping up. Everyone's head was bent in prayer. I hurried to the group standing in the back and grabbed Detective Waraday's elbow. The female investigator who'd been beside him at the funeral was gone now. He looked up in surprise and frowned, but I pointed over his shoulder at the women. "Protesters," I whispered. "Can you do anything to stop them from interrupting?"

He took off without a word, his stride purposeful. I hurried along behind him. A quick glance over my shoulder showed that the prayer was still going on and no one else had noticed Detective Waraday's departure. He met the three women at the car, still a good distance from the gravesite. Joyce and Carrie looked defiant, but the third woman began shooting glances over her shoulder and looked like she'd rather leave.

"You can't stop us, Officer," Joyce's voice carried clearly. "We have the right to assemble."

Several dark-suited men peeled off from the crowd around the gravesite and headed toward the group. I assumed they were with the funeral home or the cemetery and would help Waraday keep the women from making a disturbance.

I didn't hear Waraday's reply since he kept his voice down. The group of mourners began to disperse.

Good. At least they hadn't spoiled the graveside service.

How could Carrie and her group be so insensitive? Disturbing a graveside service had to be one of the most disgusting things they could possibly come up with, the lowest of the low. Did they really think this would sway people to their side?

Or, had Carrie suggested they come here simply out of her hate for Colonel Pershall?

I paused at the bumper of the minivan to fish my keys out of my purse. I glanced back at the ring of people surrounding the women and that was when, inexplicably, a bush blew up beside them.

Chapter Fourteen

The blast scattered leaves and sticks through the air. I blinked. Had I really just seen that?

Almost like an answer to my unspoken question, another explosion sounded, this time from the bed of a pickup parked along the gravel road. Waraday and the group of people around him hit the ground and I followed their lead, crouching down beside the bumper. We waited in silence for a few seconds and I could hear the exclamations from the graveside as people reacted to the explosions. I was cautiously inching my way to a standing position when another jolt sounded from the grassy field and this time I saw the part of a plastic water bottle, the lid and an attached piece of plastic, circling away through the air along with bits of dirt and grass.

I ducked back down and waited, my heart pounding noisily in my ears. That one had been closer than the others. I could hear raised voices around the gravesite, some with an edge of panic.

Waraday shouted for everyone to stay down and I followed his direction as I scuttled around the van, putting it between me and the blasts. We waited, tensed for another explosion. An eerie, odd silence fell, but after what was probably only a few minutes, people began to chatter and move tentatively. I released my white-knuckle grip on the minivan's grille and slowly stood up.

Mitch was sprinting across the grass, giving a wide berth to the area where the explosions had happened. He slid to a stop on the gravel. "You okay?" he asked.

"Yes, I'm fine. I think it was more dry ice bombs," I said, pointing to the plastic pieces sprayed across the grass.

"Okay, folks," Waraday's voice rang out above the chatter, "is anyone hurt?" He was standing, as were the women from the Peace Now group. He paused, and when no one responded, he said, "Stay where you are. I'm Detective Waraday from the Dawkins County Sheriff's Office. We need to get everyone's contact information. We'll have someone here shortly to check the cars and gather evidence. Those of you by the grave, return to your seats. We'll get you out of here as quickly as possible." He turned his attention back to the three women and said, "Wait here. Do not touch anything," then he pointed to one of the dark-suited men from the funeral home. "Go to the entrance and direct the officers here when they arrive," he said, reaching for his cell phone.

Mitch and I were stuck in no-man's land halfway between the group of women on the gravel drive and the gravesite. We decided to stay put, instead of walking through the grass to the gravesite. We didn't want to disturb any evidence that might be in our path. Mitch leaned against the minivan. "Well, I can't say I'm surprised to see Carrie in that group. Did you see anything?"

"Not really. Just the women getting out of their car. I realized it was the Peace Now group and figured they were here to make trouble, so I went back to get Detective Waraday."

Carrie stood with her arms crossed and one hip jutted out like a sulky teenager. Joyce had a look of resignation on her face. The last woman, who was probably in her twenties, had straight, light brown hair framing her freckled face. She nervously licked her pale lips. Her face was white, causing her freckles to look twice as prominent. Her gaze darted from Waraday to the other women. She leaned in to say something to Carrie, but Waraday's hand snapped up and he said, "No talking."

She jumped back like she'd been scorched. Carrie leveled a long, warning look at her.

Sirens cut through the air and several police cars arrived and parked at the end of the line of cars. I must say that I was impressed with the response time. Three explosions in a cemetery were pretty unusual for North Dawkins and probably had people in the houses that backed up to the cemetery calling nine-one-one right away.

Waraday sorted out the officers. They dispersed over the area, some checking the parked cars, some taking names and contact info, and others carefully photographing the bits of plastic on the grass.

We gave our contact information, but we weren't allowed to leave. Waraday separated the three women. Carrie stared at the sky a few cars away from us as she answered Waraday's question. "No, I don't know anything about whatever that was. It scared us as much as everyone else. Just because we got here right before it went off doesn't mean you can blame us."

"No," Waraday said mildly, "but it certainly doesn't look good."

"We had nothing to do with it. We're exercising our *First Amendment* right—the right to assemble. You can't stop us from doing that."

"That's not correct, Mrs. Kohl. You do have the right to assemble, but the laws of North Dawkins only allow gatherings on cemetery property for funerals. All other gatherings are prohibited."

"We *were* here for the funeral."

"Your posters, Mrs. Kohl," Waraday said, nodding to the huge white squares propped up against the car.

"We didn't use them," Carrie countered. "We were simply moving them. They took up too much space in the car."

"Then I'm sure you won't mind if we take a look at your car?"

Carrie didn't hesitate. "Go ahead."

Waraday sent one of his officers to check out the car, then said to Carrie, "Wait here, ma'am," and strode over to Mitch and me. He and Mitch exchanged nods, then he said to me, "What did you see, Mrs. Avery?"

I explained I had to leave the graveside service early and that I saw the women when I was walking to my minivan. "I'd seen them on the drive over here with their signs at the front gate, so I figured they would try to disturb the graveside service. I didn't talk to them, they were too far away. I went back to get you."

"What exactly were they doing?" Waraday asked, his gaze intense and tenacious.

"They were standing beside the car. The doors and trunk were open. They were talking, but I couldn't hear what they were saying," I said, a little surprised at how concentrated his attention was.

"Did you see them leave the car?" he asked.

"No."

"Were they carrying anything?" he persisted.

"One of them was putting on a fanny pack and they had the posters, but that was all I saw," I said.

"Did you see anyone else?" Waraday asked. "Any cars on this road?"

I looked away at the green rolling hills of the cemetery, trying to think. "There was a black car, driving toward the exit."

"What type?"

"Ah—a small two door. Not as small as a sports car, and it had a yellow ribbon magnet on the back." Waraday grimaced, but didn't say anything. I knew he was thinking that over half the cars in North Dawkins had those magnets. "I didn't notice the license plate or anything, either."

"Anything else you remember?" he asked as he wrote in his notebook.

"No, nothing el—wait. I passed Colonel Barnes. He was walking from the cars back to the graveside service."

"Colonel Barnes?" Waraday asked and I looked to Mitch. I didn't remember his first name.

Mitch said, "Lieutenant Colonel Richard Barnes. Were these dry ice bombs, Detective Waraday?" Mitch asked before Waraday could ask another question. When Waraday didn't answer right away, Mitch continued, "Because one of those went off in my car the day before yesterday."

"I'm aware of the situation." Waraday frowned and tapped his pen against his notebook a few times as he watched the officers gathering evidence. "Look, I understand what you're asking, but right now we don't know if this is connected to those incidents. There are some differences in these dry ice bombs compared to the earlier ones. We don't know if we're dealing with the same individual, a group of individuals, or a copycat. All I can really tell you now is that we'll keep you informed."

Mitch nodded and as soon as Waraday moved out of earshot, I said, "When he said they were different, I bet he means they were smaller. That lid with the edge of plastic attached to it that I saw on the grass still had a bit of the label attached. It was a small water bottle."

"So if it's the same person or," Mitch glanced at the Peace Now women, "a group of people, why the switch to smaller bottles? And if it's someone completely different . . ." Mitch's voice trailed off, then he said, "I don't know why someone would copy a stunt like that, especially at a graveside service."

"I don't either," I said, feeling lost and confused. "None of it makes sense. Even if it is the Peace Now group, why would they do something so outrageous? It'll only hurt their reputation, surely they understand that." I blew out a breath and rotated my shoulders, trying to ease some of the tension. "And if it was Colonel Barnes, why would he do it? If he really wanted Colonel Pershall's job, that's one thing, but setting off dry ice bombs after he's dead . . . that's just odd. It wouldn't help him with the promotion."

Mitch shook his head and I could tell he was as frustrated as I was. He hated not having the answers as much as I did. He wrapped one arm around my shoulder, pulling me close, and I leaned against him. A trickle of people began leaving the gravesite, the blustery wind kicking at suit coats and dress hems. Denise was escorted to the limousine, still dry eyed, but now her face had a set, angry look. I couldn't blame her for being upset.

I pulled slightly away from Mitch. "How would someone do it? Even if you had the dry ice already in the bottles, you'd have to keep the bottles cold, right? Otherwise they'd explode, especially in this weather."

"They probably packed them in a cooler with more dry ice."

"I guess they didn't find anything incriminating in Carrie's car. They're letting her leave." We watched as she and the other two women climbed in the car, then Carrie whipped the car around in a U-turn and zipped out of the cemetery.

"I'm sure Waraday will keep an eye on her," I said and leaned back against the van, only to spring away from the hot surface. "Speaking of keeping an eye on things, where's Gary? Wasn't he supposed to be watching Carrie for you? Maybe he saw something."

"I got a text from him right after you left the service. He'd followed Carrie here and he was waiting at the entrance to the cemetery. It would have been too obvious to drive in behind her. I wonder if they had time to plant the water bottles before you saw them?"

I pushed my bangs off my damp forehead. "I'm not sure. It did look like they'd just arrived." I glanced around the cemetery at the roped off portions. "Look where the explosions happened. None of those are that far from where Carrie was parked."

Mitch nodded. "Even the pickup is within tossing distance."

"So they could have arrived and tossed out the water bottles before I even saw them."

"If I had three dry ice bombs in my car, I'd want to get rid of them first thing, too," Mitch said, running a finger around his collar. I was hot in my dress, but I knew he had to feel worse in his coat. "But then why stick around for the explosions?"

"More publicity for your group?" I asked doubtfully. I looked at the scattered leaves and broken branches. "Bad, bad PR move."

"Looks like we can leave," Mitch said as the limousine with Denise and her sister began to roll.

"Oh—the reception at the O Club! I'm supposed to be there early." I gave Mitch a quick kiss and hopped in the minivan. I dropped out of the line of cars following the limousine and took a shortcut through a neighborhood to get to the front gate ahead of the funeral party. I arrived at the O Club in time to set up Colonel Pershall's picture and make sure everything else was ready to go.

Denise and her sister arrived and I hurried over to them because I didn't have long before I had to pick Livvy up at school. I told Denise again how much Mitch and I would miss Colonel Pershall.

"Thank you, Ellie," she said, almost automatically. "It means a lot to me that you're here. Thank you for taking care of the picture."

"No problem at all. You look like you're holding up really well, despite . . . everything. How do you do it?"

"This is not the time or place for me to grieve. This is for Lewis and his memory. I'm not going to become the center of attention like some people."

I recognized the subtle reference to Carrie, whose weeping had dominated the funeral service for Ryan.

I didn't know what to say to that, so I asked, "Is there anything else I can do? Do you need anything later today?"

Her mechanical manner dropped away and instead of the carefully controlled façade, I saw a moment of raw rage on her face.

I swallowed and took a tiny step back. She was still tightly controlling her anger, keeping her words low. "I want to know who disrupted Lewis's funeral."

I'd never seen Denise like this. She was always upbeat and affable. I mean, I know it was her husband's funeral and it had just been bombed, so I had to give her some leeway. "It looked like the police were doing a very careful job. I'm sure they'll figure out who did it." I realized I was using my most soothing tone, the one I used when the kids were extra cranky or hurt or scared.

"At least they can't blame it on me," she said.

Tips for Busy, Budget-Minded Moms

To streamline your time in the kitchen, create a standardized grocery shopping list with headings for:

Fresh Fruit/Vegetables
Canned Goods (Fruit/Vegetables/Beans/Soups)
Baking Items (Boxed Mixes/Dry Ingredients/ Spices)
Breakfast Items
Crackers/Chips/Snacks
Drinks (Juices/Water/Soda)
Meats
Dairy/Cheese
Breads
Frozen
Cleaning Products
Paper Products (Napkins/ Paper Towels)
Personal Hygiene Products

You can arrange the list according to the layout of the store where you shop. You can also find downloadable grocery lists online.

Make several copies and post one on the refrigerator. When you run out of an item, take a minute to add it to the grocery list. Train your family members to do the same.

Before you go to the store, make a menu and add any special ingredients you'll need for certain dishes to the list you've already started. Then, check your pantry and refrigerator to see what items are running low and add those to the list as well.

Chapter
Fifteen

And then we learned the *right* way to walk in a line," Livvy said.

I helped Livvy out of the minivan. "Really? How's that?" I asked. As I slid the door closed, I swung my latest designer purse, a red Notting Hill Design Westbourne, onto my shoulder. I'd snagged it at a good discount on eBay and felt it brought a splash of color and a bit of sophistication to my otherwise unoriginal ensemble of a black T-shirt and jeans.

Livvy braced her arms to her sides. "You have to keep your hands to yourself, look forward, and *not talk*. That's real important, the not talking part.

Mrs. Ames says that's the most important thing."

"I imagine it is." I exchanged an amused glance with Mitch, then said, "Why don't you practice walking like you do at school as you walk to Mrs. Bonnie's door."

"Okay." Livvy stepped smartly up the sidewalk, her posture stiff.

Mitch and I watched her go, then I said, "And I was worried about what I'd be missing. I had no idea we'd get a blow-by-blow account of the day."

"And we're not even to lunch yet."

"The retelling may take longer than the actual day."

I'd made it home from the funeral in time to pick her up at the school, where I'd learned that the car-rider line was a complicated thing that ran with clocklike precision and woe to anyone foolish enough to go the wrong way. Fortunately, I'd found the correct lane and picked up Livvy without incident.

She'd been so excited to have homework, a page of counting problems on one side and letters on the other, that she'd done it almost as soon as she stepped in the door this afternoon. Her enthusiasm about her new adventures in school had taken my mind off of the funeral. Livvy's constant chatter about her day had pretty much filled the rest of the afternoon, but being back in base housing, I couldn't help but think about Colonel Pershall, Denise, and Carrie.

"I thought Abby and Jeff were in charge of the supper club," Mitch said as he hoisted Nathan into his arms and passed the small yard sign that read LIEUTENANT COLONEL AND MRS. BARNES on the way to the door.

"Abby's the point of contact and she's bringing the main dish tonight. The host doesn't cook. The rest of us do," I said, holding up the plate of chocolate chip cookies I'd brought for dessert.

Nathan wiggled with excitement, "The vroom-vroom lady's house!"

"Yes, it is," I said, "but don't call her that. Her name is Mrs. Bonnie."

Mitch looked at me questioningly and I said, "He's remembering the kids' squadron Christmas party here last year." It's funny what kids remember and how they describe people. I lowered my voice so that only Mitch could hear and said, "You know how Bonnie is—constantly moving and always talking so fast. When we left that day, Nathan said Bonnie was like one of his race cars vrooming around. He had such a good time at the party, he asked for weeks when we were going back to the vroom-vroom lady's house."

"I see," Mitch said with a smile. "Here you go, big guy." Mitch angled Nathan toward the doorbell. "Push the button." His pudgy finger pressed on the bell and he grinned. Livvy frowned. She'd wanted to do it. I never thought a small thing like ringing a doorbell could cause so much contro-versy, but I knew what was coming, so I leaned down to Livvy and said in a low voice, "Since you're going to school now, Nathan needs to learn to do some of the things you've been doing." She looked like she didn't quite buy this trade-off.

Bonnie flung the door open and set her jet black hair swinging. "Come in, come in." She had pointy features, a sharp nose and chin, porcelain skin, and thin lips. Tonight she was wearing a bright red lipstick and the slash of scarlet was rather startling in contrast to her fair skin.

Her jazzy personality was perfectly suited to her job in pharmaceutical sales. She was one of the few "old guard" wives of the spouse club who'd fully supported Denise when she shook things up. But I wasn't sure *why* Bonnie had backed Denise. Either Bonnie wanted the changes Denise offered or she was savvy enough to see that Denise was going to win the battle and Bonnie wanted to be on the winning side. "Rich is still at the squadron—some big emergency—but he should be here soon."

The spicy aroma of chili peppers, garlic, onions, and cheese filled the hall. "Beautiful day, isn't it? Don't you just love this low humidity? If we'd known it was going to be this nice we could have had a cookout, but at least the kids can play. They're in the back," she informed Livvy. Mitch set Nathan down and he scurried along behind

Livvy to the sliding glass door to the backyard. I could see Bonnie's son and daughter, Sunny and Peter, who were in sixth and seventh grade, pushing the younger kids on the swings.

"Smells delicious," I said, finally managing to get in a few words.

"And these look yummy." Bonnie took the plate from me and led the way into the kitchen. "The guys are on the back patio, Mitch," she said. "Be a sweetie and tell them to come in here. The food's ready."

I followed her into the kitchen, which she had decorated with lots of blue and white Polish pottery. Abby pulled a bubbling cheesy dish of enchiladas out of the oven. I greeted everyone, then went to stand beside Megan at the counter and helped her arrange chips and dips. The guys entered the kitchen and Bonnie said, "Okay, everyone, tonight is buffet style, so help yourself and grab a seat anywhere in the living room or on the patio. There's peanut butter and jelly sandwiches for the little guys and drinks are set up in the dining room."

Mitch and I filled plates for the kids and got them settled outside at a small picnic table where they were comparing ages, which was something the kids always did when a group formed. I guess it was essential to sort out the pecking order. I returned to the house and had just filled my plate and was carrying it into the living room along with a tall glass of mango iced tea when Bonnie waylaid me in the kitchen with a folder.

"I know I keep putting you off, but I'm determined to get organized. This is such an important time for us. Everything's changing, so now's the perfect time. She shoved the file folder at me. "I tore some photos that I adore out of magazines."

I set down the plate and flicked through a few shiny pages of bare shelves and open-backed bookcases. The minimalist look was very different from her current, more traditional look. "We can do something like this, but it will be challenging in base housing. Since your rooms are already pretty small, we'll have to find ways to store things out of sight. I'm sure we can work something out. I'll look through these. The next step is for me to come over and take a look at everything you want organized. I can give you a detailed estimate with time and cost breakdowns."

"Oh, okay . . . we can do that. Maybe next week. I'll give you a call," Bonnie said.

I tucked the folder under my arm and picked up my plate again. I suspected that Bonnie was the type of person who wanted to clip photos and *think* about being organized, but she never took the essential steps to make it happen. She'd talked to me about organizing since last January, but every time I followed up with her, she put me off with an excuse. There was a fine line between being persistent and being a pest. I tried not to stray into the pest side of things and if someone didn't call me back or put me off a few times, I left them alone.

In the living room, I spotted Mitch talking to Abby and Jeff. The dining room chairs ringed the living room and I sat down in a chair placed in front of a five-foot-tall bookcase stuffed with books. Most of them were how-to and self-help books and had titles along the lines of "You Can Be a Millionaire" and "Don't Wait—Get Rich Now." I dug into the enchiladas, wondering where Bonnie thought she was going to put all those books when she switched to the minimalist look. I doubted she was planning on getting rid of them. I gave a mental shrug. Maybe that's why she never called me in for a consultation. Deep down she knew she'd have to change lots of things for a new look and wasn't quite ready to do it.

Megan was sitting in the chair next to me. Tyler, wearing a blue jean baseball cap that covered his fuzzy Mohawk hair, was dozing in his car seat at her feet. I turned to her and noticed Henry was on her other side. "Oh, hi, Henry. I didn't see you over there." Henry Fleet's brown hair, brown eyes, and medium build matched his quiet and reserved personality. Apparently, Henry kept his head down and got his work done, something Mitch appreciated. Mitch said Henry was one of the guys the squadron could count on and Mitch enjoyed flying with him, except for one thing

Henry insisted on parsing out who did each job and taking credit for every small thing he did, which ran counter to the concept that the crew was a unit and had to work together and succeeded or failed together. "So you made it back," I said. "How was your trip?"

"Good, except that Travel didn't make hotel or car reservations for us in Hawaii. I had to do it."

"Really," I said. Looked like Henry was still keeping track. That tendency would have to get annoying day after day. "So what happened? You guys didn't have to sleep in base ops, did you?"

He grinned. "Downtown, right on the beach."

"That's great. Did you get to swim?"

"No, it was a quick turn, but at least we had a view." He rubbed his eyes and said, "I don't think I'm adjusted back to this time zone."

"Mitch has done that trip, too, and he didn't get to spend any time on the beach either," I said.

Megan shot an accusing look at Henry and said, "Well, now that you're home, you'll be able to catch up on your sleep. Henry never gets up with Tyler during the night."

Henry's hand dropped away from his bloodshot eyes and he glanced self-consciously around the room, then he said in an undertone, "Not a lot I can do. You're breastfeeding. If you'd pump a bottle, I'd get up and feed Tyler."

I developed an intense interest in my enchilada. Megan pushed her food around her mostly bare plate. She'd skipped on the chips and dips as well as the fried rice. She had a teaspoon-sized portion of the refried bean dish and half an enchilada. "When am I supposed to do that? I'm feeding him all the time *and* doing everything else around the house, too."

Henry said quietly, "Maybe if you dropped one of your workouts, you'd have time." Megan's eyes narrowed as Henry stood. He included me as he spoke in a normal tone of voice, "Sorry. I'm a terrible traveler. Jet lag gets me every time. I may have picked the wrong profession." His last words drifted into sarcasm and he cut a glance at Megan before saying, "I'm going to get some of those cookies. Want one, Meg? Just one?"

"No, no cookies for me," she snapped and looked as horrified as if he'd asked if she'd like some arsenic. "I'm not going back in the kitchen or I'll want a cookie and a slice of the cake I brought. Here, take this or I'll eat the rest of it," she said, holding her plate out to him.

I watched Henry walk to the kitchen, thinking about his line about the wrong profession. The assignment to the remote aircraft must still be a sore spot. I didn't know what to think about the tension between Henry and Megan. Was it a result of the assignment or the strain of parenthood— sleep deprivation could turn anyone into an irritable, whiny person—or were they always like this?

Megan was busily rearranging the toys on the handle of the car seat. "I appreciate you getting that package for me."

"Package?" I dunked a chip into the salsa. "What package?"

"The one that's supposed to arrive tomorrow," she said while adjusting the tilt of a bumblebee with the exactness of a seamstress about to cut a very expensive cloth. "Thanks for watching out for it. I don't want it to sit on the porch for a week. I'll give you the code to the garage and you can shove it in there."

So we were going to pretend everything was normal. "Sure. No problem," I said, remembering Megan's phone call from earlier in the week. I made a mental note to run by Megan's house sometime tomorrow afternoon. She was flying to California early tomorrow morning for her sister's baby shower. Henry was scheduled to leave on another TDY that same afternoon.

She picked up Tyler's sock that had fallen off his foot and slid it back over his chubby toes. "It's just like Henry to leave on the same day I do. I still don't see why they have to stay overnight in Atlanta that first day."

I asked, "It's that medical training flight again?" She nodded and I said, "I think it has something to do with loading equipment."

"Whatever." She sat back in the chair. "It's a Fitter Fanny Exercise kit."

I chewed the enchilada slowly, a frown on my face as I tried to figure out what she was talking about. "The package, I mean." She made eye contact with me and relaxed now that we were on the safe subject of exercise. "It's got everything—an exercise ball, a balance board, cords, a step, and three videos. I've got to stay on top of my workouts. I've lost point-four pounds," she announced cheerfully. "I think the cardio really helps."

"Wow. I didn't know you could get a scale with such exact measurements."

"Oh, they're great. You should get one. Mine's digital and does body fat, too."

Just what I didn't want—my weight down to the tenth of a pound and a body-fat analysis. That would keep me from focusing too much on my weight.

I continued to shovel the salsa onto the chips as she said, "I got it at the same place I got my pedometer. That's another great thing that helps me stay on track." She tilted the pager-sized black box with a digital readout clipped to her waistband. "See, I'm already over ten thousand steps for today." She went on and told me more about her workout plan than I wanted to know. When she confided that she wanted to try a colon-cleansing product, I said, "I don't know if that's a good idea, especially if you're breastfeeding." I glanced down at Tyler. His arms jerked in his sleep, then drifted back down.

"But they say you can lose up to ten pounds in a *week*."

"You know what they say about things that are too good to be true."

"Yeah, but *ten pounds*! It's safe, too. It scrapes fat from the intestine walls—"

I caught sight of Nathan looking at a vase on an end table and interrupted her. "Nathan's about to get in trouble," I said and escaped before I could hear any more. Shouldn't colon cleansing be a taboo topic, especially during dinner?

I swept Nathan up before he could touch the vase and removed him to the backyard where the rest of the kids were playing. Nathan wanted to swing, so I pushed him until he transferred his interest to several Tonka trucks. Mitch was circulating. Now he was chatting with a group on the patio, so I went back inside and helped clean up in the kitchen.

Bonnie was setting out dessert plates and making coffee while Abby washed the dishes. I wiped down the countertops, then tied the handles of the plastic garbage bag and yanked it out of the trash can. I carried it out the kitchen door. Dusky half-light cast the carport into shadows. I looked around for their outdoor trash can, but didn't see it.

I leaned back into the kitchen and said, "Bonnie, where's your trash . . ." My voice trailed off as I realized she'd left the room.

"She's in the living room," Abby said, splashing water and soap bubbles onto the counter as she rinsed a dish. "Looking for the trash cans? Try around the side of the carport or maybe in the backyard. We can't leave our trash cans within sight of the street, that's one of the rules. You know, if they're going to tell us what type of hook to use to hang pictures, they're certainly not going to overlook telling us where to put our trash cans."

A free spirit like Abby had a hard time with all the rules in base housing, which covered just about every conceivable aspect of life. Going out of town? Thermostat should be set to fifty degrees. Want to wash your car in the driveway? Not allowed. Left your bicycle on the sidewalk? That's a notice, the first step in a chain of warnings.

"Well, I can't say that I'm surprised after the reaction to your Fourth of July display."

"Oh, don't get me started on holiday decoration regulations," Abby warned.

Since I'd already heard this rant, I said, "Wouldn't dream of it. Just don't use sparklers next year and everything will be fine."

She shut off the water and braced her damp hands on her hips. "You know, now it's like a challenge. How far can I push it? Can I find a loophole? Wait until you see what I'm planning for Halloween."

"I don't think I want to hear this. At least that

way, I can plead the Fifth when you're hauled in for violating the rules," I said before I went back to the carport.

I finally found the large trash cans tucked back behind a bush on the outside wall of the carport. I dropped the bag in and made sure the lid snapped into place—that was a rule, too, I'd learned the last time I visited Abby. Someone hadn't secured the lid of their trash can and raccoons got into it, spreading trash over two lawns. Everyone got notices and no one was happy the next day.

I heard someone walking along the concrete of the carport. The screen door creaked, then Bonnie said in a low voice, "So? Any news?"

Chapter
Sixteen

No." I recognized Colonel Barnes's voice. He spoke quietly, too, but with such sharpness that I slowed my steps. I was still on the outside of the carport. Colonel Barnes probably hadn't seen me when he walked up the driveway, since I was behind the bushes, and I didn't want to pop into the carport now.

"I can't believe General Crabtree hasn't done anything about the position. He's got to know that it would be better to get someone in as commander instead of leaving everyone in limbo. Did you call him?"

"No."

"But, you said you would," Bonnie's voice took on a familiar whiney tone that I'd heard so often in my conversations with Livvy and Nathan.

The scent of citronella from the tiki torches drifted on the air as Colonel Barnes said, "He's TDY and won't be back until next week. There's nothing I can do about that."

"So he's going to let it go . . . let everyone hang for another *week*?"

"Yes, apparently so," Colonel Barnes said, and I heard his footsteps move across the carport to the kitchen door.

"Where's he TDY? If you knew where he was, you could call Lodging and—"

Colonel Barnes stopped walking. "Bonnie, I am not going to badger the man. He may not want to intervene in the process at all. He might let things run through normal channels."

The command handled the assignments at the squadron commander level, but I knew that sometimes people with influence, like a general or colonel, could have input on assignment decisions.

"But you're the best person for the slot—he's got to know that. You're here. You're already acting as temporary commander. You know the squadron and everyone in the wing. It would be a seamless transition."

I couldn't see Bonnie, but I knew she was

ticking the items off on her fingers as I'd seen her do many times at the squadron coffees.

"And the slot really should have gone to you instead of Lewis in the first place," she added.

"Bonnie . . . I don't want to talk about it right now. It's been a long day. We've got guests. Let's put it on hold at least for one night."

I glanced behind me to see if anyone on the block had noticed me standing motionless by the hedge, but the street was empty for the moment.

"If we let this opportunity slip through our fingers, who knows when we'll get another one?" Bonnie said. "You said yourself when Lewis got this commander slot that you had to take care of yourself because no one else was going to do it. I'm not going to slack off on this. I think I might need to give Gina a call."

"Don't do that," Colonel Barnes's voice was weary. "Calling his wife would be the worst way to do this."

"But—"

"I'll find out where he is," Colonel Barnes said, his voice resigned, "if you promise not to call Gina."

Bonnie huffed, then said, "Okay, but you've got to do it soon. Time's slipping away."

"I'll do it tomorrow. Now forget about this for a while." The screen door creaked as they went inside.

I stayed where I was. I didn't want to follow

Bonnie and Colonel Barnes inside right away, so I leaned against the carport wall and scanned the shadows lengthening over the neighborhood's perfect yards. Lights began to glow in windows as twilight waned. After listening to that conversation, it seemed Bonnie was much more concerned about the move to squadron commander than Colonel Barnes. Was she the ambitious one, not him? Or maybe they were in it together? Had they worked together to create an "opportunity" for Colonel Barnes to move up in the squadron? I shuddered in the warm evening. I didn't want to go back inside and have to put on a smile and pretend everything was fine.

I saw a movement down the street. I only noticed it because I'd been standing outside long enough that my eyes had adjusted to the growing darkness. The slight shift of a figure near the trunk of a magnolia tree down the street made me uneasy. I watched the deep shadows for more movement, then reminded myself that it was a safe neighborhood. Abby didn't think twice about jogging at five in the morning when it was still dark during the winter. Parents felt comfortable enough to let older kids play up and down the street and even walk to the Shoppette by the gas station without adult supervision.

So why was I staring at the murky outlines of the tree, feeling wary? Nothing moved. The tree was in the front yard of a house with its windows still wide open, the lights inside a bright contrast to the growing darkness. It was dark enough now that I could see inside the house and even pick out the couch, a bookcase, and a lamp with a cream shade. Wait. I knew that room. That was Denise's living room.

I scanned the front of the house again and confirmed that it was Denise's house. I hadn't recognized the exterior of the house in the darkness from this angle. I suddenly remembered the encounter I'd had with Colonel Barnes earlier today in Denise's house. The graveside service had been so weird that'd I'd completely forgotten about it. I had to tell her about it.

I saw movement again. A figure meandered down the strip of concrete that ran from the front door to the sidewalk for a few steps, then the person circled back and rambled toward the house. I could tell it was a woman. I squinted as she stepped into the pool of light from the window and stood for a moment, gazing in the window. Light reflected off a pair of oversized glasses and I recognized the short haircut and the statuesque body type. It was Denise.

There was a burst of laughter from the backyard and I heard Mitch's voice. I hurried around the carport and entered the backyard.

Mitch stood with a group of guys on Bonnie's patio. Nathan and Charlie were attempting to throw balls into a miniature basketball hoop. I touched Mitch's arm and pulled him slightly away from the group. I told him what I'd seen and that I was going to check on Denise. I looked at the time and said, "I won't stay long. We need to get back home. School night and all that."

"Okay. How about I wait fifteen minutes, then round up the kids and pick you up at Denise's house?"

"Sounds good," I said with relief. I wouldn't have to cross paths with Colonel Barnes tonight.

Denise was still in her front yard when I arrived. I walked up the sidewalk and stepped into the grass beside her. She held a royal blue shawl loosely around her shoulders over a cotton robe printed with daisies. Her fuzzy yellow slippers stood out against the dark grass. I recognized the weave of the shawl, which was shot through with silver thread. Denise had been knitting it during one of our spouse coffees and about half the group wanted her to make one for them. She'd laughed and said she didn't know if she was ready to go into the knitting business. Abby had looked at her and said, "Honey, you already are. At the pace you're going, you could crank out a couple of those a week and have a nice little side income."

Denise hadn't said anything else at the time, but about two months later, she'd announced that her Web business, Yarn Crazy, was up and running and she was taking orders to make shawls, sweaters, and throws. She also began teaching knitting classes at Wool Works.

"Denise," I said softly. I didn't want to startle her. She didn't respond at all. "Denise, are you doing okay?"

"Ummm?" She jerked toward me and looked delighted when she focused on me. In a dreamy voice she said, "Oh, Ellie, look at that." She pointed to the window. "Doesn't it look nice? All warm and shining. From outside, it all looks normal, doesn't it? Like someone, a family, lives there and they'll be home in a few minutes."

The living room did look cozy with the soft lamplight bathing the reds and browns of the cushy chairs. Another shawl like the one Denise was wearing was draped over the arm of the leather couch, but this one was a pale yellow shot through with gold thread and was only half-finished. A mug sat next to a jumble of books and magazines on the coffee table.

I patted her shoulder. "It does look nice. Do you want to go inside now?"

"No," she said with a huge sigh. "Once I get inside I can feel it—it's not right in there." Her words were slow and breathy. "Lewis isn't coming home. It looks so much better out here." She took a step and stumbled on the uneven ground. "We used to have some chairs out here . . . don't remember where Lewis put them . . . I wanted to sit out here and look inside . . . maybe they're in the back."

I wondered if she'd been drinking. This slow, rambling demeanor was so far from her normally whip-sharp personality. "I know it's not the same, but why don't we go in there and sit down?"

I'd expected her to resist, but she meekly said okay and let me guide her up the steps. The front door was unlocked, so I steered her into the living room and she plopped down on the couch.

I picked up a mug from the coffee table. It contained tea and was cold to the touch. "Do you want some more of your tea? I can warm it up."

She plucked at the yarn in the shawl. "No. It's not doing a thing to make me sleepy. That sleeping pill isn't working either," she said, gazing vaguely around the room.

"It might be working better than you think," I said, relieved to know she'd at least been trying to get some rest. "How long ago did you take it?"

She shrugged. "Don't know. I stared at the ceiling for at least an hour, so I thought I'd get up and make some tea. Isn't that what you're supposed to do if you can't sleep? Or is it warm milk?" She shuddered. "That sounds awful. No warm milk. I've never had trouble sleeping before. My head touches the pillow and I'm out. I always thought people who couldn't fall asleep were . . . namby-pamby. They just didn't do enough during the day . . ." She trailed off, staring at her reflection in the opaque window.

"Let's get these curtains closed," I said as I moved

around the room closing curtains, then I picked up her mug and warmed it in the microwave. I returned it to her and she absently sipped from it.

"Is your sister here? Is Nancy here?" I asked.

"No. She had to go. Joey set the kitchen on fire last night—left a grocery bag on the stove." Denise grinned, her gaze focused on the floor. "That kid is always eating, my nephew. He's a teenager . . ."

So Nancy had left and Denise was alone. No wonder she was having trouble sleeping. I sat down in the chair beside her and said, "Denise."

She looked up at me, eyebrows raised as if to keep her eyes open. I told her about discovering Colonel Barnes in her house today. I didn't know if she'd be coherent enough to talk about it, but I figured it was worth a shot. I was here, after all.

"He was here? Inside?" she asked, as she leaned forward, then drifted backward.

"He said he and Bonnie had brought in your mail for you. That's how he knew where the key was."

She nodded. "Yes . . . last summer." She gazed around the room, her vision shifting bumpily from one piece of furniture to another, then she snapped back to me. "We're not out of town now. He didn't need to bring in the mail today."

"No. He said he needed something and didn't want to bother you."

She frowned. "What could he need? Except for

Lewis's job," she finished bitterly. The surprise must have shown on my face. "Oh, they think I don't know, but I do. I know Rich wants the commander position. Well, at least I think that's what he wants. I *know* it's what Bonnie wants and therefore," she stumbled on the word, but managed to get it out before concluding with "it's what Rich wants. Whatever Bonnie wants, Bonnie gets," Denise said, pointing her finger at me for emphasis. The mug tilted crazily, but she righted it and took a sip. "You know, I think this might finally be working. I'm off to bed. Will you let yourself out?" She stood and took a moment to make sure she had her balance.

"How about I walk you back there?" I wasn't sure she'd actually make it into bed.

We were shuffling through the living room, when the doorbell rang. "You get it," she said and gripped the back of a chair.

I looked through the peephole, then asked, "Were you expecting Detective Waraday?"

Tips for Busy, Budget-Minded Moms

Meal Planning Made Simple
- Plan meals during the week that have similar ingredients.
- Double the ingredients that can be used again in another recipe—that way you cook once and eat twice.

For instance:

Monday—Spaghetti with red sauce. (Make a double batch of red sauce and save half for the next meal.)

Tuesday—Baked chicken. (Bake double the amount of chicken you need for the meal and save half.)

Wednesday—Baked ziti. (Use leftover red sauce.)

Thursday—Use cooked chicken to make chicken salad sandwiches, a chicken casserole, or toss chicken with a salad of romaine lettuce, dried cranberries, walnuts, and crumbled bacon bits.

Friday—Tacos with ground beef. (Make double portion of ground beef.)

Saturday—Use extra ground beef for a Mexican casserole, burritos, or taco salad.

Chapter
Seventeen

Denise looked at the door uncertainly. "No . . . I don't think so, but everything is so bleary now."

I opened the door and Detective Waraday's face registered surprise. "Mrs. Avery. What are you doing here?"

"Looks like I could ask you the same thing," I said. Before he could say anything else, the female investigator who'd been with him at the funeral walked up the sidewalk and stepped in front of him.

"Special Agent Kelly Montigue," she said. "And you are?" Her flyaway brown hair was cut in a no-nonsense bob around her elongated face. She had wide gray eyes and a thin build and still wore a pantsuit with a blue and white striped shirt. She looked like she was probably in her early thirties, but I had a feeling that she might be another of those people who tended to look younger than their actual age, something she and Waraday had in common.

"Ellie Avery, a friend of Denise's."

Waraday added, "Mrs. Avery is the one with the theory about the squadron coins."

"Ah." There was plenty of meaning in that one sound. Basically, it translated, "Oh, so you're the crackpot." Aloud, she said, "No wonder your name sounded familiar." Her gaze traveled around the small living room and settled on Denise, who was still clinging to the back of the chair and seemed to be drifting to one side.

I explained that I'd been at a supper club down the street and had seen Denise in the front yard. "I came down to check on her. I was worried. She's taken a sleeping pill and I think it's just now kicking in."

Montigue and Waraday exchanged a look, then Montigue walked over to Denise and said, "Mrs.

Pershall, I'm Special Agent Kelly Montigue. Do you remember me? Detective Waraday and I are investigating your husband's death."

Denise nodded, but didn't seem to care. "I think I'll sit down," she said and carefully gripped the arm of the chair as she stepped around it. She sank into it, fighting to keep her eyes open.

Montigue handed her a piece of paper. "This is a search warrant. It gives us the authority to look around your house."

"Fine," Denise said vaguely. She didn't even open the paper, just put it in her lap and stifled a yawn.

I hurried over and scanned the document, plowing through the dense legal text until I found what I was looking for. "Denise, this says they have the right to look for . . . knitting needles?" I handed the warrant back to Denise and turned to Waraday.

Before he could say anything, Denise waved her hand at the couch, "Over there in my knitting basket."

Montigue snapped on gloves as she walked to the couch. She examined a large round basket placed between the arm of the couch and a small end table. She carefully pulled out balls of yarn in a rainbow of hues and lined them up on the coffee table. Long metal needles clicked as she placed them beside the yarn. Denise yawned and her jaw cracked. She was the only one in the room unaware of the tension. I told myself to relax. There was nothing to worry about. Denise was innocent and they wouldn't find anything. And why were they looking for knitting needles, anyway? Colonel Pershall hadn't been stabbed.

Montigue sat back on her heels and I could tell by her expression of satisfaction that she'd found what she'd been looking for. She took a camera out of her jacket pocket and clicked a few photos, then pulled out a short, thick metal stick from the basket. A slender metal wire connected to the end of the stick uncoiled as she raised the stick in the air. She held it as if she were handling a venomous snake. As she raised her arm, I could see a matching stick attached to the other end of the wire. "Mrs. Pershall, I'm going to take this with me," she said.

A soft snore sounded beside me. All my attention had been focused on Montigue. I shifted around to Denise. She was curled up in one corner of the chair, her head tilted to one side and her feet tucked up under her. The search warrant had drifted to the floor.

I glanced from Denise, her face smooth and vacant in sleep, to the thin cord connecting the needles. I'd seen them before. What had Denise called them? Circular needles, that was it.

My thoughts flittered through information. They had to be searching for the murder weapon. Abby had said at the hospital that Colonel Pershall had been strangled, but there had been no word about what had been used to strangle him. Megan had heard he'd been strangled with a kudzu vine, but even at the time, I'd thought that was probably a rumor. Since the sheriff's department hadn't released the information about what had been used to strangle him, they were either keeping that bit of information to themselves for a reason or they didn't know yet. As I watched Montigue put the needles in an evidence bag, I got the feeling it was the second option. Their interest in the circular needles seemed to indicate that the murder weapon was a wire and that would mean Colonel Pershall had been garroted.

"There's more," Montigue said, examining a rolling bag propped up near the couch. I recognized the brightly patterned bag. It was the one that Denise loaded with her knitting supplies and took with her when she was out of the house. She'd been working on a sweater at the last spouse coffee. Montigue clicked off more pictures, then began transferring more circular needles to evidence bags.

Mitch poked his head in the still-open front door and said, "Ellie? You ready—" He broke off when he spotted Waraday and Montigue.

Mitch stepped inside the door and nodded to the investigators, saying, "Evening, sir, ma'am." Then he raised his eyebrows as he looked at me.

I hurried over to the front door. "Mitch, they're

searching her house. Denise took a sleeping pill and it's finally kicked in, but I can't leave her now."

"Let me get Abby to come stay with her. It's getting late," Mitch said.

"We do need to get the kids home and in bed," I agreed, "but I need to tell them about Colonel Barnes." I hadn't been able to talk in much depth to Denise about why Colonel Barnes might have been in her house, but she certainly hadn't known he was there, and now there was no need to warn her that the police might show up since they were already on the scene. "Why don't you go ahead? I'm sure Abby or Jeff can run me home."

He paused and I could tell he was running through other options. He must not have been able to come up with a better one. I said, "I'd rather trade with you and take the kids home, but I'm the one who saw Colonel Barnes."

Waraday joined us. Montigue was moving around the room, checking drawers and cushions. "Saw who, Mrs. Avery?" he asked as Montigue disappeared down the hallway toward the bedrooms.

Mitch glanced at Waraday, then said to me, "Give me a call when you're done so I'll know you're on the way home." He gave me a quick kiss on the cheek and whispered in my ear, "Be careful."

I wasn't sure if he meant be careful what I told Waraday or if it was a more general warning. I felt a little annoyed. Of course, I'd be careful. I knew weird things were going on and I wasn't going to take any chances. And if I wasn't safe with two law enforcement professionals in the same room, well, I was in big trouble. Montigue emerged from the hallway and said, "Nothing in the bedrooms."

Mitch pulled the minivan away from the curb and I turned to Waraday. "I came by here today . . ."

I broke off as Denise shifted in the chair, then rubbed her eyes. She blurrily surveyed the room. In her groggy state, I could tell it was too much for her to take in. "What's going on? Detective . . ."

Her voice trailed off and Montigue, who was still carrying the first set of circular needles, said crisply, "Mrs. Pershall, your circular knitting needles—"

"Go ahead. I don't need them," she interrupted as she leaned forward and focused with an effort. "Not mine, anyway. The length is too short. Mine have a longer cord, at least twenty-nine inches. I'm going to bed," she announced and tottered unsteadily out of the room.

The three of us exchanged a quick glance, then I volunteered, "I'll go make sure she's okay." I followed her back to the bedroom and found her sleeping soundly under the covers still in her robe. She was sleeping as hard as Nathan, my championship sleeper. I clicked off the light and shut the door, glad that at least she'd get some rest.

When I returned to the living room Waraday already had out his pen and notebook. He was sitting in the chair Denise had vacated. Montigue had moved into the kitchen. "You had something you wanted to share?" Waraday asked.

"Yes." I sat down on the couch, my gaze traveling over the balls of yarn still ranged across the coffee table and the gaping bag of knitting supplies. "I came by here before Colonel Pershall's funeral." I explained about Denise's request to pick up the picture. "When I got here, Colonel Barnes was already in the house."

Waraday frowned. "Inside?"

"Yes. In the bedroom they use as a study. I could hear him moving around back there, but I didn't know it was him, so I was moving toward the door when a gust of wind blew it closed and he came out to see what the noise was." I gave Colonel Barnes's explanation of why he'd been there and Waraday wrote it all down.

"Did he have anything with him?" Waraday's pen drummed out a quick beat on the notebook.

"He was holding a stack of papers."

"Anything else?" Waraday said in an even, almost bored tone.

Did I have to spell it out for him? I scooted forward to the edge of the cushion. "It's no secret that he's ambitious. He wants the squadron commander position." I paused for a moment, not sure if I wanted to mention Bonnie's name. She might actually be the more ambitious one of the pair, but he was the one who'd benefit the most from Colonel Pershall's death, if he became the next squadron commander.

"Anything else?" Waraday repeated.

"Isn't that enough? He was at the golf course when Colonel Pershall died. He could have used the needles to kill Colonel Pershall and then planted them here to incriminate Denise—he was here in the house alone and would have had time to arrange everything so that Denise would look guilty. And he was around the cars at the graveside service. Don't you see? He has connections to all the incidents and he's trying to benefit from Colonel Pershall's death. He wants to be the next squadron commander. In fact, he thinks he should have had the job in the first place instead of Colonel Pershall."

Waraday said blandly, "Interesting."

I'd been leaning forward as I talked, but at Waraday's tepid response, I threw myself back against the pillows. "You don't think Colonel Barnes is involved." It was a statement, not a question.

Waraday gazed at me for a moment, then said, "I didn't say that."

"Well, you certainly don't seem very excited by what I've told you."

"I could be leaping up and down inside for all you know," Waraday said, deadpan. Then he cracked a small smile. "Playing everything close to the vest is part of the job, ma'am."

He closed the notebook and leaned back in his chair. "I'm not saying that what you've told me isn't interesting. It will be investigated, but there are other . . . issues that we have to pursue, issues that indicate the investigation is progressing in the right direction." He tapped the side of the notebook with his pen. The sound of cabinet doors opening and closing came from the kitchen in the silence, then Waraday said, "Were you aware of any conflicts between Colonel Pershall and Mrs. Pershall?" When I didn't respond right away, he added, "Any disagreements? Fights?"

"I never saw them fight or even argue," I said carefully.

"Any rumors going around about their marriage?"

"No. None." At least that question I could answer unequivocally. He was actually giving away more information than he was getting from me. I intended to keep my answers as short as possible on this topic.

Waraday adjusted the arm cover slightly as he asked, "Did Denise ever say she was leaving Colonel Pershall?"

"No," I said, but my heart sank. They knew. Again, technically, I wasn't lying. Denise had told me she'd made preparations for a divorce, but she'd never announced she was leaving Colonel

Pershall. "I'm sure they had their issues, but I'm also sure they loved each other. Are you saying they had marriage problems?"

Waraday studied me for a moment and I had the urge to squirm, but I forced myself to stay still. "*I'm* not saying anything, but *the evidence* indicates she was planning to leave him."

I pretended shock as I said, "I find that hard to believe." I still had trouble wrapping my mind around the concept, so it wasn't that hard to fake the emotion. I realized Waraday's gaze had dropped to my hands, which were clasped together in my lap. I relaxed my grip. He'd only asked the questions to see my reactions, I realized. He already suspected that Denise had confided in me. Had I just sabotaged any chance that the investigation would look at anyone but Denise? "You will look into Colonel Barnes, right?"

His gaze snapped back to my eyes and I thought I saw a trace of a smile. "Yes, ma'am. All leads are pursued, but let's look at the things you mentioned one at a time."

"He was with Colonel Pershall on the course. True. He admits to being there, but no one can place him in the parking lot at Colonel Pershall's car where the attack occurred. That's not to say he wasn't there, but we have no eye witnesses or forensic evidence to place him there."

He'd been holding up one finger and now he raised a second finger. "Second, he was around the cars shortly before the explosions. Again, true. He admits to being there, says his wife needed a tissue and he went to get one for her from their car."

He tapped his third finger as he said, "He was in this house. Okay. If that's true, then we'll probably be able to confirm it with a neighbor—military neighbors are so good about keeping an eye on things—so, fine, but let me also point out that you've admitted being in this house, too."

"But I wasn't trying to plant evidence or search for something or whatever he was doing," I said, irritated that Waraday had paired me with Colonel Barnes.

"No, I don't believe you were doing any of those things, but you do have an agenda, helping your friend stay clear of murder charges," he said, his gaze boring into me.

I sat up straight in the chair. "Yes, because she *didn't do it*. I know Denise and I know she'd never murder her husband."

"Well, Mrs. Avery, I hope for your sake that you're right," he said as he stood, and suddenly his voice and his face looked older. "I hope you're not disappointed and your faith isn't misplaced."

I stood, too, and Montigue came back from the kitchen. I realized I hadn't heard any sounds from the kitchen for the last few minutes and I suspected that she'd finished her search and had stayed out of the living room so Waraday could finish questioning me.

"Looks like we're finished here, Mrs. Avery," Waraday said as Montigue picked up the evidence bags.

"I'll go out with you," I said. There was no need to stick around for Denise. She wouldn't be awake for hours, but I would ask Abby to check on her in the morning. "I'll dead bolt the front door behind you and then leave through the kitchen door that leads to the carport. It locks automatically."

I left Denise a note on the kitchen table, turned off the lights, then stepped into the carport and pulled the door closed behind me.

A dark form moved out of the shadows of the carport and I started, jumping backward.

"It's me, Mrs. Avery," Waraday said as he reached passed me to check the door, then stepped back to allow me to precede him down to the sidewalk where Montigue stood impatiently at the curb beside a base security police car.

"Would you like a ride to your friend's house?" Montigue asked.

"No, thanks, it's just over th—"

A loud noise, like a clap of thunder, resounded through the air. Montigue looked around, frowning, but I recognized the noise.

"That was a dry ice bomb," Waraday and I said at the same time. Another explosion rocked through the air and almost simultaneously a high-pitched scream cut through the neighborhood.

Chapter
Eighteen

The scream continued, a thin wail. "It's coming from around the corner," Waraday said. We were all ducking down, low to the ground beside the car.

Montigue scuttled around to the back and opened the trunk. She placed the evidence bags inside, then made a radio call. I couldn't understand the abbreviations or the garbled voices, but I assumed she was calling for backup.

"Let's go," she nodded to Waraday as she closed the trunk and drew her gun. Waraday already had his out.

"You stay here, Mrs. Avery," Montigue said. "Stay low."

They didn't have to tell me. I was practically one with the pavement.

They took off, crouching low and moving carefully down the street. Porch lights began to flicker on and curtains twitched.

The wail tapered off, then the sound shifted. I thought the cry was coming from a person, but the horrible keening sound was so distorted I couldn't make out any words.

A few front doors opened and people stepped outside. Montigue and Waraday continued their careful progress down the street. The sound grew louder. A woman came around the corner at a run, one arm extended stiffly in front of her. There was something dark on her hand. Her cries echoed down the street. She saw Montigue and Waraday and headed for them full speed, her cries shifting to sobs. I made out the words "help me."

As she ran under a streetlight, I realized it was Carrie and her hand and arm were covered in blood. Montigue put away her gun and moved to Carrie. She gripped Carrie's shoulders and spoke in a low, soothing tone as she helped her sit down on the curb. Waraday still had his gun drawn as he scanned the street.

I glanced around at the neighbors who'd emerged from the houses. Bonnie was standing on her porch and Colonel Barnes was leaning out the front door. A few people had walked down to the sidewalk. I recognized the young woman who'd been with Carrie and Joyce at the cemetery. Her straight hair was caught back in a ponytail and flicked back and forth and she looked up and down the street, searching for someone, anyone. I moved closer to her and said, "Do you know what's going on?"

"She did it again. I can't believe she did it again." She wasn't really speaking to me, just talking aloud.

"What did she do? Do you know what happened? I saw you at the cemetery earlier, didn't I?"

She focused on me and said, "She did it again," then put both hands over her face and shook her head back and forth for a second. She shifted her hands to the sides of her face and said, "I knew something like this would happen. I didn't understand at first, but when I saw those explosions, I knew I couldn't do it anymore."

"Are you okay? Do you want to sit down?" I asked, genuinely concerned. Even in the dim light, I could see her freckles standing out against her pale face.

"Yeah, good idea," she said and plopped down on the grass.

I squatted down beside her and said, "Should I get someone for you? Your husband? Is this your house?" I asked, half-standing, but she gripped my arm and pulled me back down.

"No. I'll be fine. If Tim sees me like this . . . no. I'll be fine. It's just the shock of seeing the blood. I've never done well with blood."

I sat down beside her in the grass. She looked toward Carrie, but a huddle of people blocked her from view. A siren sounded in the distance. "I knew someone was going to get hurt. I didn't think those little bottles could be dangerous—that's what Carrie said—no big deal, just a little pop to get attention. But when I saw them go off myself, I knew someone was going to get hurt eventually."

"It was Carrie who placed the dry ice bombs a

the cemetery?" I asked, thinking that if it was true, my theory about Colonel Barnes being involved was wrong.

"I didn't do anything. It was Carrie and Joyce. They'd done it before, but I didn't want to touch the bottles and when I saw the explosions," she shuddered, "I knew I wasn't going to have anything else to do with Carrie."

The grass pricked my bare legs. People continued to move around us, but no one noticed us. "How did she get the dry ice there?" Maybe Colonel Barnes was involved in some indirect way?

"Oh, she didn't bring it. She had a girlfriend keep it in an ice chest in her car. Her friend met us at the cemetery and they grabbed the bottles out of her car and placed them real quick. Her friend left and we stayed with the signs, to raise awareness, you know. But they exploded so fast. There was supposed to be time to get farther away, but they went off a couple of seconds after we got back to the car."

"So it was just you, Carrie, Joyce, and the person who drove the other car? No one else from Peace Now is involved?" I asked, to be clear. I was also reluctant to let go of my favorite suspect, Colonel Barnes.

"No. Stephanie is adamant about that. No violence. Nothing that could turn people off and now I see why. Carrie convinced me that they needed more people to make a bigger impact. She'd set off some dry ice bombs on her own, but then Joyce found out and Joyce loved the idea. They convinced me to join them and I knew I shouldn't do it. Deep down, I had a feeling it was going to go bad—" she broke off and focused on me. "Hey, who are you? Why are you asking so many questions?"

I think up to that point she'd been talking and hadn't cared who was listening, but suddenly she was on guard.

"I'm Ellie Avery. I'm curious because one exploded in my husband's car earlier this week."

"Oh, God. Was he hurt?"

"No, he wasn't in the car, but it could have gone off when he was driving home and if it had . . ."

She shook her head as she watched a fire truck arrive. "He could have been hurt or even lost control of his car and hurt someone else. Oh, this is too horrible. How did I get myself involved in this?"

"How did you?" I asked as I waved away a tiny bug buzzing near my face.

"I wanted to make a difference," she said miserably. "I don't like the violence and dying I see on the news. I want it to stop and this seemed like a concrete way to get my voice heard. They'd have to listen to us. Carrie said if we set off some of the explosions in random places, they wouldn't be able to catch us and they'd be forced to listen to us or else we'd keep setting them off. It was just supposed to be property damage. No one was supposed to get hurt."

"So the first set of explosions? Carrie set those?"

"Yes. Your husband was one of the unlucky ones, I guess," she said and I noticed she'd been plucking blades of grass and had created a neat pile of them by her knee. "Carrie said she walked through the squadron parking lot and found a couple of unlocked cars and put in the bottles. Then she had some dry ice left, so she made a few more bottles and put them in the shopping cart return at Wal-Mart. She put another one in some business office lobby."

The front door to the house we were in front of opened and a man stepped onto the porch. "What's going on, Faye? You okay?"

Faye scrambled to her feet, then reached down and pulled me up, too. She gripped my hand hard and said quietly. "Please don't tell anyone I was involved with Carrie."

"But the investigators already have your name from today at the cemetery."

Her grip tightened. "Please," she said before turning and running lightly up the steps.

I studied the scene around the fire truck for a moment. Carrie was being loaded into an ambulance that had arrived. She wasn't sobbing, but her face was tear streaked and she looked terrified. Waraday and Montigue were talking with more security police who'd arrived. I walked in their

261

direction. I wasn't going to rat out Faye. Waraday already knew she was at the cemetery and had her contact information. I bet he'd be in touch with Faye again soon, but I felt I should pass along the information about the car to him. If the cemetery had any sort of video surveillance at its gates, then it shouldn't be too hard to get the license number for it.

The ambulance pulled away. I walked to the edge of the group of people gathered at the side-walk. As the ambulance left the neighborhood, the situation seemed to wind down and neighbors moved back toward their houses.

I spoke to an officer stationed at the edge of the sidewalk. I told him I had information for the detectives, which didn't impress him at all, but when I mentioned specific last names and told him I'd been questioned earlier, he reconsidered. A few minutes later, Waraday strode over and said shortly, "Yes, ma'am?"

"Just wanted you to know that I heard—in the crowd—that Carrie had someone in a car drop off the dry ice bombs at the cemetery."

His impatience disappeared as he flipped back through his notes, then he said, "You mentioned you saw a black car pass you on the road shortly before the explosions."

"Yes, that's right."

"Okay. Thank you, Mrs. Avery. Who in the crowd mentioned it?"

The sirens were off, but the pulsating emergency lights continued to flash, giving Waraday's face a red cast. "Umm . . . just someone talking," I said hurriedly. "I don't think I could point them out or anything, but I thought you'd want to know."

He gazed at me for a long moment, then said, "Yes, we'll check it out. So how does this," he said, gesturing over his shoulder to the fire truck that was parked in the street and the milling crowd, "impact your theory about Colonel Barnes?"

I sighed. "It blows it out of the water." I could admit I was wrong and, clearly, I'd been on the wrong path.

"Afraid so. Look, Mrs. Avery, I know you're 'trying to help,' and you've got an inside track with some of the people involved, but this is a murder investigation and you'd be smart to not involve yourself in it."

Anger fired through me. "Not involve myself?" I sputtered, trying to grasp my surging thoughts. "How can I not be involved? There was an explosion in my husband's car! I—my family—we're all involved whether or not we want to be!"

At my outburst, Waraday's chiding expression didn't shift and his voice grew sterner. "All the more reason to stay out of it. There's dangerous stuff going on . . . people who wouldn't think twice about hurting you or your family if you get in their way."

I stared at him in amazement, surprised that

even though he looked like he wasn't old enough to order a beer without getting carded, he could sound like my dad. "I know there's a murderer out there, you don't have to remind me of that. Believe me, I've been thinking about it a lot."

"That's what I'm afraid of," Waraday said under his breath.

I spun on my heel and pushed through the crowd, doing some muttering of my own. I couldn't turn my back on a friend. And you'd think he'd be happy that I'd passed along information that might be helpful. I gritted my teeth, thinking I should have pointed those things out to him. I'd never been a good debater—or arguer—I came up with my best points only after the whole thing was over. In the heat of the moment, my thoughts tended to be a jumbled mess and it was only when I was away from the situation that I thought of zinging comebacks. And there still was no explanation for why Colonel Barnes had been in Denise's house.

"Ellie," a familiar voice called. "What are you mumbling about? Everything okay?"

I turned to find Abby standing beside me with a concerned frown on her face. I was in the mix of people in Bonnie and Colonel Barnes' front yard. "Oh, I'm just trying to work things out and nothing is making much sense at the moment."

"Well, good to see you're operating as normal. You wouldn't be you if you weren't trying to sort things out into a logical and orderly arrangement," Abby said. "Where's Mitch and the kids?"

"He took them home to get them to bed early. Can you or Jeff give me a ride home? I stayed here to check on Denise. She was wandering around her yard." I summarized the situation with Denise and asked Abby if she'd check on her in the morning.

"Poor thing. Of course, I'll look in on her. And, what's all the commotion down the street?" Abby asked and I realized she was guiding me like I'd guided Denise earlier.

"It looks like Carrie is the mysterious dry ice bomber," I said as we stopped beside her car.

"Really? Carrie?" Abby asked, her voice rising in surprise.

"Yep. Apparently, one went off in her hand. They're unpredictable."

Abby was nodding her head. "You know, I can see her doing it . . . she had to channel all that anger into something. What a shame it was blowing things up. She's lucky that the only person she hurt was herself."

Tips for Busy, Budget-Minded Moms

Getting a Handle on the Paperwork
Despite trying to be a paperless society, we seem to have more paper than ever. Here's a few ideas on how to establish some routines for the paper chase in your life.

- Don't let mail pile up. Open and sort it as it arrives, trashing junk mail and shredding anything with your personal information that you're not going to keep. Create a folder or in-box for bills to be paid.
- Request electronic billing to reduce the amount of paper you receive. Paying bills with electronic bank transfers cuts down paper and eliminates mailing costs.
- Create a system to deal with the paper your kids bring home from school. A notebook with pocket dividers labeled with each child's name is an easy way to store field trip permission slips, receipts for fund-raiser purchases, and school picture order forms.
- You can add more pocket dividers to the notebook for takeout menus and coupons.
- Label plastic storage crates for each child's graded homework papers. Go through kids' backpacks at the end of each week and help them clean out papers they don't need. Save graded papers and tests until the end of the quarter, semester, or school year, in case a grade wasn't recorded or they need old tests to review. At the end of the year, you can throw everything away or go through the crate with your child and pick out several examples of their work to store in a memory box.

Chapter
Nineteen

I know it's short notice, but if you could make time for me, I'd appreciate it," Bonnie said. I pressed the phone into the crook of my shoulder as I shoved a juice box into Livvy's lunch box.

"Mom, I can only find one shoe," Livvy called, her voice near panic level. Rex circled the island with his tennis ball in his mouth and managed to nudge my calves with his head as he passed me.

I glanced at the clock, wishing I'd had the sense to let the answering machine pick up the call. Seven forty-five. We could still make it to school if I got off the phone, but with Bonnie that was no small feat. If only it had been my cell phone. Calls get disconnected on cell phones. Too bad I was on my landline. I covered the mouthpiece and called, "Check under your bed."

Bonnie rattled on as I shoved the lunch box into Livvy's backpack, reached to pick up Nathan, and grabbed the tennis ball from Rex's mouth as he trotted past me again. I flicked the ball across the living room and he lunged after it, his paws skidding and slipping on the kitchen floor. I stood, boosting Nathan onto my hip. He needed a diaper change before we left to take Livvy to school.

Bonnie said, "Since my meeting's cancelled, this morning would be the perfect time. You have no idea how ready I am to get this project moving. Simplify. Streamline. I'm ready to get the clutter out of my life, to go green, to work out more. Things are changing for Rich and me. We have to be ready to go with this new phase . . ."

Livvy's impatient and increasingly frantic wail overpowered Bonnie. "Mooomm, it's not there."

Our late night last night had thrown us off schedule this morning. I made a mental promise to myself to always pack lunches and lay out clothes the night before. Livvy had already checked the other usual places where her misplaced shoes usually turned up. Rex sat waiting expectantly at the door to Nathan's room with the tennis ball clamped in his mouth.

"So you can see why it's so important to get started on organizing now. I want to eliminate distractions and have a more peaceful—"

"Bonnie," I said, interrupting and probably disturbing the Zen vibration she had going, but I couldn't stay on the phone any longer. "I'm in the middle of something right now." I taped on a new diaper. "Let me see what I can do. Will both you and Colonel Barnes be there?"

"Oh, no. He left for the squadron today at five this morning. He's so dedicated, you know. He's the one who's holding everything together since Colonel Pershall . . . anyway, I was just saying the other day how crucial, how integral, he is to the squadron—"

Bonnie was making her pitch to the wrong audience. Since I had no input or control over who became the next squadron commander, I had no idea why she was talking him up to me. Habit, maybe? I cut in again. "I'll call you back within the hour and let you know if I can make it."

I weighed my options. I didn't want to turn down a potential client, but I had no idea if Colonel Barnes was involved in Colonel Pershall's death. I thought back to Waraday's lukewarm response to my information about Colonel Barnes being in Denise's house. He'd said it would be followed up, but he certainly hadn't seemed excited or even very interested in it.

Perhaps a little time alone poking around their house would be productive, if I actually got in. Bonnie's past wishy-washy actions had left me in the lurch. She'd set up appointments and cancelled moments before, so I wasn't going to drop everything to run over to her house right this minute. Of course, she could be serious about getting organized. She certainly sounded like she'd had some sort of epiphany.

I set a clean and ready-to-go Nathan on his feet and went to help Livvy. A quick scan of her room didn't reveal a hidden shoe.

"Mom, I don't want to be late."

"We still have a couple of minutes," I said as I opened her closet door. "Look, here it is, right where it's supposed to be. Amazing!"

• • •

An hour later I rang Bonnie's doorbell, quickly flipping through the folder of pictures she'd given to me at the supper club. My go-to sitter was on a field trip to the science center, so I had to break down and call my neighbor Dorthea. I hated to impose—it was such short notice—but she'd been thrilled with the idea of Nathan spending an hour with her. Nathan loved to go to her house. I think it had something to do with the ice cream bars she handed out.

The glossy pages Bonnie had torn from magazines were all of slick, minimalist-style rooms. Not the easiest thing to achieve in base housing.

Bonnie opened the door. "Hi, Ellie. I'm so pleased you could make it today."

"Glad it worked out, too. I was looking through the photos you clipped," I said, stepping inside as Bonnie closed the door. I followed her, flicking to the last sheets at the back of the folder, which were white copy paper. Maybe she'd made some notes of her ideas.

I slowed my steps. No, the papers were copies from a book with dense text and lines highlighted in yellow. I frowned. The section heading STRANGULATION seemed to jump off the page. I skimmed the page, more amazed at each word. *Hanging. Ligature. Manual strangulation. Garroting.* The words jumbled together in my mind.

"So what do you think?" Bonnie asked.

I snapped the folder shut and swallowed hard. The pages had to be from a forensic-type book. Why would someone have that info with the section on strangulation highlighted?

"Ellie?" Bonnie asked.

"What?" Why hadn't I looked through this folder at home? Why had I waited until I was on the doorstep?

"What do you think?" She pointed at the folder. I stared at her. "Of the magazine pages," she said pointedly.

"The pictures. Right. Ah—they're great ideas," I said, playing for time. I realized I was gripping the folder so hard I was bending it. I made myself relax my grip. I put the folder in my Kate Spade tote bag. I couldn't run out the door a few seconds after I'd arrived. That would look odd and I didn't want to do anything that might let Bonnie know that I knew she had an unhealthy interest in the details of strangulation. I had to stay for a few minutes, but I vowed this would be the quickest consultation ever.

I pulled out the paperwork I needed to get started with the consultation. "Here's my brochure," I said.

"Do you want a cup of tea or coffee before we get started?" Bonnie asked.

"No," I barked. I realized I sounded odd and tried to moderate my tone. "No, thanks. I have another appointment so I can't stay too long. In fact," I extemporized, "I'm meeting Mitch."

"Okay," Bonnie said uncertainly. I told myself to calm down. Obviously those papers weren't supposed to be in that folder and Bonnie didn't know I'd seen them.

"Well, why don't we start in here," Bonnie said, motioning for me to sit down on the couch. I dropped the tote at my feet and perched on the edge of the cushion, feeling as skittish as a kid in a doctor's waiting room. Why would she have those copies? If you wanted to know something about strangulation, wouldn't you just go look it up online? Well, probably not. You especially wouldn't do that if you didn't want anyone to know what you were researching. Everything left a trail on a computer. Probably the only place you could go and not leave a trace was the library, especially if you didn't check the books out, just *made copies* of the relevant information.

"So what do you think?" Bonnie asked again, bringing me back to the conversation.

"Right. Living room." I had to buckle down and concentrate on organizing for about ten minutes. "Well, the style you like might be more of a challenge to achieve in base housing with the tight quarters. We'd have to find ways for everything to do double duty with the storage. You know, things that function for storage and as furniture, too, like hollow ottomans."

"I like it. What else?"

"Well, if you want to totally change your decorating style, you're going to have to do some thinning. The looks you like are very streamlined and clean," I said, glancing around the heavily furnished and knickknacked room.

Bonnie looked at the bookcases doubtfully. "I don't know. What would we do with all of these books?"

"Well, you'd have to decide which ones were essential, the ones you really wanted. Then we'd find a place for those. The rest you'd give away, maybe to a library, or you could sell them online."

"Oh," she said, her voice small.

"What I usually do at this point is ask you some detailed questions and look at what you want organized, so I'm sure we're on the same page. I'll write up an estimate for you," I said, pulling out my paperwork, ready to make notes. "So tell me, what areas of your life and home would you like to be more organized?"

"Um . . ." Bonnie looked around the room, frowned, and then said uncertainly, "Well, everything, really."

"We'll need to narrow that down a bit. Think about the different areas of your house. Are there any areas that don't function well for you?"

The crease between Bonnie's eyebrows deepened. She had that panicky look of a game show contestant who doesn't know the answer to the question. The air conditioning clicked on and it was so quiet I could hear the air whooshing out of the vents. It was the longest I'd ever seen her go without talking.

"There's no right or wrong answer, just think about what's working in your house and what isn't," I prompted.

"Well, there's the dining room. It isn't really a dining room anymore," she said at last. "Rich has taken over in there. Here, I'll show you." She jumped up and I followed her into the room.

"See, it's only been a week since Rich cleaned up his mess and he's already dragged it all out again."

I hadn't been paying attention last night to the dining room. I only remembered Bonnie had drinks set up in here, but now the long table was covered with stacks of paper and books. A laptop was positioned on the table with a printer near it. More thick books, reams of paper, and boxes lined the baseboard on the far side of the room.

"So you'd like this room to function as a dining room?" I said, pacing around the table.

"Well, yes . . . although we usually eat in the kitchen at the bar," she said uncertainly.

"Do you have another place for a home office?"

"No, it's just a three bedroom, so there's no spare bedroom." She pulled on the hem of her lemon shirt.

I glanced quickly around the house. There didn't seem to be any extra space for a home office. The living room was cramped as it was and space was already at a premium in the kitchen. "We could probably come up with some way to use this room as an office, but still have the option of using it as a dining room, too," I said, thinking of concealed storage spaces and a drafting-type desk that folded down from the wall. Maybe something that could fold back up and attach to the wall with artwork on the bottom so that it looked like a painting when it was folded up. Something unframed and very modern would fit the look she liked. But before I got too excited about my idea, I asked, "So this is Rich's work area?" Bonnie nodded and I said, "Well, I'll have to talk to him before I do anything in here."

I felt the surge of excitement that came with the first glimmer of an idea at the beginning of a project, but I didn't want to get too deeply involved here, especially in light of the copies I'd just found.

"Oh, sure," she said as she tugged at her collar. "He'll be home for lunch so you can talk to him then."

"I can't stay," I said quickly. "Let me ask you the rest of my questions and then I really have to go. I'll talk to him later."

Bonnie moved some stacks of papers and we sat down at the table. I ran through my list and got more rambling answers from her. Except for the dining room—and she'd been vague even about that area—she really didn't know what she wanted. She liked the idea of being organized, but she couldn't pinpoint another specific area that she wanted help with.

"What about routines? Are there times of the day or week you'd like to be more organized, like the rush in the morning or paying bills?"

Bonnie shifted in her chair and straightened the hem of her yellow shirt again. "I don't know," she said almost irritably. "Everything seems to work okay with those things. Do we have to go through all these questions? Can't you just make my house look like those pictures?"

I put my pen down. "Bonnie, I think you need an interior designer."

"What?" Her hands dropped to the table, motionless.

"For a completely new look, you need to find an interior designer." I had a knack for organization, but I knew my limits. Bonnie really didn't want me picking out furniture for her. "I can help you thin your belongings to fit your new style."

Bonnie sat there, frowning, and I could tell it wasn't the answer she wanted. She wanted her new look and she wanted it now. Bonnie always did move at warp speed, so I was slowing her down and she wasn't happy about it. "Well, do you have any names?"

"I can have some for you by the end of the day," I said, thinking of my online network of organizers. They would have contacts with interior designers I could pass on to Bonnie. And I also had business cards from several people I'd met at chamber of commerce meetings.

"Fine," Bonnie said, standing abruptly. "I'll check into it." Her cell phone rang. She hurried into the kitchen, saying, "Sorry, but I have to take this. I've been waiting for this call."

I stood and shuffled my papers together. So much for a new client. I doubted Bonnie would call me back after I gave her the interior designer names. I gave a mental shrug and told myself it was better not to have a client than to take on a job without clear goals. I gazed at the dining room table, thinking I would have enjoyed the challenge of the office-slash-dining room. I mentally tucked away the fold-down desk idea for future use and capped my pen. I really didn't want to be interacting with Colonel Barnes right now, so it probably was better that the Barneses weren't going to be my next organizing job.

Bonnie chatted on the phone, confirming a time. I picked up a stack of typed pages, one of the piles of paper she'd moved earlier, and put it back on the table, figuring I'd do a little cleaning up while I waited for her. I grabbed another stack and replaced it, only to stop and stare at it after I put it on the table.

More yellow highlighted text caught my attention. It was another photocopy from a book with the subheads highlighted. The page on top of the stack was about poisons.

Chapter Twenty

I flicked through the rest of the stack, my gaze skipping from one yellow stripe of highlighting to another: poisonous plants and toxic drug combinations. Bonnie said these were Colonel Barnes's papers. What was he doing with all this information? Why did he need it? And why was he methodically highlighting this stuff, as if he was studying it? I wanted to run, get out of there, but it was like knowing I should stop eating so much chocolate. I couldn't stop. I couldn't step away. With a sick feeling, I thumbed through the rest of the stacks. *Gun specifications, blood spatter patterns, bomb components.*

"Ellie," Bonnie called, her voice cheery. I could hear her shoes tapping toward me from the kitchen as I dropped the papers back into place and patted the edges to line them up, with trembling fingers.

"I am so sorry, but I have to go. That was a client, an orthodontist. We have some great products that I know he'll love. I've been trying to get in to see him for ages and ages, and he'll only see me today in half an hour, so I have to leave." She shrugged into a black jacket that went with her pants and I had to push away thoughts of bumblebees.

"That's fine." I grabbed my papers and pen, then picked up my tote bag from the living room. It had fallen over and I shoved the loose papers that had spilled under the couch back inside with one hand. "I need to leave, anyway. I have an appointment, too," I said, practically sprinting toward the front door. "No, you don't have to go with me. I know the way. I'll e-mail you," I called, already on the porch. I shut the door firmly behind me as she said good-bye.

Once in the minivan, I took a deep breath to try and calm down. I pulled out my cell phone and called Mitch. Of course, he didn't answer. He was probably in a meeting. I left a message for him, telling him about the papers, and said I'd be at the Base Exchange, if he wanted to meet for an early lunch. Then I called information and got the phone number for the county sheriff. As I was being transferred from one extension to another, Bonnie pulled out of the driveway in her black Volkswagen GTI and zoomed by me with a wave.

It took a while, but I finally got through to Waraday's voice mail and left him a message about the papers I'd seen in the dining room. "I have some of the pages. I'm not sure how they got in the folder Bonnie gave me." I described what I'd seen, then left my phone number.

A car pulled up beside me and I was relieved to see it was Jeff. I rolled down my window as he powered down the passenger window on his car. "Hey, Ellie. How's it going?" he asked.

"Oh, fine," I said, with forced cheerfulness. "Just making some phone calls." I waved my phone.

"Yeah, don't drive while you're talking on the phone. The no-cell-phone policy on base has been pretty hard on Abby. She always forgets about it. She's gotten two warnings in the last month."

"So what are you doing?" I asked, inhaling the scent of freshly cut grass.

"Home for lunch. I'll let you get back to it," he said, pulling away. He drove a few houses down and pulled in the driveway.

I decided I'd better try and call Montigue as well. I knew the phone number for the base operator by memory, thank goodness, so I started with that and began the convoluted process to get her extension at the OSI office. Two women I recognized from the squadron walked by on the opposite side of the street. They were in workout clothes, their arms and legs pumping as they power-walked. They waved to me. My window was still down, so I waved to them, glad they didn't stop.

I began to see why Mitch hadn't wanted to live on base. Could you do anything without someone noticing?

An airman transferred my call and then a crisp voice said, "Montigue."

"Agent Montigue, this is Ellie Avery. I've just left a message for Detective Waraday about some papers I have that belong to Colonel Barnes."

Over the clatter of a printer and a cavalcade of voices, she said, "Papers?"

"Yes, from Colonel Barnes. He's been doing . . . I guess you'd call it research, into strangulation, poisons, guns, explo—"

"You have these papers in your possession?" she asked sharply.

"Yes," I said, reaching for my tote bag. "Well, I have some. Bonnie—that's Colonel Barnes's wife—she wanted me to do an organizational consultation for her. She gave me a folder with pictures and sketches from magazines . . . well, never mind, that's not important. What is important is that in the back of that folder were some papers, photocopies from a book about . . . strangulation . . ." I said, my words slowing down as I shifted through the papers in my tote bag. I didn't see the file.

"Strangulation? *Exactly* what does it say?" Montigue's voice was still sharp, but there was a layer of interest that hadn't been there before.

I pulled out my brochures, my notepad, my calculator, then dug through my billfold, sunglasses, toys, a plastic bag of animal crackers, and a single spare diaper.

I fell back against the seat with a thump. I didn't have it. It had to be under Bonnie's couch in the living room. It must have slipped out when the tote bag fell over and I didn't see it in my rush to get out of there.

"Mrs. Avery, are you still there?"

"Yes, I'm here, but I don't have it with me. It's inside their house," I said, frustrated. "But there's more in the house. I saw more copies from books about poisons and guns and—"

"We searched Colonel Barnes's house and car, Mrs. Avery," Montigue said, and I could tell she was losing interest. "I don't know what you think you saw, but there was nothing like that in their house."

"It's there now. Can't you search again?"

"I'm afraid not. I can't get a search warrant for what you think you saw, at least not from the person I'd have to go to."

"So you're not going to do anything?" I asked, amazed.

"Unfortunately, I can't, Mrs. Avery, and at this point we have other persons of interest that we have to pursue. Thanks for your call, ma'am. I'm making a note of your information."

She hung up and I snapped the phone closed. They were focused on Denise. I bet they were waiting for analysis of the circular needles they'd taken from her house last night. If they could prove any of the cords connecting the knitting needles had been used to kill Colonel Pershall, then Denise was in deep trouble. With the evidence of her divorce preparations, she'd look guilty, never mind that Colonel Barnes could have planted the murder weapon.

I dug out a chocolate kiss from my purse and popped it in my mouth. There had to be some way to get those papers back.

I chewed my lower lip for a moment, considering alternatives. I could drive away and try to forget about it, but I didn't want to do that. What if Colonel Barnes found the folder later and Bonnie told him she'd given it to me? Then he'd know I'd seen it.

I opened my phone and dialed Bonnie's number. She answered on the first ring, sounding impatient as always. "Yes?"

"Hi, Bonnie." I had to work to make my voice sound casual. It was especially hard since my heart was pounding. "It's me, Ellie. I left some papers in your house—"

"I can't come back there to let you in," she cut in.

"No, that's fine. I wouldn't want you to miss your meeting. I was wondering . . . do you have a key hidden somewhere or with a neighbor? I could pop in and get the papers and you wouldn't have to come all the way back here. I hate to bother you, but I really need—"

"Yes, fine. Taped under the mailbox. I'm going into the meeting right now, so I won't be answering my phone. If you can't find the key you'll have to wait until this afternoon."

She didn't say good-bye, just hung up on me. Well, that must be some meeting if she wasn't even going to answer her phone. I had a couple more Hershey's kisses to fortify me as I checked the street. There were a few kids riding bikes, but they were the only movement. I decided I better go before anyone else I knew arrived and wanted to chat.

I hurried across the lawn, reminding myself I had Bonnie's permission to do this. It's not like I was breaking and entering. I was *entering*, but with permission. Then why did I feel breathless and could practically hear my own heartbeat? I felt like I did during the stroller brigade workout when I'd climbed the steepest hill in the neighborhood. I ran my fingers under the mailbox, pulled away a thick layer of tape, then peeled the key off the tape and inserted it in the lock.

I turned the key and shoved the door open. I was stepping across the threshold when a deep voice asked, "Can I help you with something, Ellie?"

Tips for Busy, Budget-Minded Moms

Storing paperwork
- Create a filing system. Have one set of folders labeled with individual accounts like utilities, insurance, retirement accounts,

store and charge cards, and charities. After a bill is paid, file it in the appropriate folder.

- Make another set of files for long-term storage: mortgage or lease contracts, tax returns, warranties and receipts, and personal documents.

- It's a good idea to create a file for each family member with birth certificate, passport, social security card, shot records, school transcripts, and resumes. Keep this file in a fireproof safe or safety-deposit box. Small document safes can be purchased at discount stores.

Chapter
Twenty-one

Colonel Barnes stood on the porch behind me with a quizzical look on his face. He was in workout clothes—a sweat-drenched T-shirt, shorts, and running shoes. His shaved head glistened with sweat. He wiped his arm across his forehead, then said, "Seems we're destined to run into each other at empty houses, Ellie. Bonnie's not home."

"I know. I met her here earlier." I'd completely forgotten that Bonnie had said he would be coming home.

"She told me about that—organizing thing," he said with the same vaguely suspicious tone that

I'd heard many times from spouses of people who wanted to hire me. Sometimes I had to sell organizing services twice—once to each spouse. Of course, that wasn't the case here, since I wasn't going to organize anything for them.

"I left some of my stuff here by accident, so I called her and she told me where the key was." I held it up, like it was evidence that I hadn't picked the lock.

"Sure, fine, go ahead," he said as he reached by me and opened the mailbox. He took out several envelopes. "I'll wait until you're done before I head back to the squadron."

I paused. "You ran all the way from the squadron? That's on the other side of the base."

He shrugged as he looked through the envelopes. "It's not that far, only about three miles." A little of my anxiety at being alone with him eased. He was preoccupied with opening one of the envelopes and wasn't even looking at me. He didn't seem to care that I'd been about to enter his empty house.

I hurried down the hallway and into the living room where I leaned down and ran my hand under the edge of the couch. The file was a few inches back. I pulled it out and quickly checked to make sure the photocopied papers were in it.

Colonel Barnes had stepped inside the door. He tossed the mail on a stack of magazines and envelopes on a small table near the door.

"I found it," I said as I waved the file and hurried past him. "Thanks, Colonel Barnes."

I was already in the grass of the front yard when he called out. "Ellie, the key."

"Oh. Of course. Sorry." I met him on the porch and held out the key. In my hurry to get out of there, I let go of the key a second before he grabbed it and it pinged to the concrete. "Oops. Sorry," I said and picked it up. "Here you go."

He took the key, then said, "Wait," his gaze fixed on the folder I had firmly clutched to my side. I glanced down and saw the papers had come loose when I bent down. Now the edges of the papers where fanned out, peeking over the edge of the folder, the highlighted lines glowing almost neon in the sunshine.

He quickly reached out and plucked a photocopied page from the folder. "Where did you get this?"

I took several steps back. "That? Oh . . . I didn't even realize it was in there. Haven't seen it before." I took another step back. "I've got to go—"

He closed the distance between us and gripped my arm above the elbow. The sharp smell of sweat enveloped me. Obviously, he hadn't bought my never-seen-it-before ploy, maybe because I kept inching away from him. "Where did you get this?" he demanded again.

"It was in the folder Bonnie gave to me, but I'll

forget I ever saw it, really, if you'll let go. You're hurting my arm."

His tight grip eased, but he didn't release me. "I have to show you something," he said, and began marching me to the front door.

"No." I straightened my legs, resisting.

He pulled harder, practically dragging me. "I just want you to see something."

"No." I squirmed, fighting to break free of his grip. I realized I still had the folder in my other hand and started hitting him in the face with it. "Let me go." I twisted around, but couldn't break free, so I dug my feet into the soft grass.

He stopped and released my arm. "My God, you're afraid of me, aren't you?"

I would have turned and sprinted to the minivan, but his voice, a mixture of incredulity and—surprisingly—fear, held me still.

"I'm not going inside that house," I said. My hands were trembling and I was breathing hard. I stepped back and saw a trail through the lawn where my heels had ripped up the grass and exposed dark streaks of earth.

"Okay, okay," he said and backed away, his hands in the air.

A car cruised down the street and we both noticed the driver watching us. Colonel Barnes put his hands down and said, "Look, I only want to show you something. I apologize for grabbing you, but you've got the wrong idea—I know it looks bad, but I—just wait here, okay? Please don't leave, all right?"

I'd never seen this pleading, almost nervous side of Colonel Barnes. I glanced around and saw the kids on their bikes at the end of the street and a dog walker heading our way. Another car was turning onto the street.

What could he possibly have to show me? Part of me wanted to get out of there, but part of me— the curious side I never seemed to be able to quite squelch—wanted to stay. His attitude was so weird. "I'll stay as long as there are people on the street and I'm in sight of them."

He glanced quickly up the street and saw the car and the woman walking her dog. He nodded and backed slowly away. At the porch, he stepped inside the door, which was still open, then reappeared outside in a few seconds.

"Here, take a look at that," he said, holding out an open envelope at arm's length.

I took it and he said, "Go on, read it."

The return address read, "Pomeroy & Associates." I pulled a single sheet of paper from the envelope and quickly scanned three lines of text, a preprinted form letter. *Thank you for your query. Unfortunately, I am not taking on new clients at this time. I wish you the best in finding representation.*

A scrawl in blue pen across the bottom read, *Sorry, but I already have several thrillers on my list and there was nothing in your query to indicate your work would stand out in an already crowded market. Best of luck.*

The only thing I could make out in the scribble of a signature under the personal note was an enormous *P* at the beginning of the last name.

I looked up from the letter. "A thriller? As in a book? A novel?"

"Yes. I have seventeen more rejection letters inside, if you'd like to see them," he said.

Seventeen. Wow. That was a lot of rejection, but instead of looking embarrassed or depressed, he had an eager look on his face as he pointed to the letter. "See that? I'm getting handwritten notes on mine, not just form letters—that's a good sign."

"You're writing a novel?" I asked again, still stuck on this surprising bit of news. Colonel Barnes glanced at the dog walker who was almost even with us, then stepped closer and said, "I've already written it, all ninety-two thousand words. That page you saw—that was research."

Research. Who would have thought that? And from Colonel Barnes. He was about the farthest from a literary-type guy that you could get with his blustery personality and focus on promotion. I thought back to what I'd seen in the dining room. Besides the stacks of photocopies, I'd also seen a three-inch-thick stack of double-spaced pages. If I hadn't been so focused on the photocopies, I might have paid more attention to the other papers. My thoughts circled back to the photocopies. "I still don't understand about all those papers. Why would you copy that information? Doesn't everyone do research on the Internet these days?"

"Nah—I'm old school. I like to have a hard copy and you can't trust everything you read on the Internet, anyway. Books and magazine articles are much more reliable."

"So everything in the dining room—all of those papers—it's all research?" I asked.

"You saw that, too? No wonder you looked petrified. Yes, that's all research. I have terrorists in my novel killing people, blowing up things. I have to be accurate. Could you please keep quiet about this? I know what you were thinking —that I was somehow involved in Colonel Pershall's death, but I did that research months ago and it has nothing to do with his death."

Why would he care if people knew he was writing a book, even a book with terrorists in it? Unless . . . "Someone's strangled in your book, aren't they?"

He sighed, resigned. "Yes."

"Who? What character?"

"A commander."

"So when Colonel Pershall died, you panicked and hid your book and research." Bonnie had said the dining room had been cleaned out and Montigue had said they hadn't found anything like the papers I described.

"I know it looks bad," he said, reaching out for the rejection letter. I handed it to him and he added it to the highlighted paper he'd pulled from the file, which he still held in his hand. He continued, "I was with him at the golf course. I knew they'd check me out. Who's going to believe that it's a coincidence—that I wrote a scene with strangulation and then my commanding officer is strangled?"

He was using the word strangled, not garroted, so maybe he didn't know how Colonel Pershall had died, or maybe he did know and was covering by using the wrong word. "So you hid everything? Where did you put it? You've got a lot of papers in there," I said, shifting so that I could glance up and down the street. A car paused at the four-way stop, then continued on.

"I rented a second locker at the gym. No one noticed when I made a few trips to the gym with heavy duffel bags. It took me three trips to move all that paper. But it was worth it. If the police had looked at me more closely—searched my laptop—they'd find out, but since they didn't find any initial evidence that I was involved, they didn't look deeper."

"Writing a novel with a scene like that is a long way from actually committing murder. I still don't see why you'd want to hide your writing. If the only evidence is that you've *written* about strangulation, then you're not in trouble."

He rubbed his hand over his mouth and looked at me thoughtfully, then said, "It's hard to explain. I want to keep the writing thing quiet. You're the only one who knows now."

"Bonnie doesn't know?" I asked, incredulous. How could you keep something like that from your wife? "Didn't she see you working on it, or notice all your research papers in the dining room?"

He made a dismissive gesture with the letter, wiping away my comments like they were nothing. "When I'm writing, she thinks I've brought work home from the squadron. Besides, she's too wrapped up in her own world to notice what's going on in mine."

That was an amazing statement that I couldn't let go. "How could a wife not know her husband was writing a novel—wouldn't the extra stacks of paper tip her off? And what about your computer? Wouldn't she see your files on there?"

"She never goes in the dining room—that's where I work. We don't eat in there and we have separate laptops."

"What about the mail? Wouldn't she see that letter?" I persisted, pointing at it.

"Why do you think I ran over here today before lunch? Most of my queries are e-queries anyway, so there's only a few I have to watch for in the mail. But even if she did see one, she'd probably just hand it off to me and keep plowing through her routine. She's got tunnel vision—her job and the kids are what she focuses on. I'm on the periphery. At least, I was until Colonel Pershall died and she decided I should be squadron commander," he said wearily.

"And you don't want it?" I asked.

"No. I want to write and get published and write more books. I'd rather write novels than be a squadron commander."

"Well, you've certainly done a good job hiding what you really want to do. I think everyone in the squadron thinks you want to be a general." Something about what he'd said earlier was bothering me and I suddenly realized what it was. "Colonel Pershall knew, didn't he? You said I was the only one who knew about your writing *now*, like someone else had known about it."

He smiled weakly. "Yes, Lewis knew. He picked up on all my jokes about promotion. I think it was a case of protesting too much. He realized I didn't want it. I told him what was going on and he was supportive. He even read the first chapters of my manuscript—that's why I was in Denise's house. I had to get those manuscript pages back before Denise or the police found them."

If he was telling the truth—and I did believe him—then his reason for being in Denise's house wasn't as sinister as I thought. The power-walking ladies turned the corner and headed in our direction.

"So," he said, his voice shifting from the confessional tone to a let's-wrap-this-up tone, "since you know what's going on and know it has nothing to do with Lewis's death, will you keep it quiet?"

"No, I can't. I've already called the detectives investigating Colonel Pershall's death and told them what I saw."

He looked scared and I thought maybe I'd made the wrong assessment of him. Perhaps his writing was an elaborate ruse to cover for a murder? He slapped the letter against his leg. "That's it, then—everyone will know."

I felt the wariness rise in me again and I began easing back a few steps. "They'll know what?"

"That I'm a writer."

"Why do you care about that?" Shouldn't not becoming a murder suspect be his real concern here?

"Don't you see? Most agents and publishers reject ninety-nine percent of the material they see. It's a long shot. If I don't get an agent and don't get the book published—it's another failure and now, if that happens, everyone will know."

I picked my words carefully, thinking of how he'd said *another failure*. Was he talking about his air force career? I didn't see how he could consider himself a failure. Reaching the rank of lieutenant colonel was no easy thing, but if your aspirations—or your spouse's aspirations—were much higher than that, well, I suppose you could see yourself as a failure. Finally, I said, "I don't think people are going to look down on you, if you don't get your book published. In fact, I'm impressed that you've written one while you've got another full-time job."

"Thanks, that's nice of you to say, but I doubt everyone will see it that way."

He glanced at the house and I knew he was thinking of Bonnie. Remembering their conversation that I'd overheard last night, I could pretty much imagine what her response would be. I bet she'd be upset he'd poured his time into writing a book instead of focusing on his air force career. Yep, she'd be mad. I could almost understand his attitude. "Well, if it's any consolation, the OSI agent I talked to wasn't very interested when I told her about the papers I'd seen. She may not even follow up on it."

"No, that's too much to hope for," Colonel Barnes said, his gaze fixed behind me. I turned and saw a security police car pulling to the curb.

A security police officer emerged from the driver's seat and Montigue stepped out of the passenger side. As they crossed the grass, the officer said, "We had a call about a possible domestic disturbance at this address. Is there a problem?"

I glanced at Colonel Barnes to see his reaction. He looked down at the highlighted paper he still held in his hand along with the letter from the literary agent. He pressed his lips together as he studied the papers, then raised his head.

"Special Agent Montigue, I have something that appears to have drawn some attention." He glanced at me as he added, "And raised some unfounded suspicions." He gave her the high-lighted paper.

She shot me a long glance before she said, "Well, we better clear this up."

Chapter
Twenty-two

By the time I'd explained my involvement and extricated myself from the scene at Colonel Barnes's house, it was almost noon and I hadn't heard back from Mitch, so I decided to run by the squadron on my way home. I tried to shake the feeling of unease that had settled on me. There was probably a completely normal and reasonable explanation for Mitch's silence. I repeated that thought to myself and then forced myself to con-centrate on Colonel Barnes.

When I'd left he'd been repeating, for about the third time, that he was writing a book and the notes and papers were research. He was sticking to his story and I thought it was the truth. He'd really been scared that I would broadcast his secret. Now, of course, there wouldn't be any way to keep it quiet.

I pulled into the squadron parking lot and headed for a side door. Unlike Mitch's last squadron building, which had been a converted Cold War–era alert facility, the three-story squadron building here at Taylor was new and had even escaped the blah-yellow paint that covered many buildings on air force bases. The squadron building was red brick, a nice change from the usual bland yellow exterior.

I went in the side door, glad that it was unlocked during the day, and quickly climbed the staircase. I passed one of the squadron's trophy cases on the landing between the first and second floors. Stuffed with every type of sports trophy, it glittered with metallic statues, plaques, medallions on ribbons, and team pictures. Most squadrons fielded some sports teams and this one was no exception.

Despite the new building, the 233rd Refueling Squadron had been in existence since World War II and, although they hadn't always flown air refueling tankers, they'd always played sports. Sometimes when the kids and I were waiting for Mitch to finish up some paperwork, I'd bring the kids down to look at the trophies as a distraction. Some of the trophies dated from the forties. They'd actually run out of space inside the case and many of the newest trophies perched on top. Livvy's favorite was a shiny, angel-like winged creature on a five-inch marble base. Nathan's favorite was a stuffed animal, a hawk—the squadron's mascot—that someone had stuck on top of the case.

I wasn't sure why Colonel Pershall had the trophy case set up in the stairwell. Usually it would have gone in The Nest, the squadron's break room. I thought of Bonnie and her desire for a streamlined look. Maybe he'd been going for cleaner lines in the break room, which would have been an aberration for most squadron break rooms.

Except for the break room and high security cipher locks on some doors, the building looked like your average office space with low-pile gray carpet and offices with cubicles. Only the break room was different from what you'd find in most work places. Flight squadrons always seemed to have elaborate break rooms, which usually resembled a bar. Liberally decorated with beer posters and a big-screen TV, it was a room where people ate their lunch, or, on Friday afternoons, had a beer. Not like any office I'd ever worked in, that was for sure. But with the new building, the break room had a more generic feeling—there was a single beer advertisement, a full-size cardboard cutaway of a blonde in a bikini, and a smattering of souvenirs from the squadron's deployments, which were an odd mishmash ranging from the typical group photos in restaurants to a deer head mounted on the wall near the pool table.

I pushed open the door to the third floor and hurried down the hallway to the flight training office, which was where Mitch worked when he wasn't flying. The office was empty, but his computer was on, papers were spread across his desk, and his gym bag was beside the rolling chair. He was around somewhere. I should have tried The Nest first, I decided, and retraced my steps to the stairwell because the break room was on the ground floor.

I tried calling his cell phone again as I walked through the squadron. I breathed a sigh of relief when he answered. "Sorry I couldn't answer earlier. I was in a meeting. Are you still on base?"

"Yep, in the squadron, in fact. I'm on the first floor," I said, deciding all my news could wait until I could talk to him face to face.

"Okay, I'm leaving the conference room now."

"I'll meet you on the stairs," I said, retracing my path. "See you in a second."

I swung open the stairwell door and heard Mitch's heavy flight boots tromping down. Instead of climbing the stairs again, I decided to wait at the bottom for him. He rounded the stairs at the landing in front of the trophy case. I looked up to greet him and saw one of the taller trophies wobble, then fall.

"Watch out!" I yelled, pointing over his head.

He looked back over his shoulder and the heavy marble base smacked his forehead. He reeled back like he'd been punched and blood spurted from the gash it left.

I raced up the stairs. "Are you okay?" I asked, even though I could tell he wasn't. He pressed his hand to his forehead, but blood was already seeping between his fingers.

"I'm fine," he said, as he stood back up, then swayed slightly, his face pale and washed out.

"Here, sit." I pushed him onto one of the steps and when he actually obeyed me without complaining that I was fussing over him, I felt a thread of fear run through me.

I didn't have anything to press on the cut. It was so hot I wasn't wearing a jacket and, for once, I didn't have the diaper bag—which was practically a survival kit—with me. A rivulet of blood flowed quickly from his fingers down over the back of his hand and soaked into the edge of his flight suit. I needed paper towels, but the bathrooms and the break room were on the other side of the squadron. I spotted the stuffed hawk still perched on the top of the case and grabbed it. "Here, use this."

Mitch took it without a word and pressed it to his head. Blood blossomed through the furry cover so quickly that I pulled out my phone.

"I'm calling nine-one-one," I said.

"No." Mitch grabbed my arm. "I think it's slowing down."

"I don't think so," I said and punched in the numbers.

"Ellie, wait, I'm serious. Don't call."

I paused with my finger on the *send* button and looked at him. The stuffed animal looked like something from a horror movie, blood soaked and matted, but his color was returning to normal and the cut wasn't spurting blood now. "Head wounds bleed a lot, trust me, this happened to me a ton of times when I was a kid. I'm going to be fine," he said as he removed the stuffed hawk. "I just need something else . . ."

Now that I could see the cut, it wasn't very big and he did look better. "I'll go find some paper towels, Mr. Tough Guy," I said. These macho pilot-types never wanted to go to the doctor for anything. They were afraid that anything that went in their medical files might impact their flying.

"It's not that," Mitch said. "Look at the trophy." He shoved it with his toe and I saw a thin string tied around the foot of the statue where it connected to the marble base.

"What is that?" I asked, leaning closer.

"Ellie, about those paper towels," Mitch said, pulling away his fingers, which were still covered in blood.

"Right." I stood up, reluctant to leave him alone. "Wait," I said and dug around in my tote. "I have a diaper." I pulled it out with a flourish and handed it to him.

"You've got to be kidding," he said, but he opened it and pressed it against his head.

"Diapers are extremely absorbent." I went back to the string that was tied around the trophy. "It's dental floss." I tugged on the long strand that trailed away from us. It was threaded through the open treads of the stairway above us. "Why would someone use floss?" I asked.

"It's strong—much stronger than thread and small enough not to be noticed," Mitch said as he reached out and jerked on it. It fell in a large pool on the stairs beside him. "That's enough to go to the third floor." He tentatively pulled the diaper away from his head.

The bleeding had slowed. "It's not bleeding much. Keep applying pressure," I said and pressed the diaper back on his head.

"I hope no one sees this. I'll never live this down if they do."

The door on the third floor clanged open and footsteps echoed down the stairs. Mitch made a move to get up, but I shoved him back down just as the door on the ground floor opened and a swath of sunlight illuminated the shadowy staircase. It threw the bloody stuffed animal and shiny trophy into a spotlight glare as a group of flyers returned from lunch. Jeff was the first one in the door and I could see Mitch cringe as Jeff asked, "What happened to you?"

I could tell he wanted to be anywhere but sitting on a step with a diaper pressed to his head. "Just an old war wound," Mitch joked.

"Looks like that hawk put up one heck of a fight," Jeff said, nodding to the stuffed animal. "Man, where's a camera when you need one?"

"I've got my cell phone," Henry said.

I knew an image like this would end up on the squadron bulletin board and that would be the very last thing Mitch would want. "He's hurt. This is not the time to make fun of him, Jeff," I scolded and Henry put away his phone. "Look at that trophy. The base has to weigh at least ten pounds. That could have caused some serious damage. And it looks like—"

"It was on the edge of the case," Mitch said, interrupting me. He gave a slight shake of his head, warning me off the subject of how the trophy fell. "The vibrations of everyone going up and down the stairs eventually made it fall."

Henry moved to the front of the group. "Let me take a look. I had some EMT training." He tilted Mitch's head and said, "Well, I don't think you'll need stitches. It doesn't look too bad."

Footfalls had been echoing down from the upper floors as we talked. They were right above us and I looked up to see Denise rounding the landing above us, carrying a cardboard box. She had on jeans and a polo shirt and her sunglasses were propped up on her head. She looked so much better than she had last night. She had makeup on and her gaze was sharp as she scanned the scene below her, then said, "My goodness, Mitch, are you all right? I knew that trophy case should have gone in The Nest." She came down the steps and handed the box to Henry. She examined the cut on Mitch's head, then grabbed his elbow. "Come on, let's get you to The Nest. There's a first aid kit in there."

Jeff made a move to take Mitch's other elbow, but Mitch waved him off as he stood. "I'm okay."

"Of course, you are," Denise said. Mitch hadn't been able to disengage himself from her since she had her arm tucked through his elbow. "We'll get you cleaned up and you'll be fine." I trailed along and filed into the break room behind them. Assessing a situation and taking charge still came naturally to Denise. Those were skills I'm sure she'd used often as a commander's wife.

She found the first aid kit and turned to Henry, who'd dropped to the back of the group and was entering the room. "Did you say you've had some experience with this sort of thing, Henry?"

"Yes, ma'am," he said, taking the kit from her after he put her box down on one of the tables that were scattered around the room. He cleaned the cut and applied a small bandage. It was hard to believe that small cut had produced so much blood, I thought as I looked at the cuff of Mitch's flight suit, which was now crusty with dried blood. A few drops also spotted his flight suit and patches. "Looks like you'll be fine. It's not a deep cut," Henry said.

"Probably because it didn't hit me straight on. When Ellie yelled I saw it and ducked but couldn't get completely out of the way."

"Well, you're lucky you saw it coming. A solid blow from that thing to the back of the head . . ." Henry shook his head. "That wouldn't be good." He stepped back and closed the first aid kit, then wadded the bandage wrappers into a pile. "That'll hold you for now, but you could still have it checked out, to make sure it doesn't leave a scar." Henry glanced from Mitch to me. "Do you want to take him to the hospital or the flight doc?"

"There's no emergency room on base, so it would have to be the hospital in North Dawkins," I said.

"I'm fine," Mitch said rather crankily. "You heard him, Ellie. It's not deep. I'm fine," he repeated firmly and I knew there was no way he was going to get any more medical attention. I wasn't the only one in the family with a stubborn streak. Mitch stood up. "I need a new flight suit, but other than that, I'm all right. Let's go clean up the mess in the stairwell."

Jeff and Henry left to get ready for their flight and Mitch and I returned to the stairs. Denise was already ahead of us there. She was on her hands and knees wiping up drops of blood. "Wow, Denise, you're fast," I said.

She sat back on her heels, and tossed a wet paper towel into a plastic trash bag that contained the ruined stuffed animal. "It looked like Henry had things under control in there, so I came back here."

"Is there anything I can do to help?" I asked as I picked up the plastic trash bag and the remaining stack of paper towels she'd set down on the floor.

"I think I got it all. I didn't want someone to slip and fall. Feeling okay?" she asked Mitch.

"I'm fine." He said it politely enough, but I could tell he was already tired of the question.

The trophy was still on the floor where it had fallen. Denise reached over and picked it up. Mitch and I exchanged a quick puzzled glance as Denise twisted it in her hands. "Not a scratch on it, which is not surprising, considering how heavy it is." The trophy weighed down her arm and she braced her hand on the stair handrail to leverage herself up.

"Here," Mitch said, jumping forward. "Let me." He took the trophy from her and then held her arm as she stood.

"We really should request a new case," Denise said. "It could go in The Nest . . ." Her voice trailed off and I realized she'd forgotten for a few moments that she wasn't the squadron commander's wife anymore. She forced a smile and said, "Of course, that will be up to the new commander."

"I'll make sure it's at the back of the case where it won't fall," Mitch said. "That'll take care of it for now."

She nodded and seemed to brace herself as she pushed her shoulders back. "I'll take that bag and throw it away on my way out," she said and I handed her the trash bag.

"Denise, how are you doing? Feeling better?" I asked.

"Yes, much better. I'm fine." she said with a quick nod and jogged down the stairs. The stairwell door clanged shut behind her.

I turned back to Mitch, who was carefully examining the trophy. "Lots of people are 'fine' today," I said. "She obviously doesn't want to talk about anything right now."

Mitch shrugged. "Let her have her space. Maybe she's embarrassed about last night."

"Could be." She had been wandering around her front yard in her robe. I know I wouldn't want to be caught doing that.

Mitch carefully set the trophy at the back corner of the case.

"Where's the dental floss?" I asked.

"I don't know," Mitch said. He checked around the case. "Well, it's not under it or behind it. Was it in the trash bag?"

"No, I looked. There wasn't anything in there but a few paper towels and that awful-looking stuffed animal."

We looked at each other for a moment, then I said, "That means someone came back here while we were in The Nest and removed it."

Tips for Busy, Budget-Minded Moms

How long to keep paperwork
- Tax paperwork—seven years.
- Debit and credit card receipts—keep until the charges appear on the account statement and accounts are reconciled or paid, unless they are needed to support tax filings.
- Receipts and warranties—keep as long as you own the item and the warranty is active.
- Bills and credit card statements—keep for one year, unless they are needed to support tax filings.
- Cancelled checks—if you still receive cancelled checks, keep them along with check registers for one year. Keep checks that support tax filings for seven years. Hold onto bank statements for one year, unless you need them to support tax filings, then keep them with your tax paperwork and store seven years.
- Paycheck stubs—one year.
- Investment paperwork—check with your tax professional.

Chapter
Twenty-three

I rubbed my forehead. "Do you take these stairs every day?"

"No. I *did*, until we had those strange incidents. After the dry ice explosion in my car, I switched to parking in the lot out front where I could see my car from the windows in my office. And I started taking the front staircase. These stairs aren't as busy as the ones up front and I've been avoiding deserted places lately."

We'd gone several days without any incidents, as Mitch called them. I'd felt like I was holding my breath, waiting for the next horrible thing to happen. As the hours passed and nothing happened, I'd begun to relax slightly. Maybe it was over and nothing else would happen? But now, I felt the cold grip of fear seize me again. There were so many places where Mitch was vulnerable in his daily life. Just walking down the stairs was dangerous, for crying out loud. We couldn't live like this. Knowing that Mitch had assessed this staircase as a risky place and avoided it made me feel a little bit better. He was taking all these incidents very seriously. That also scared me.

"Why did you take these stairs today?"

"I got lazy. I should have used the front staircase, but I thought you'd be coming in this way—

you usually do—and I'd relaxed since nothing had happened lately."

"So this is the first time you've taken these stairs since the dry ice bomb went off in your car?"

He nodded. I swallowed, my throat suddenly dry. "Someone had to be watching you, waiting for you to take the stairs. This 'accident' was engineered specifically for you." I sat down on one of the steps, feeling weary and overwhelmed. "And now we know it couldn't have been Colonel Barnes or Carrie. Who else could want to hurt you?"

"How do you know it couldn't be Colonel Barnes?" Mitch asked with his dark gaze focused intently on me. "We didn't see him today, but he could be upstairs. Anyone could have tied floss around the trophy, waited until I took these stairs, pulled it down on me, then returned to their office upstairs. Or they could even have left the building using the front stairs."

"I know. That's all possible, but I know Colonel Barnes isn't in the squadron because he's at his house. Remember, I went to meet Bonnie this morning for an organizing consultation?" This morning seemed so long ago. "Colonel Barnes showed up right after she left. There were some papers that Bonnie accidentally gave me . . . well, it's a long story, but the bottom line is that Colonel Barnes doesn't really want the commander position."

"What? Of course he wants it. It's practically all he can talk about."

"Then he's putting up a good front." I explained about the papers I'd seen and the encounter I'd had with Colonel Barnes.

"*Colonel Barnes* has written a book?" Mitch said, then shook his head. "No way. Not possible. The guy can barely sit still for the commander's call. There's no way he'd be able to sit down and write a book."

"I wouldn't have believed it either, but I saw it in their house. Reams of double-spaced pages. Of course, I didn't realize what it was at the time." I noticed several tiny red dots on the stair step beside me. Blood. I ran my finger lightly over one. It was already dry.

"That's amazing," Mitch said, shaking his head.

"And we know Carrie didn't have anything to do with this because she's still in the hospital," I said.

"You know that for sure, or you're assuming she's still in the hospital?" Mitch asked.

"I called her at the hospital as I drove over here. I know what she did was stupid and she armors herself with her anger, but I know she's got to be hurting, too."

"What happened when you called?" Mitch asked.

"She hung up on me."

A small smile crossed Mitch's face. "Typical."

"I know, but I had to try."

"So she's still in the hospital?"

"Yes. After she hung up on me, I ordered a plant for her and checked with the reception desk at the hospital to make sure Carrie would still be there to get it. She's not being released today." I scratched at a dried blood drop with my fingernail.

"Well." Mitch sat down slowly on the step beside me and I pulled my hand away from the faint blood traces. He pulled a sheaf of papers from the pocket of his flight suit and handed them to me. "I did some research of my own."

I unfolded the thick stack of papers and raised my eyebrows. He shrugged. "Slow day. I plugged every name we've tossed around into a search engine and printed out what looked significant." He tapped a photo on the top page. "Look at that. I think you're right. We can mark Carrie off our list."

The photo accompanied an article from the *North Dawkins Standard* about the protests Peace Now had staged outside Taylor's front gate. "That's Carrie, alright," I said. Even in the dim light of the stairwell, I could make out her small figure. The camera had caught her with her mouth open, probably shouting a slogan, and her balled fist raised in the air. I quickly scanned the article, then frowned. "This doesn't tell us anything new. We already knew she was involved in the protests."

"See the bank clock in the background?" Mitch pointed to the edge of the photo.

"Yes." The digital readout from the bank down the street from the base was visible behind the line of protestors. "So it was five minutes after two when this photo was taken." I still didn't see what Mitch was getting at.

"Look at the date." He pointed at the dateline at the top of the story.

"Last Saturday. I still don't see—oh." I stopped because I finally understood. Last Saturday was when Colonel Pershall died. "But are you sure about the time? She could have slipped away for a while."

He pulled the next paper from the stack, the article about Colonel Pershall's death, also from the local newspaper. The golf course confirmed that Colonel Pershall had returned his golf cart at one-forty, bought lunch at the restaurant, then exited the building. Another golfer called nine-one-one from the parking lot at ten after two when he discovered Colonel Pershall's body beside his car.

"So she had nothing to do with it. There's no way she could have gotten from Taylor to Five Pines in that amount of time." I slapped the stack of papers against my leg, frustrated that we'd been sidetracked. "We've spent so much time thinking about and focusing on Carrie and Colonel Barnes. Now it turns out neither of them had anything to do with Colonel Pershall's death." I rubbed my forehead because there was a minor ache behind my eyes. "I need some medicine and chocolate, not necessarily in that order," I said, digging in my tote for a chocolate kiss.

"Hey, I'm the one who's supposed to have a headache here," he said, pointing to his bandage.

"You're going to milk that for all it's worth, aren't you?" I said.

"Of course." His upbeat tone faded with his smile. "You're sure Colonel Barnes won't still be a suspect?" Mitch asked as he waved away my offer of chocolate. His good eating habits never failed to amaze me.

"Pretty sure. He was genuinely upset about Colonel Pershall's death and he really doesn't want the commander position," I said, retracing the crease in the papers.

"He still had the opportunity. He was there, at the golf course," Mitch countered.

"I know, but I think we're leaving something out. What's the link between you and Colonel Pershall? Why would someone want to harm both of you? Carrie had a reason—she hated Colonel Pershall because he didn't pull Ryan off the deployment and I thought she was upset with you because you sort of represented the squadron to her. You said she went ballistic when you tried to give her Ryan's organizer and then the dry ice bomb went off in your car, so I thought she was still angry at the squadron and she'd transferred her fury from Colonel Pershall to you. It's still hard for me to take in that it was a random thing. It's amazing that she picked your car out of all the ones in the squadron parking lot."

"Well, even if she recognized it and put it in there on purpose, she didn't have anything to do with Colonel Pershall's death and we know she didn't pull that trophy down on me," Mitch said as he touched the bandage and winced. "And now Colonel Barnes is in the clear, too."

Mitch looked so disheartened that I shifted around so that I could rub his shoulders. "We just have to keep looking," I said, using deep strokes to knead out the tension in his neck. "We'll go through that stack and see if there's anything else we missed. There's got to be something and I think we're on the right track. We have to stay focused on anything that will link you and Colonel Pershall, that's the critical point that we've been overlooking."

He nodded, head down. I gave his shoulders a few final passes, then kissed him on the cheek. "There you go. That should help."

He caught my hands before I pulled away and twisted around to give me a real kiss. He stood and pulled me up. "Come on, let's go home," he said as he picked up the papers. "We can look over this stuff, and I think I do feel a headache coming on. I might need to lie down."

I rolled my eyes as we walked into the parking lot. We were about to separate to go to our cars when I noticed a group of people gathered around a hulking SUV. "What's going on over there? Isn't that Denise's SUV?" I asked, squinting against the contrast of the bright sunlight after the dimness inside. "Hey, that's Montigue," I said. "And Waraday." There were a few other people in the group I hadn't seen before, including a security police officer. As we got closer I heard Waraday say, "Denise Pershall, you are under arrest for the murder of Lewis Pershall. You have the right to remain silent . . ."

Chapter
Twenty-four

It happened so quickly. I was still stunned into speechlessness as the car left the parking lot with Denise handcuffed in the backseat. I swiveled toward Mitch and tried to shake off the paralysis that held me. "They arrested her. Denise! Denise did not kill Colonel Pershall. Should we follow them? Meet them at the sheriff's office? Or would it be the OSI office?"

"Ellie, they're not going to let us talk to her," Mitch said gently. "She'll call a lawyer. That's the only person who can help her right now." Mitch looked after the car, then glanced back at the squadron building. "Ellie, I know you're her friend and I know how loyal you are, almost to a fault . . ." His voice trailed off and he gave me a pitying look.

"You think she did it?" I couldn't believe it. "Mitch, we're talking about Denise. Denise! Denise, who went to bat for the wives so we didn't have to do those stupid things that were 'traditional' for spouse clubs. Denise, who loved her husband. Denise, who didn't want to turn over those hateful letters from Carrie because she wanted to protect Carrie. There's no way she killed Colonel Pershall."

Mitch sighed and said, "Think about it, Ellie. They're not going to arrest her on a whim. They have to have some solid evidence. I know you want to defend her, but we've considered every other possibility. Don't discount her, just because she's your friend. What if she is the one?"

"Mitch," I began again, but he put his hand on my arm.

"Just think about it on the drive home. I'll meet you there." He kissed me quickly and headed to his car.

I stood there, fuming. How dare he be so logical and . . . and . . . measured . . . when a friend was in trouble. Didn't he see that Denise needed help and support, not condemnation from us? I watched him walk down the aisle to his car, then carefully check around it, even getting down on his hands and knees to look under the car. When I saw him do that, I blew out a breath and went to the minivan, some of my irritation draining away. I slammed the door shut and watched in the rearview mirror as Mitch started his car and backed out. It was boiling hot inside the minivan and I pushed the air conditioner to the max, angling the vents so they hit my face.

I pulled out of the parking lot. Okay, Mitch seemed to think my support of Denise was based on feelings. It was—she was my friend and I couldn't take my feelings out of the equation, but I could show him, logically, that it didn't make sense to suspect her.

Following the train of thought I'd been on earlier, I tried to think of something that would link Colonel Pershall and Mitch, something that Denise would care enough about that she'd murder her husband and then try and hurt or kill Mitch.

I covered five miles of state highway as I wracked my brain for something to connect that triangle, but in the end, I had nothing, which was a strong argument for her innocence, in my book.

So what evidence did the investigators have that gave them so much confidence that they'd arrested Denise? Mitch was right on one point. They wouldn't arrest her unless they had hard evidence. Waraday liked physical evidence and he wouldn't move unless he had something solid.

I frowned as I entered the shadowy portion of

the road where Mitch's car had run off the road. I slowed down and carefully navigated the swoops in the road as the sun and shadow flicked over the windshield. When I was back on the straight portion of the road and out of the copse of trees, I called Mitch.

"I can't decide if 'Wind Beneath My Wings' is better or worse than 'Danger Zone,'" he said, referring to the new ringtone I'd set on his phone.

"Worse. Much worse," I said, smiling briefly. "Hey, I'm thinking things through your way— only to prove to you that I'm right, of course—"

That made him laugh. "Of course," he agreed.

"So, I think you should call Gary and see what you can find out about Denise's arrest. You're right, they have—"

"What was that? Did you say I was right?" Mitch teased.

"Yes. I can even say it again." I could be magnanimous. "You're right. Now, keep in mind that I'm not saying I'm wrong, just that you're right on *one point*," I said lightly. I brought the van to a stop for a red light.

"Oh, I see. Should have known there'd be conditions," he said.

I turned serious. "We need to find out what evidence they're basing the arrest on. Is it those knitting needles? Because if it's those, Denise said they weren't hers. Someone could have planted them in her house. Not Colonel Barnes, it wasn't him, but apparently it wasn't too hard to find out about that key they had hidden outside. Anyone watching the house when they were out of town could have figured out where it was and used it to get in to plant evidence."

The light changed as Mitch said, "That's true. I'll call Gary and see if he can tell us anything."

I hung up and turned into the neighborhood, trying to look at the case against Denise from the investigators' point of view. They'd see evidence of a woman who'd made preparations for divorcing her husband, a woman who didn't have an alibi. Carrie's insinuations that Denise was having an affair had been false, so Denise had nothing to worry about there. I shifted in my seat, remembering how Denise had carefully stepped around the truth when Abby and I first arrived at her house after our "stake out." Denise had been protecting the boy she was tutoring, but if she could have worked it out where she didn't have to tell us about him, she would have. That thought made me uncomfortable.

I slowed as I drove through our neighborhood. An image of Denise at the funeral popped into my mind, her face set and unemotional. She hadn't shown an ounce of grief at the funeral and that couldn't look good to the investigators, but I knew she was grieving for her husband in private. How she handled her grief shouldn't have an impact on the investigation.

I pulled into the garage beside Mitch's car and walked inside. Since I'd caught several red lights he'd arrived first and already picked up Nathan from Dorthea's house. Nathan ran to me and clutched his arms around my knees. I swept him up in my arms and asked him if he'd had fun.

He nodded and wiggled, ready to get back to his game of chasing Rex around the living room—good thing all our low tabletops had only unbreakable things on them. Mitch was in the kitchen, still in his flight suit, but with the sleeves rolled up, making peanut butter and jelly sandwiches.

"I had to promise him food. It was the only way I could get him to leave without crying."

"He does like Dorthea. I'm surprised she didn't feed him."

"Oh, I think he ate a zoo's worth of animal crackers," Mitch said, pulling slices of bread out of the bag.

Since Mitch seemed to have lunch under control, I poured milk in a sippy cup for Nathan, then tall glasses of iced tea for us.

"Okay, approaching this logically—and rather coldly, I might add—I can see why Montigue and Waraday are interested in Denise, but I think they're missing something—the link between the things that have been happening to you and Colonel Pershall," I said.

Mitch shrugged as he twisted the lid back on the

peanut butter. "I can't think of any connection I have with Colonel Pershall that would drive Denise to kill him and then want to kill me, so that's a point in her favor, at least with us," Mitch agreed reluctantly.

"Why was she in the squadron today, do you think?" I asked. "She had that big box . . . maybe she was picking up Colonel Pershall's things?"

"Could be. I didn't see her until she came down the stairs. I didn't even know she was there," Mitch said, replacing the jelly in the fridge.

"But isn't the squadron commander's office on the second floor?" I asked as I leaned against the kitchen island.

Mitch stopped and looked at me. "It is."

We stared at each other for a few seconds. The hum of the refrigerator sounded loud in the quiet kitchen. I shook my head. "There are plenty of reasons for her to be on the third floor. There's a storage closet up there. She could have been picking up something she'd left there. Or maybe she needed to see someone up there. Or drop off something."

"It was deserted up there. We were all at the meeting." Mitch finally put into words what we were both thinking. "She was the first one to come down the stairs after the trophy fell."

I sighed, hating to even think she had something to do with it. "She could have been the person who set up and pulled the floss." I admitted.

"And who was the person who led the whole group to The Nest?"

I didn't like where these thoughts were headed. "Denise. And then she was the first one back to clean up the mess. She could have removed the floss before we got back there."

"Did you notice she handled the trophy, too? Her fingerprints will be all over it."

I closed my eyes for a moment. I didn't want to think Denise was involved in this. "There has to be some other explanation." I pulled out a bar stool and took a seat, feeling exhausted as I tried to sort through these confusing and uncomfortable thoughts. "Any word from Gary?" I asked.

He stopped slicing a sandwich and looked at me. "Yeah. Of course he couldn't tell me much and if anyone asks, we didn't hear it from him. He said they found Denise's prints on the murder weapon, those weird needles."

"But she said those weren't hers."

Mitch shrugged and cut carrot sticks to go with the sandwich. "That's what he said."

I frowned. "But . . . why would she kill Lewis?"

She didn't want a divorce anymore. Or *that's what she told me*. The thought popped into my head and I wanted to immediately reject it, but I forced myself to examine it. Could she really have wanted to be free of Colonel Pershall all along and she'd lied to me? Had her "reconciliation" been an act? I didn't want to think so, but if her fingerprints were on the cord that killed him . . . I jumped up and began to pace around the kitchen. I didn't want to think these thoughts. A divorce could mean possible alimony and splitting their assets while his death would ensure everything went to her. And there would be survivor benefits, insurance, things like that. What if there was a large life insurance policy on Colonel Pershall? Something beyond the standard policy that all military personnel had? Denise would be the beneficiary. I began to see why the investigation had focused so closely on her.

"You okay?" Mitch asked as he picked up Nathan and washed his hands before settling him at the table for lunch.

"No," I said. "I don't want to think that Denise might be capable of any of this, but I can't help but see there's a possibility . . ."

"I know. I can tell you're upset—you're eating a carrot."

I hadn't realized I'd taken one from the cutting board and had been munching on it as I paced. I smiled ruefully and leaned back against the counter. "I still don't see the connection between you and Colonel Pershall—that's the one thing that keeps me from believing Denise did it."

"Waraday and Montigue don't care about a connection between me, Colonel Pershall, and Dan. They're only looking at Colonel Pershall's murder. They're not trying to link his death to any of the things that have happened to me."

I sagged against the countertop. "If you looked only at the murder, then Denise is a very viable suspect, but if you throw in the 'accidents,' and the coin—the coins! I almost forgot about them. They have to fit into this somehow. That shows there's more going on here than they're taking into account."

"It looks like that, but I don't think anyone's really interested in the coins." Mitch checked the time and said, "I have to change and get back. Henry and Jeff have an afternoon show time and I'm covering the office." His mental focus was already shifting back to work.

Ten minutes later, Mitch was wearing a fresh flight suit and on his way back to the squadron. I pushed away my sandwich after a few bites. I couldn't eat, with my thoughts racing between all the things that had happened. I kept thinking of Denise, wondering if she was being questioned, if she'd been able to get a criminal attorney, if she was—hopefully—out on bail. I called her house and left a message, then vowed that if she wasn't out by the next morning, I was going to try and visit her. I needed to at least make the attempt.

The rest of the afternoon took on a weird fractured kind of reality. On the surface, I went through the motions—I put Nathan down for a nap, I loaded the dishwasher, sorted the laundry, and replied to an e-mail from a potential organizing client, all very normal day-to-day stuff, but I wasn't able to give anything my full attention, because my thoughts skittered from one strange incident to the next.

Nathan woke from his nap grumpy and irritable, which was unusual. I wondered if he was coming down with something since he was so fussy. He wasn't happy with anything—refusing to play with the mini-basketball hoop or his block set, two things he usually loved. Every time I tried to set him up with a game or activity, he abandoned it and climbed into my lap with a board book. I spent the rest of the afternoon reading books to him and trying to read the pages Mitch had printed, but didn't make much progress.

When three o'clock came, I strapped Nathan in his car seat and headed to the school where I took my place in the long car-rider line. Nathan settled down in his car seat and I was able to read through the pages while we waited for school to let out. I wasn't surprised to see that Denise belonged to several online knitting discussion sites. Her name also came up occasionally in the local newspaper, usually in connection with something related to the base. There was a photograph of her and several other military spouses and a local high school senior, a scholarship recipient.

I had to smile at a mention of Henry Fleet that Mitch had found. Another pilot from the squadron, Paul Roanoke, complained in his blog that Henry had ditched him in Atlanta on the first day of one of their trips, taking the crew's rental car and stranding Paul at the blocky, chain-hotel with an overpriced restaurant. I didn't think pilots were supposed to have blogs that described their activities, but apparently the information in this blog wasn't sensitive enough to warrant it being shut down, or else the military hadn't run across this one yet.

The last set of pages was about Colonel Barnes. He must not have expected to win a writing contest, because he had entered under his real name, and anyone who searched for his name online would be able to discover his secret.

A honk sounded from behind me and I looked up to find the line of cars was moving. I inched forward until it was my turn. Once Livvy hopped in the car, her excited chatter about her day didn't stop until we reached home.

The afternoon continued its semblance of normalcy—the kids had their snacks and I signed the paperwork that Livvy brought home for me—she was quite insistent that it had to be turned in on Monday and we had to do it this afternoon so we didn't forget it. I chopped onions and melted butter for a barbeque sauce recipe I was trying out, while Livvy gave Nathan a school lesson. She'd set him up at the coffee table with paper and crayons, and wrapped her hand around his chubby fist to help him form the letter *N*. Something about that picture made me pause, and not just in an oh-my-kids-are-so-cute way. A memory stirred faintly, but I couldn't quite grasp it. It was like overhearing bits of dialogue at the table next to you in a restaurant, a few words caught here and there, but the meaning of the conversation was undistinguishable. I shook my head at myself, knowing it would come to me later. I added Worcestershire sauce and brown sugar to the pan and stirred until it bubbled and filled the house with a tangy-sweet aroma. I drenched a brisket with the sauce, tucked the whole thing in the oven, and set the timer.

Nathan pushed Livvy away. "Do it myself," he announced.

"But you're not doing it right," Livvy said in a bossy voice, and I had to intervene before things got out of hand. Livvy's friend Geneva, from down the street, rang the doorbell and asked if Livvy and Nathan could play at her house. Since they were hardly ever invited over to Geneva's house, I said they could go.

Geneva brushed a braid off her shoulder. "My mom says you can come get them at five-thirty. I have dance."

"Fine," I said, a bit shortly because Geneva played at our house for hours on end. "Have fun," I called as the three kids trooped down the street to Geneva's house. I went back inside and again picked up the pages Mitch had printed out earlier.

I was about a third of the way into the stack when Mitch came home, gave me a quick kiss, and said, "Smells great in here," as he disappeared into our bedroom.

"I'm trying out a new barbeque sauce recipe. We're bringing the main dish to the next supper club," I called after him. He emerged a few minutes later in his running clothes. "You're not going running, are you?"

He propped his foot up on the dining room chair to tie his shoelace. "Yes," he said shortly. "I didn't get to run today during lunch and the indoor running track at the gym on base is being resurfaced, so I can't run there." He saw the look on my face. "Ellie, I know what you're thinking—that it's not safe—but it is."

"How can you say that? Whoever killed Colonel Pershall and tried to hurt you is still out there."

He adjusted his music player, which was strapped to his arm, then gently put his hand on my shoulder. "No. The person who killed Colonel Pershall has been arrested. You have to accept that. It's over. As much as you don't want to believe it—well, there it is. She did it."

I rolled the papers into a tube as I said, "Mitch, what happened to you? At lunch you were agreeing with me that there's no connection between you and Colonel Pershall that Denise would care about."

"I thought about it a lot this afternoon. She had the opportunity and the murder weapon was in her house."

"But there's no connection to you," I repeated as I broke free from his hand. "And what about the coins?" I asked, pointing the tube of papers at him accusingly.

"I think she's a little unhinged. I don't know why she'd single me out. Maybe she's out to get anyone associated with the military, but I'm sure that the police will figure it out."

"So she's just crazy—there's no explanation," I said, my grip tightening on the roll of papers.

"I'm afraid so."

"What about the coins?"

Mitch shook his head. "Ellie. The coins aren't that important. She probably sent them. Maybe Colonel Pershall had some extra around the house and she added that skull and crossbones thing, then sent them to the people she'd tried to take out."

I tossed the papers on the table in frustration and crossed my arms. "She mailed one to herself?"

"See, unhinged. You can't make it make sense when the person doing it is . . . mentally disturbed."

"Fine. Okay. Whatever," I said, pacing into the kitchen and back to the dining room, my arms still tightly crossed. "You think she's the murderer and she's in police custody, but I still don't want you running today." I wished I'd bought him that treadmill for Christmas instead of a watch.

His voice became even quieter as he unwound the cords of his ear buds. "It's full daylight and

I'm not going to be kept prisoner in my house. I've been through survival training courses and threat reduction courses. I think I can handle a jog through my neighborhood."

I tried another angle. "You shouldn't run after a head injury."

"It's a scratch, not a concussion," he said.

He'd replaced the large bandage with a smaller Band-Aid and, while I wouldn't call it a scratch, it certainly didn't look like anything you'd run to the hospital about. But I had to try and keep him home. "You don't know that. You could have a concussion."

"Ellie," Mitch said warningly as he ran one hand through his short haircut, causing it to spike up. His exasperated tone verged on anger, something I rarely heard from him.

I flung my arms out. "Okay," I said, backing off. Mitch could be as stubborn as . . . well, me. "Just take your phone."

"Already got it," he said, pointing to his waist-band where the phone was clipped. He tucked the ear buds into his ears and headed out.

I snatched up the papers and unrolled the tight tube. I sat down at the table and tried to concentrate on the pages. There had to be something to show Denise wasn't a murderer. I read through everything again, taking frequent breaks to look out the window. I read the last page, then flipped it over onto the stack on the table.

I sat back, frustrated. Nothing. There was nothing there to help Denise.

A large brown delivery truck rumbled past the dining room window. I pushed myself out of the chair. I might as well go check for Megan's package. By the time I did that it would be almost time to get the kids from Geneva's house and, Lord knows, I didn't want to be late. They wouldn't receive another royal summons if I made Geneva's mom mad.

I tucked the piece of paper with the garage code that Megan had given me into my pocket with my cell phone, put Rex in his kennel, and punched in the code to close our garage door. It seemed like a waste of gasoline to drive over to Megan's house since it was only a short distance away and a walk would be good for me.

I hesitated a moment in the driveway. I hadn't wanted Mitch to jog around the neighborhood alone, but here I was heading out by myself. Maybe I should wait until he got back. I dismissed the thought. No one was after *me*.

I strode past the pond and around the curve to the newer section of the neighborhood, then climbed the incline that was the toughest part of the stroller brigade workout. I was always relieved when we reached the top where the trees fell away for a short stretch and there was a view down into the rest of the neighborhood. Of course by then my thighs were screaming and it was hard to enjoy the view, but the rest of the workout was easy going. The road flattened out and followed the plateau-like ridge that swept around in a curve, then gradually dropped off in gentle dips back to the valley and the cluster of houses that make up Magnolia Estates.

I caught my breath after the climb and thought about Dan. This was where he'd been shot at, where the ambulance and crowd had been. I usually didn't think about it, probably because I was normally in a group of chatting women and the commands from Tina kept me focused on the workout, but today in the quiet afternoon, I couldn't help but think of how scary that day had been. I hurried by the gap in the trees and felt better as the road flattened and the trees closed in around the mix of finished houses and houses still under construction. There were two moms at the small park where the stroller brigade often stopped to work with elastic bands or do push-ups using the benches ringing the playground equipment.

Today there were two empty jogging strollers parked at the curb and the moms were relaxing on the benches watching their kids play. The normal scene steadied me and I shook off the uneasiness I felt. I hurried on, glad there were no push-ups in my routine today. I walked up the sidewalk to Megan's porch and saw the medium-sized cardboard box standing beside the front door.

I carried it to the garage where I set it down while I found the code, then punched it in. The door clanked up, revealing an empty garage with plastic bins scattered around, some with the lids off. It looked like Megan was in the middle of putting away clothes that Tyler had outgrown or were too warm.

I carried the cardboard box over to the door that led into the house. I intended to hit the button to close the garage door and scurry back outside, skipping over the invisible beam that would automatically reopen the door if it was broken, but I glanced into a plastic bin near the wall that was full of baby clothes, shoes, and a blue blanket. A few balls of blue yarn were shoved in along the edge.

My steps slowed. I'd seen that blanket before. It had fallen out of Tyler's stroller during a stroller brigade workout, but I'd seen it before then. I stopped with my hand on the garage door button, thinking. Where had I seen it?

At the spouse coffee, I realized. It was like a replay running in my head, the memory was so clear. Megan had been working on knitting the blanket and had gotten stuck on the last few rows. Denise had helped her, putting her hands over Megan's to show her how to make the stitch—that's why watching Livvy guide Nathan's hand to write letters had stirred a memory.

After a few attempts, Megan had said, "Oh, I

messed it up again," and handed it back to Denise. "I'm so frustrated with this." Denise had taken the needles, circular needles, I remembered as my heartbeat sped up. Denise had finished the blanket, then removed the needles. She'd wound them together in her hand, then said, "Here, let me get you a plastic bag to store these. That way they won't get tangled. That's what I do." She'd hurried off, then returned with the needles tucked inside a plastic zippered bag.

The day the blanket fell out of the stroller during the workout, Megan had told me she'd never knitted again. I stood motionless. If Megan had never knitted again and she'd kept the needles in that plastic bag, then they would still have Denise's fingerprints on them. If someone wanted to implicate Denise in a murder, they could use the knitting needles. My heartbeat was racing as I stood in the quiet garage. As long as the murderer only grabbed the cord with gloves and used that to strangle Colonel Pershall, then Denise's fingerprints would remain on the needle portion.

Even though the garage was blazing hot, I felt shivery. Who could be that cold and calculating? Megan? Somehow I didn't think she cared about anything as much as her diet and exercise program. Henry? Hardworking, always dependable Henry? That didn't fit either.

I don't like things that don't fit together. It's the organizer in me—I have to shift and sort until everything matches up neatly. There was something here that bothered me.

"Atlanta!" That was it. Megan had said Henry would be in Atlanta today. My thoughts skipped to the printout from Paul's blog that I'd read earlier today. Paul had complained that Henry ditched him in Atlanta . . . and Megan told me that Henry was out of town the weekend that Colonel Pershall was murdered. But Henry hadn't been that far out of town—it was the medical support mission, the one that overnighted in Atlanta, so Henry would have been in Atlanta the afternoon Colonel Pershall was killed.

My legs felt unsteady and I sat down on a nearby plastic bin, trying to work out if it was possible. Had Henry killed Colonel Pershall? If he was in Atlanta that day, he could easily have driven back. North Dawkins was less than two hours away from Atlanta and if he took the rental car as Paul complained, it would give Henry anonymity to move around town without anyone knowing he was here. It was an excellent alibi. And Colonel Pershall played golf every weekend. It wouldn't be that hard to find out which course he'd be playing that weekend—a question or two during the week at the squadron would uncover that information.

But why would he go after Colonel Pershall? I ran my hands over my face. What had Denise said Henry was upset about? A promotion thing. I sat up straighter. Megan had mentioned the same thing when she was talking about their reassignment to the unmanned reconnaissance squadron. Henry wanted the school slot instead of the position flying the unmanned aerial vehicles.

I stood up and circled around a few steps. Henry wanted the school slot, the slot that Mitch had. He wanted Mitch's school slot! There it was, the connection between Colonel Pershall and Mitch—and it was Henry Fleet, of all people! And hadn't Megan told me Henry knew about Denise being the last person to handle the knitting needles? Yes, she'd mentioned it when she offered to give me her knitting supplies, I was sure of it.

I paced around, trying to figure out what to do. I should call Waraday. I reached for my phone but stopped. Would Waraday believe me? I knew he'd listen, but what did I have that would convince him that the wrong person had been arrested? I had a blog entry, which I didn't even have with me, a memory of Denise handling Megan's circular knitting needles, Henry's reassignment, and his desire to go to a military school "in residence." Somehow I didn't think that would be enough to convince Waraday that Henry was a murderer.

I stopped pacing and pushed my bangs on my sweaty forehead. I needed more. Waraday was a hard-evidence type of guy. He didn't want hearsay and with Denise under arrest it was going to take a lot to convince him Henry was involved.

I glanced at the street. There were no cars on the road. My car wasn't in the driveway. No one would know I was here. I glanced at my watch. If I was going to do it, I had to do it quickly because I had to pick up the kids soon.

I took a deep breath and punched the garage door button. As it clattered down, I pulled on a pair of gardening gloves from the labeled bin Megan and I had created. The door to the house might be locked. Mitch and I never locked the door from the garage into the house, but Megan and Henry might have locked theirs since they were both going out of town. I flexed my fingers in the stiff gloves and gripped the doorknob. It turned smoothly and the door swung open. I was enveloped in a gust of cool air-conditioned air, scented with lemon furniture polish.

Tips for Busy, Budget-Minded Moms

Keep these documents indefinitely
- Education transcripts.
- Loan discharge papers.
- Wills and living trusts.
- Insurance paperwork.
- Mortgage deeds.
- Paperwork associated with automobiles—title, registration, and warranties.

- Birth certificates, marriage certificates, adoption papers, divorce decrees, and military discharge paperwork.
- Social security cards.
- Retirement benefit paperwork.

Chapter
Twenty-five

I'd never been inside Megan and Henry's house before. Megan and I had spent all our time organizing the garage. I stepped into a kitchen of pale wood cabinets and cream countertops. A package of rice cakes sat on the counter next to a collection of low-fat, low-calorie cereal boxes. I moved across the tiled floor into the breakfast nook between the kitchen and the living room. The house was a combination of contemporary furniture in the colors of the ocean—lots of blue, beige, and white accented with exercise equipment and baby paraphernalia.

I stepped around an ExerSaucer and baby swing next to a treadmill and surveyed the open floor plan, feeling at a loss. What could I hope to find when I wasn't even sure what I was looking for? I spun in a slow circle, looking for anything that might be off or odd, but everything looked like the typical family home—slightly messy with mail and magazines on the coffee table and baby toys on the couch.

Now I felt a bit silly, but I was in and I might as well walk through. I took a quick tour through the living room around the pale blue sectional couch, then walked into the formal area of the house by the front door. A dining room and formal living room flanked the front door, and each room was perfect. No one lived in these rooms. A quick scan of the china cabinet revealed nothing except pale gold-rimmed china.

I walked to the bedrooms, flexing my fingers in the stiff gardening gloves and feeling more awkward by the minute. A linen closet contained nothing but sheets and towels. Tyler's room was all boy with pale blue walls and a baseball-themed wallpaper border.

Megan was using the second bedroom as storage for more workout equipment. Bare white walls, no curtains, and mirrored sliding closet doors gave it a gym-like appearance. A stationary bike along with three weight-loss contraptions that I recognized from television infomercials filled one side of the room. A weight machine took up the rest of the floor space.

I entered the master bedroom last, feeling worse and worse. What was I doing poking around in this house? I wasn't a trained investigator and I wouldn't know what I was looking for, much less have the time to do an actual search. What if by just being here, I'd compromised the scene? I glanced around the room and didn't see anything that screamed "murderer lives here."

The king-size bed with a beige bedspread dominated the room. There was a dresser and two nightstands in blond wood. A doorway at the far side of the room led to a walk-in closet and master bath with a large garden tub and separate vanities. I stood on the threshold of the bedroom, debating whether I should leave. But I was also thinking about an interview I'd seen with a thief who'd served his time and now worked with a local television station for a segment called "How Safe Is Your House?" On the most recent segment, he'd broken into a house—with the homeowner's permission—in under twenty seconds and headed straight for the bedroom, saying that most people keep the really valuable stuff close to them, in their bedroom or closet. So the master bedroom was where Henry would be most likely to hide something he didn't want found.

I checked under the bed and found flat storage boxes of pictures and papers, including various certificates from military training classes. I paused over one, a marksman award for accuracy from a local shooting range. Each pilot had to spend time on the firing range and pass a shooting test. The fact that Henry was an accurate shot wasn't going to help me. I replaced the document in the box and shoved it under the bed.

It was difficult to open the nightstand drawers

wearing the gloves, but when I did slide out the drawers, I found only a phone book, notepad, and calendar in one and an assortment of socks and undershirts in another. I pulled open each dresser drawer and saw clothes. I didn't want to move things around too much, so I poked and prodded at the edges. As far as I could tell, the dresser only contained clothes.

I went to the walk-in closet and patted the top shelf. At the back, my gloved hands touched something rounded behind the shoe boxes. I dragged a step stool over from the corner of the closet and stepped up. I moved a few of the shoe boxes, exposing the long barrel of a rifle. My breathing sped up, but I told myself to calm down. A gun in itself was not that surprising. Lots of people hunted. But this was a rifle and I couldn't help but wonder if Henry had aimed it at Dan in a mistaken attempt to shoot Mitch.

I didn't touch it. I stared at it a moment before I stepped down and replaced the step stool in the corner. The closet was narrow with two tiers of rods running its length. Megan had taken over most of the space and I looked through the clothes quickly. There was nothing except the normal clothes, shoes, belts, and ties. The cabinets in the bathroom held towels and toiletries.

I walked back into the bedroom and removed the gloves, my hands sweaty. I might as well leave and try to figure out some way to tell Waraday about the rifle in the top of the closet. I walked toward the door, giving the room once last glance. A glimmer of gold in the change holder on top of the dresser caught my eye and I walked closer.

Amid the copper and silver of the pennies, dimes, and quarters, there was definitely a flash of gold. I put one glove back on and pushed the change out of the way. There were three squadron coins at the bottom of the dish. I had to work to get the thick finger of the glove under the edge of the coins, but I flipped them over, one after another. Each one had the familiar tiny black blob on the side with the replica of the squadron patch. When I leaned closer and squinted, I could see the black strokes formed a skull and crossbones. I pushed one coin out and picked it up by the edge. A movement at the window caused my head to jerk up. I closed my gloved hand around the coin and took a step closer to the window that looked out on the front lawn of the house.

A figure was walking to the front door, a man with a cell phone pressed to his ear. I shoved the coin in my pocket and stepped closer to the window. It looked like . . . I frowned. It couldn't be Henry. He was in Atlanta. I leaned sideways, trying to see the man as he trotted up the front steps.

I heard the distinctive metal clicks as a key shifted the dead bolt from the locked position. The front door opened and I felt the subtle change in air pressure as the sheer curtains stirred by my face. It had to be Henry.

My first instinct was to hide. Where? The bed was a low profile and hugged the floor and I didn't think I could get under there with the boxes. There were no heavy curtains to hide behind like in the movies. These were wispy, gauzy transparent things over blinds.

I spun around, practically flapping my hands as my breathing went choppy. The bathroom? No, the shower was a clear glass cube and the cabinets were far too small for me to get into, even if they weren't already full. I could hear his voice, a one-sided conversation, as he walked down the hall.

Should I brazen it out? Meet him in the living room, tell him Megan asked me to come over and pick up the package, but I heard a noise inside? I discarded the idea even before it was fully formed and scooted toward the closet. It had to be the closet. I wasn't glib at the best of times and right now I was so stressed he'd probably take one look at my face and see something was up.

I stepped into the closet, shoved some clothes aside, and ducked under the double rod. I tried to squeeze myself into the back corner. At the last minute, I realized the closet light was on, but I didn't dare move because Henry had entered the bedroom.

From my corner, I could see out the door of the closet to the mirror over the dresser. In the reflection, I saw Henry standing in the middle of the room. "It was fine. A typical flight," he said into the cell phone. He was in civilian clothes, khaki carpenter shorts, a collared green short-sleeved polo shirt, and sandals.

He walked over to the dresser and bent down. I couldn't see what he was doing. He stood up, holding one of the gardening gloves. I massaged the fabric in my hand and only came up with one glove. Shoot. I must have dropped it when I saw him coming up the walk. He frowned at the glove, then tossed it on the dresser. He didn't even look at the coin dish and I breathed a tiny sigh of relief.

The closet was hot and stuffy. Beads of sweat were forming along my hairline and between my shoulder blades. I snuck my hand up and patted my forehead with the glove. It smelt dusty and sweaty. Of course, the section of clothing I was hiding behind was Megan's winter clothes and a scratchy wool fabric brushed against my arms and face, making me feel even hotter.

Henry listened for a moment, then said, "No, I'm still in Atlanta."

Liar, I thought, gently pushing the arm of a wool jacket away from my nose.

"Well, I'm glad you made it to California. Sure. Right. Okay. I'll call you from Hawaii. Bye."

He ended the call and stepped into the closet. I averted my gaze to his feet in a childlike effort to not attract his attention. I prayed he wasn't able to either smell the sweat that seemed to be pouring off me or hear my heartbeat, which was pounding in my ears.

I watched his feet as he dragged the step stool over and climbed on it. He pulled the rifle down, replaced the step stool, then left the closet. He returned almost immediately and began rummaging through the clothes on the other side of the closet, muttering to himself about where something could be.

I swallowed as he transferred to the side I was on. I scrunched down the wall and tried to roll myself into a ball. What would I say if he found me? There really wasn't an explanation that I could give him. His hand flickered through the clothing on the rack above me until he reached the end of the rack. He braced his feet and went back a few feet to the area where he'd just looked, but this time he went slower, moving each item individually, and I nearly had a heart attack as the moving hangers parted closer and closer to me, sending a shaft of light down into my hiding place.

He moved down to the lower rack. I was toast. What to say? What to do? Push him? Try and hit him?

"Finally," he muttered, and snagged several hangers a few inches from my nose. As he left the closet, I saw he had camouflage clothes in one hand and a pair of stout boots in the other. I could hear him moving around in the bathroom, then he walked through the bedroom. I didn't have the nerve to stand up again and watch him in the mirror. I strained to listen for more sounds, but there weren't any.

I stayed where I was for another full minute, counting the seconds off in my mind. My legs were beginning to cramp. I worked my way up the wall into a standing position and rotated my feet one at a time until the pins-and-needles sensation died away. Once my legs were functioning again, I took a deep breath and eased out from between the clothes, bending over double to get out from under the lower rack.

I gently put the hangers back into place, then moved as silently as possible to the doorway of the closet and peered out.

Silence. I hadn't heard the front door close. It was possible that I hadn't heard it because I was in the depths of the closet, or Henry might still be in the house. The clothes he'd been wearing were dumped in a heap on the bathroom floor next to the sandals. I couldn't stay in the closet any longer. The fact that he'd taken the rifle and changed into camouflage scared me.

Carefully, I stepped into the bedroom, then inched my way toward the door. I paused, scanning every inch of the house that I could see. Unfortunately, that encompassed only the linen closet door and the other two bedrooms. I waited for a few more seconds and listened to the air-conditioner unit run. I swallowed and eased out the door and down the short hallway. A quick peek around the corner as I came to the end of the hall assured me Henry wasn't in that part of the house. With the open floor plan, I could see the living room, breakfast nook, and kitchen. All were quiet and still.

Everything looked exactly as it had when I arrived, except the door that opened onto a deck in the backyard was open. There was a screen on the door and it was closed. I inched over to the door. My gaze ran quickly over the empty deck, then to the stairs that descended to the woods behind the house. The house was situated on the ridge that ringed the valley. The land, covered in thick woods and undergrowth, dropped away steeply behind the house, then widened into the bowl-like valley that contained most of the houses of Magnolia Estates. From the deck, I could see through several gaps in the trees to other parts of the neighborhood, including the sliver of an opening at the peak of the road where Dan had been targeted.

My heart began to hammer.

He was going to try it again. Just like last time. He had an alibi—everyone thought he was out of town. And Mitch would be running through the newest part of the neighborhood soon. It was the last part of his run. I hurried over to the windows, searching the hillside below the deck, but I couldn't pick out a figure of a man anywhere. In the thick brush, Henry could hide anywhere. It was no use to stand here and try and find him. It was like looking for a tiny object in one of the kids' seek-and-find books.

I licked my lips and checked my watch. Maybe Mitch was already back home. I squinted through the gaps in the trees, searching for any movement on the road at the base of the valley. Two cars drove sedately down past, then I spotted Mitch, striding down the street. He flicked into view for a second, then disappeared behind the next thick clump of trees. He was almost at the base of the steep road that would bring him up to the open section at the top.

I grabbed the handle to the screen door, about to step outside, then stopped. Henry could still be close enough to see or hear me. I'd be an easy target on the deck. I stepped back from the door and hurried through the house. I had to warn Mitch. He was close, but I probably had a minute, maybe two, before he reached the top of the hill where Dan had been shot. Until he got to that wide gap in the trees, he'd be safe from Henry, because the trees were too dense to get a clear shot off until Mitch came to the clearing at the top.

I called Mitch on my cell phone. It rang four times, then went to voice mail. I slammed the phone closed with sweaty hands. He had on his ear buds and was listening to his music.

I raced to the front door, unlocked it, and slowed down enough so that I didn't slam the door. I tossed the single gardening glove I was still carrying on the front porch, then took off at a run down the sidewalk to the street, with my cell phone still gripped in one hand.

My feet slammed against the pavement, sounding loud to my ears. In my shorts and T-shirt, I hoped I looked like a normal jogger, not a frantic woman.

I slowed my pace slightly and settled into a rhythm, surprised that my breathing didn't become labored right away. I guess those stroller brigade workouts were helping me get in shape. Either that or it was the adrenaline. Definitely adrenaline, I decided as my feet flew across the asphalt. I sprinted by the little playground, veering around the strollers parked near the street. As I reached the end of the flat section of the road, I slowed down, not wanting to run through the gap in the line of trees. I was sure Henry was in the woods with his gun-sight trained on the opening. I stopped while the trees and houses still sheltered me. The road twisted back on itself at the bottom of the steep slope. From above I could see bits and pieces of the road through the thick foliage. A flicker of white flashed through the gaps at a steady pace, a runner's pace.

It was Mitch. I couldn't see his face, but I knew it had to be him. And I couldn't get down there to warn him. Even if I plunged down the steep wooded slope, I wouldn't reach him in time and I'd probably get a broken ankle or poison ivy, at the very least. What should I do? I scanned the street . . . if there was a car . . . but it was quiet in this new section of the neighborhood. My heartbeat accelerated, like I was still sprinting. I spun in a slow circle. There was nothing but pallets of bricks in dusty yards and low plastic black fencing around the new construction sites. No good. The few completed houses on this stretch were quiet. No time to try and rouse anyone and even if I convinced someone to help, there wasn't enough time. The bright colors of the strollers caught my eye.

The strollers! I shoved my phone in my pocket, sprinted to the park, and grabbed the handles of the red one.

One of the moms stood up. "Hey—"

"Sorry. I need to borrow this." There was a diaper bag tucked into a pouch on the back. I transferred it to the front, strapping it in to weigh down the stroller.

"You can't take that."

"Sorry," I yelled as I ran down the street, pushing the stroller in front of me. It was beautifully balanced with its big front wheel. It rolled smoothly and felt lighter than any stroller I'd ever pushed. Before I came even with the gap in the trees, I shoved the stroller and sent it flying down the slope.

I didn't like being on the street, even with the trees and houses around me, so I stepped over the low plastic fence and went over to a pallet of bricks in the yard of one of the unfinished houses.

After a few seconds of silence, I heard an exclamation.

A muted crash. I cringed. That would probably be the stroller, hitting . . . something. Hopefully one of the fancy bricked mailboxes and not a car or a person.

I whipped out my phone and dialed Mitch. Maybe at the sight of an unmanned stroller zipping by him, he'd pull out his earbuds . . .

The phone rang twice, then Mitch, his breathing labored, said, "Ellie?"

"Mitch. Do not come up the hill." My breathing sounded worse than his and I hadn't been running for a few minutes.

"What?"

"Get off the road. It's Henry. He's got a rifle and he's waiting for you to hit the clearing at the top of the hill. He's going to shoot you, like he tried to shoot Dan."

There were a few beats of silence broken only by Mitch's ragged breathing. "Where are you?" he finally asked.

"I'm up the hill from you—at the top where it levels out. I'm in front of . . ." I twisted around and saw the house numbers spray-painted on a piece of plywood nailed to a stake in the yard, "1303. Beside a pallet of bricks in the front yard."

"Stay there. I'm coming to you."

"No. Don't come up the street," I practically screamed into the phone.

"Trust me," he said, his voice calm. "I'm not coming up the street. So the stroller was a warning from you?" His breathing was more even now and I could hear a hint of a smile.

"Yes. Best I could do," I said, looking over my shoulder. "The mom I stole the stroller from is standing in the street watching me. She's clearly debating whether or not I'm some sort of deranged lunatic she should avoid."

There was silence on the line. "Mitch?" I glanced down the street, but didn't see him, then looked back over my shoulder. The mom wasn't staring at me anymore. She was carefully backpedaling to the park. I followed her gaze and saw Henry, rifle tucked in the crook of his arm, casually walking across the street toward me.

Chapter
Twenty-six

Henry stepped into the yard and strolled toward the pallet of bricks. I scrambled backward, away from the tip of the rifle, and tripped over the uneven ground, dropping my cell phone.

"Ellie," he said, his tone chiding. "No need to look so scared. You're not my target."

I grabbed the phone, but it had flipped closed, ending the call with Mitch. I hoped Mitch had heard Henry's voice. Then at least he'd have some warning. I did an awkward crawl for a few feet, backing away as he closed the distance. I stood, the phone gripped in my hand, wishing I was good enough at texting that I could send a message without looking at the keypad, but Henry was close enough he'd hear the sounds from my phone if I punched the keys.

He was too close. I shifted around to the other side of the pallet and he followed. I stepped back again, clinging to the next side of the cube of bricks. Part of my mind fixated on what a strange picture we made. Were we going to play some crazy Ring-Around-the-Rosie game until we were too dizzy to stand? This was Henry in front of me. Good old, dependable Henry. Henry with a rifle. I felt a giggle bubble up and firmly told myself to get a grip.

"That's far enough," Henry said and my stress-induced hysteria faded at his flat, conversational tone. How could he be so . . . normal? He looked the same. His face, his posture. Nothing was different about him. Well, except for the rifle. That was the major difference. I realized my breathing was coming in short puffs and my hands were gritty with dirt from my sprawl.

"I assume you were chatting with Mitch when I arrived and he'll be along shortly?"

I glanced around and realized that Henry had positioned himself behind the pallet of bricks, which shielded his rifle from the street. Anyone driving past would see only his upper body. The bricks would block the view of the rifle pointed at me. And my back was facing the direction that Mitch would arrive from. "He's on his way," I said, playing for time. I gripped the phone tighter in my hand, trying to think what to do. I had to get back on the other side of the bricks or shift around so that I could watch for Mitch. Maybe give him some sign. He'd be here any minute.

In fact, he should have been here by now. Maybe he'd heard Henry's voice or seen what was happening and he'd cleared out so he could call the police. As soon as the thoughts formed, I discarded them. Mitch wouldn't run. He said he'd meet me here, so he'd be here. He was probably taking his time. He'd said he wasn't on the street, so he must be keeping to the cover of the trees and houses.

"Why so quiet? Afraid he won't show?" he taunted. "Don't be. You're a sickeningly devoted couple. He'll be along," Henry said, sweeping his gaze along the street and trees. The barrel of the rifle remained steadily trained on me.

A flicker of movement in the woods beside the half-finished house caught my eye. I tried to focus on it without giving away to Henry that I was staring at something over his shoulder. No. Nothing. Just a branch moving in the wind.

I glanced up the street. The mom was gone. I hoped she'd called the police, but in this day of random shootings, I'm sure her first instinct was to get her kid out of the area. Then maybe she'd called the police, but it would take them a good ten or fifteen minutes to get to our secluded subdivision. I licked my lips, trying to think of something to say to Henry. He seemed so blasé. His hands weren't gripping the rifle and they weren't shaking with nerves either.

I felt a bead of sweat trail along my hairline and reached up to wipe it away. Unlike Henry, my hand trembled. "Henry, why are you doing this?"

He reacted to the movement of my hand. His attention, which had been focused on the woods, whipped back to me. He noticed my shaking hand. "I told you, Ellie. You have nothing to worry about. My quibble is with Mitch."

"But why? What's Mitch done to you?" I asked.

His casual attitude dropped away. "He's got my slot."

"The school slot?" I asked.

Henry's eyes narrowed and he enunciated each word slowly as if I didn't speak the language. "It's *my* slot. Colonel Scofries promised it to me. It's mine."

Colonel Scofries had been the commander when

we were first transferred to Taylor, but had moved on after a few months, and Colonel Pershall took over as the commander. "But if Colonel Scofries promised you the slot, then he's the one you should be upset with, not Colonel Pershall or Mitch." Promises in the military are like airline tickets—they're not transferable. You couldn't count on promises to be passed on from commander to commander. If someone said they'd do something for you, then you'd better hope they were still in the position to do it when the time came. Mitch found this out the hard way a few years ago when it was time for him to upgrade from copilot to aircraft commander. His squadron commander had told Mitch he was next in line to upgrade, but when the time came, that commander was gone and a new commander put several other guys in for upgrade before Mitch. Mitch had eventually gotten his turn, but it wasn't what had been promised.

"Normally, yes, that would be how it worked, but Scofries told Pershall about the slot and Pershall agreed to send me."

"Well, what happened? Colonel Pershall was a man of his word." I couldn't believe that Colonel Pershall wouldn't follow through. It would be like Mitch deciding he didn't want to watch the Super Bowl.

He muttered something, looked away.

"Something must have happened," I persisted

and risked a glance over my shoulder. I didn't see anything.

"It was a misunderstanding. I explained the whole thing, but he blew it out of proportion. Said because I'd done it, he wasn't sending me. Said it showed poor judgment on my part." He snorted. "Poor judgment. *He* was the one with poor judgment. I deserved that slot. I was the one who came in early, who stayed late, who picked up the slack when everyone else was goofing off. That slot is mine and something as insignificant as a charge on my credit card can't outweigh everything else I've done."

"So you charged something on your government card? Something other than official travel or expenses?" I asked. Another shadow seemed to shift and I slowly turned my head a few degrees.

"No. It was a bogus charge," he said, all righteous indignation. "I told Pershall that, but he refused to believe me."

The empty house behind Henry had plenty of places to hide. Maybe Mitch was inside the house. I thought I saw a shadow trace across a wall inside, but when I looked closer, I couldn't see anything.

"So you .. ."

"Killed him, yes," he said matter-of-factly. "It was laughably easy, actually. Just wear the right clothes, pull the hat low, and drop off the drink at the table. They were so deep in conversation—important squadron business, I'm sure—they didn't glance at me. Once he'd drunk it . . . well, the rest was easy. He hardly put up a fight at all. You can stop gaping at me like that. Yes. I did it, but it wasn't cold-blooded murder. He refused to listen to me, so I removed him. Colonel Barnes is much easier to work with. He's acting squadron commander, you know. He's got the power to fix things. A suggestion here and a nudge there. He likes me. I've pulled him out of hot water often enough—he owes me a few favors. He can't do jack in PowerPoint and every slide presentation he's given to the general in the last year, I've done for him. He's agreed that I should have the next school slot."

"But what about your assignment? The UAV squadron?" A tiny no-see-um bug hovered near my eyes, but I resisted the impulse to wave it away. No sudden movements on my part.

"Barnes can take care of that for me." I blinked a few times, at a loss for words. I didn't know if Colonel Barnes could get Henry's assignment changed, but Henry clearly thought it was going to happen.

"So it's simple, really. I remove Mitch from the picture and it bumps me up. Barnes sends me and I'm on my way up again."

"So this whole time . . . it's been you," I said, working it out as I spoke. "That shot, the one that barely missed Dan. You thought he was Mitch. You were trying to kill Mitch."

"Yes. Quite frustrating, your family reunion and plethora of relatives. But it was only a temporary setback. It simply postponed the inevitable."

His casual tone paired with his truly creepy words frightened me. He was so offhand. He really didn't think killing someone was a big deal. I pressed my free hand into the rough edges of the bricks, to see if I could work one loose. To distract him from what I was doing, I said, "When that didn't work for you, you set up a few more things—the leaf blower. You did that, didn't you?"

He half-shrugged a shoulder in acknowledgment, then said, "Now, we must get down to business. I can't stay around here all day—"

The bricks were packed too tightly for me to slip one out without him noticing. "Not very effective, the leaf blower, I mean," I said, interrupting him. There was no way I was going to let him "get down to business" if I could help it. The miniscule bug had drifted to my ear. I tried to ignore it.

A spark of anger flashed in his eyes. "Your stupid family was crawling all over your place and then you've got that big lug of a dog. It's amazing I was able to get to the leaf blower and the tire on his car. I was on a time line."

"You had to get back to Atlanta," I said.

"Considering my limitations, not bad." He swatted at his ear and muttered, "Dang bugs."

"But why all the convoluted setups?" I licked my lips and said, "Why didn't you take care of Mitch like you'd taken care of Colonel Pershall? Why didn't you garrote him?"

He lowered the barrel of the rifle a faction of an inch. "Because then they'd be linked. I'm not that stupid." His tone indicated that he thought I was an idiot for even asking the question. "I did my research. I didn't want the cops to think they had a serial killer on their hands. They'd call in all their experts and the media might pick up on it. No, one garroting and one death from a stray hunter's bullet wouldn't be connected. Of course, I went to all that trouble to make them different and then Carrie almost did my job for me. Too bad her little dry ice bombs didn't get Mitch." He sounded sincerely regretful. "It really would have saved me so much trouble."

"But that doesn't make sense. Why go to all those lengths and then send everyone the slightly altered squadron coins?" I truly didn't understand. The tiny bug drifted off. I thought I heard an engine and tensed, but then I realized it was far below us in the area of the neighborhood where our house was.

He shook his head. "Because it was too easy to fool them. Everyone thinks getting away with a crime is difficult. It's not. It's easy. Planning and intelligence are all it takes. All their high-tech equipment, the fingerprinting, DNA analysis, and computer databases. They'll never put it together. That's why I sent the coins. My signature, if you will."

"To let them know you're smarter than they are?" I asked slowly as I considered yelling for help. But would anyone get here before he could shoot me? No. I abandoned that idea.

"Now you're beginning to understand," he said in an encouraging tone, like I was a student who'd answered a difficult question correctly.

"But even in that, I laid down a false trail." He lifted the barrel of the gun slightly as he leaned forward in his eagerness to explain on his cleverness. "When I realized it wasn't Mitch that I'd shot at, I knew I had to send a coin to Dan, too. It wasn't hard to find his name. A call from a 'florist' to the hospital confirming a delivery was all I needed to find out his name."

He swiped at another bug, this one by his nose, and I jumped at his unexpected movement. Then he said, "I asked Mitch a question or two and I knew he had cousins in Alabama. Then, a Web search for Dan Avery brought up his address, and I had all the information I needed. If any investigator ever tracked down the coins and made the connection between the three incidents, the coin to Dan would negate any speculation. A rather brilliant red herring, don't you think? There wouldn't be a pattern in who had received the coins. Investigators love patterns, which would automatically make them discount the coins' significance."

He raised the barrel again and checked his watch, then barked, "Mitch, I know you're close." I jumped at the sharp shout. "You've had plenty of time to get here and I'm sure you're planning some sort of heroic ambush." He raised the rifle, aimed it at my face. "But let me assure you, you don't want to do that. Show yourself or I'll put a bullet between her eyes."

I swallowed and felt my heartbeat go into overdrive. Leaves rattled somewhere to my left and Mitch stepped into the yard, his arms bent up at the elbows, hands raised and empty.

"Ah, there he is, the fast burner, the golden child."

I'd never seen Mitch look so strained. He spoke slowly, calmly. "Henry, this is between you and me. Let Ellie leave."

"Interesting proposition, considering that you have nothing to bargain with. I hold all the cards here, Mitch."

I noticed that Mitch was slowly edging closer to me.

"This is ridiculous, Henry," I said. "You can't just . . . just shoot Mitch and go on your merry way. This isn't happening in a vacuum. I'm here, for one thing, and—"

"Well, in that case, it seems I may have lied. I may have to remove you as well," Henry said, positioning the rifle at his shoulder.

The first notes of "Livin' On A Prayer" sounded and for a second we all looked at each other in confusion. I realized it was my cell phone going off in my hand. Three things happened almost simultaneously.

I chucked the phone at Henry. Mitch covered the distance between us and took a flying leap at me as Henry fired the rifle. Mitch's body hit mine and took us to the ground.

There was a rush of feet and a flurry as several people in dark clothing erupted from the foliage and the house. There were some shouts, but I wasn't paying attention because I was more focused on the primary sensation of an aching knee and the taste of dirt in my mouth. But I figured if those were the main things I felt, that was a good sign, and it meant there were no bullet holes in me.

My cell phone stopped ringing and I heard a stern voice telling Henry to keep his hands where they could be seen. Mitch rolled off of me with a groan and I twisted around to check on him. "Are you okay?" I asked, looking for blood.

"Yeah. When you threw the cell phone, he flinched and fired in the air." He propped himself up on his elbows. "But you can keep patting me down, if you'd like."

I realized I'd been running my hands up and down his legs and arms, looking for broken bones or worse.

I leaned back on my heels. "I can see you're fine."

"Don't worry, I'll return the favor later," he said with a smile.

"What's going on?" I realized the people swarming around were law enforcement and most of them were wearing bulletproof vests. A veritable alphabet soup of acronyms identified them. I recognized the Georgia Bureau of Investigation "The GBI? And the DEA? Where did all these people come from?"

Mitch sat up and crossed his legs. "It seems that this new part of Magnolia Estates is a perfect location for drug deals."

"What? No! It can't be. This is one of the best neighborhoods in North Dawkins."

Mitch glanced around the lot and said, "I think all these people have a different opinion."

"I believe this belongs to you?" The voice came from behind my shoulder.

"Gary!" I took the phone and said thanks. He was dressed in dark clothes and bulletproof vest.

Mitch said, "Ellie thinks our neighborhood is too nice to be a hotbed of crime."

Gary glanced around and said, "Don't think so. Not that it's not a nice neighborhood but, hey, a drug house is a drug house."

"A drug house! We have a drug house in Magnolia Estates?" Another gnatlike bug floated near my face and I swatted it away.

"Well, not a specific house per se, but this new part of the neighborhood is usually a quiet area. Mostly deserted at night. Plenty of places to hide and it's easy to set up a meeting here. A couple of cars parked on the street for a few minutes wouldn't draw much attention because, well, there's hardly anyone around to notice it. And the half-finished houses provide a place to wait or cover if the weather turns bad."

"But the park up the street . . . and what about the construction workers during the day?"

"Sure, during the day there's occasional traffic on this road, but at night, this stretch and the two streets that branch off of this road don't have a single finished house. So at night, no one's around."

"I'm amazed. Drug deals going on in Magnolia Estates."

"Don't feel bad. We've been working on busting this ring for two months."

"So the North Dawkins Police Department is working with the GBI and the DEA?"

He nodded. "The interstate is a corridor for shipping drugs north from Florida. Little North Dawkins is just one pit stop on the route up the East Coast."

"Wow. I guess that explains Waraday hanging around our neighborhood and the strange people Megan saw in the empty houses." I leaned back against the pallet of bricks. "Did Henry ruin everything for you?"

Gary scanned the area. A sheriff's car had already pulled to the curb and Henry was being escorted to it. Either a police photographer or a forensic technician was clicking away with a camera. Gary checked the sky before replying. "I think we'll fold this up before our targets—our original targets—get here. We've been watching them for months and they usually show up after dark. We'll probably be able to get this area cleared and everyone repositioned before then."

It was the last of the long muggy days of summer and sunset was still hours away. I looked at Mitch and said, "So when I called you, you got off the street and . . . ?"

"Practically stepped on a DEA agent in the woods. Once he understood what was going on, he alerted everyone and they moved into place."

"What were they going to do?" I asked, thinking of how I'd stood in the open, so afraid and feeling so alone.

Gary said, "We were going to do what we do best—take out the bad guy."

"Well, what were you waiting for?"

"You had him on a roll. He confessed to Colonel Pershall's murder and we were pretty sure you were safe until he had Mitch. He had to have you. You were his guarantee to draw Mitch out, so we knew he wouldn't hurt you. If he'd closed the distance between himself and you or made a move to shoot you, we'd have taken him out."

My phone sounded again, playing the same Bon Jovi song. I flipped it open and saw I had a voice mail. I listened to it and began laughing.

"What is it?" Mitch asked, concerned. I'm sure laughter was the last thing he expected from me at this point.

"That was Geneva's mom. She's very upset that I haven't made it back to pick up Livvy and Nathan." I mimicked her annoyed tone as I said, *"You've inconvenienced me and been very inconsiderate. You could have at least called, if you were held up."* I took a deep breath and calmed down. "I don't think Livvy and Nathan will be playing with Geneva much from now on."

"That may not be such a bad thing," Mitch said.

Tips for Busy, Budget-Minded Moms

Don't forget to add household and car maintenance routines to your planning calendar, including:

- Oil changes and routine service for your cars.
- Changing the filters on your heating and cooling systems.
- Changing the batteries in smoke detectors.

Chapter
Twenty-seven

W ell, I think that's the last of it," I said, pulling the roll of tape across the top of the cardboard box. I noted the contents on the side and top in bold red marker, then carried the box to the small U-Haul trailer in the carport. Denise's SUV was parked at the curb and was already stuffed with boxes except for one section that had been carefully reserved for the last minute addition of her Boston fern and spider plant.

I returned to the kitchen and looked around. Even though the movers wouldn't arrive until tomorrow, the house already had that un-lived-in feeling. Cabinet doors gaped open, stacks of miscellaneous debris sat on the countertops, and in the living room, Denise's packed suitcases waited by the door. After I'd dropped off Livvy at school and Nathan at his Mother's Day Out class, I'd spent the morning helping Denise get ready for the movers. Even though the movers do most of the heavy lifting and major packing, there were still things that Denise wanted to hand-carry or pack herself. She'd spent her time packing all the sensitive paperwork she didn't want to lose, like old tax returns and insurance information. I'd packed her photos and special keepsakes, like the china bowl that had belonged to her mother, then moved on to taking the pictures down from the walls and removing stuff from the attic. The movers didn't climb attic stairs and everything had to be out where they could get to it.

I could hear Denise humming as she made her way down the hall. It was good to see her . . . *happy* wasn't the right word, relieved or calm came closer to describing her disposition. It was certainly the complete opposite of her state of mind before Henry was arrested. The tension and worry that had etched deep lines around her mouth and given her dark circles under her eyes had faded. I knew she was still grieving for Colonel Pershall, but with Henry making his way through the judicial system, the threat of being tried for the murder of her husband was gone. Henry had been arraigned and was awaiting trial. Megan was still in California. She was living with her parents and it didn't look as if she was going to return to Georgia. She maintained that she hadn't known what Henry was doing and I was inclined to believe her. She and Henry seemed to live in separate spheres, despite being married.

"I finally found it," Denise said, waving a real estate flyer as she came in the kitchen. "I knew it was around here. Take a look. My new home."

It was a small condo painted canary yellow with a bold blue door and a pink flowering vine trained up around the door frame.

"It's only two bedrooms, but that should be all I

need. Prices there are astronomical, but it's on the water and I can swim every day."

"It's beautiful," I said. "I can picture you there."

"The strange thing is, I can picture myself there, too. Settling down and never moving again. Hard to believe. I'm going to be a homeowner. No more base housing for me. I'll be grousing about having to fix my leaky pipes in a few weeks, but I'm never going to have to cut my lawn to meet regulation again." She smiled, her eyes twinkling. "They maintain the grounds, so all I have to worry about is keeping that vine alive, and knitting. I've got enough requests to keep me busy for a while."

"So you're going to keep your online store? I want to be able to order one of your gorgeous vests."

"Of course. Thank goodness Nancy is a wiz at all the technical stuff. She's always taken care of it for me and now we won't have to talk long distance about my Web site." Denise had picked a condo not far from her sister's house.

"Well, I hope you don't get too busy to answer knitting questions. I'm still working on that scarf, you know." I'd seriously underestimated the time it would take to make the scarf. I'd be lucky if I finished it before Christmas.

"I'm just an e-mail away. And speaking of knitting . . . wait here."

Denise returned with a white box. "This is for you. To say thank you."

"Oh! You didn't have to—"

"Yes," she said firmly. "Yes, I did. It's the least I could do and the best way I know how to say thank you."

I pulled off the lid. Nestled in tissue paper was a cream-colored fisherman's sweater. "Denise, this is amazing. I love it," I said as I pulled it out and held it up. Thick with texture, the intricate patterns of the cable stitching boggled my mind.

"Good. I know you won't get to wear it much here, but you'll be moving on someday."

"Thanks," I said as I gave her a hug.

"You're welcome. It doesn't compare with what you did for me. It scares me to think that I dragged you into that mess and it almost turned out terribly."

I leaned on the edge of the cluttered kitchen table, the sweater draped over my arm. "We were already involved in it but didn't know it, so there's no need for you to feel guilty. Henry had his sights set on Mitch even before you asked me to help. There's something I've been meaning to ask you about Henry." I wasn't sure if she'd want to talk about him, but she nodded, so I said, "Henry said something about a mistaken charge on his government card. Was that true?"

Denise snorted. "There was no mistake about it. He charged a big-screen TV, at the Base Exchange of all places, and expected Lewis to look the other way. Henry lied and said his card had been stolen."

"So there was no identity theft?"

"No. He went out and used it the next week. I guess he didn't think Lewis would check on it. Henry expected Lewis to forget about the lie." She swallowed and shook her head slightly. "Lewis wasn't one to look the other way."

"No, he wasn't," I said quietly. Colonel Pershall always tried to do the right thing. I traced one of the diamond patterns in the sweater, feeling guilty for suspecting Denise had murdered her husband and was out to get Mitch.

Denise began moving around the kitchen, efficiently closing cabinet doors. "He could no more change his personality than I could stop knitting," she said with a sad smile. "Why do you think Henry sent the coins?" Denise asked me. "It's been bothering me, wondering why he did that."

I frowned. "It's so weird. It seems it was a way for Henry to thumb his nose at the investigators and throw them off the trail. For someone who thought he was so smart, it seems like a stupid move to send your victims and potential victims something that could be traced back to you. I think he was too clever for his own good."

Denise picked up several rolls of packing tape and stacked them on the counter. "Lewis did say that Henry always kept track of everything," Denise said. "Henry was a hard worker, but he was a bit obsessive about making sure everyone knew *exactly* how hard he worked."

"Mitch always said Henry would have loved it if the squadron had a sticker chart like the one we use to keep track of Livvy and Nathan's chores."

Denise laughed. "That's true. How's Mitch?"

"Quiet," I said with a sigh. "He's usually so upbeat and positive, but now he's withdrawn." Once the adrenaline had faded, Mitch's attitude had turned more somber.

"Give it time," was all Denise said, and I thought she was giving herself advice as much as she was passing some along to me. "It has to be disconcerting to know someone tried to kill you. He was targeted at home and at work."

"Oh, you heard that the 'accident' with the trophy was no accident?" I asked. I wasn't sure how much the detectives had shared with Denise.

She shoved the packing supplies into a box as she nodded. "Yes. I wanted to know everything. Well, everything they'd tell me. I didn't notice any string tied to the trophy that hit Mitch."

"It was floss. He'd run it from the trophy up the side of the stairs and it was so thin, no one noticed it. He must have been feeling pretty desperate to try something that was so inaccurate, but he wanted Mitch out of the way and he wanted it to look like an accident." The thick, warm fabric of the sweater weighed heavily on my arm. I shifted it to my other arm.

"So how did he do it? How did he know Mitch

was there?" Denise asked as she tucked several black markers in with the packing supplies.

"He must have been keeping a close eye on Mitch at work because Mitch said he hadn't used the back staircase until that day. Henry watched Mitch go into the stairwell upstairs. He must have caught the door before it closed and waited for the right moment to pull the line of floss so the trophy would hit Mitch on the head."

"But I thought Henry came in the door from the parking lot," Denise said, her brow wrinkled.

"As soon as he pulled the trophy down, he left the stairwell, went across the third floor to the front stairwell and left through the front doors. He circled around to the back of the building and came in from the parking lot with the group of flyers that included Jeff."

"But the floss. It wasn't there when I went back to clean up," Denise said.

"I know. Henry was the last person to come in The Nest when we took Mitch in there to bandage his head. Henry took advantage of the confusion to lag behind us, then double back to the stairwell and remove the floss before he entered the break room. Detective Waraday told me they found the floss wadded up in a pocket of his pants, which were in his clothes hamper."

Denise shook her head slowly, "He really is disturbed, isn't he? I keep thinking if I find out all the details, I'll understand why he did it, but . . .

he's . . ." her voice trailed off and she shrugged.

I remembered his conversational tone and the rising panic I'd felt as I looked at him holding a rifle aimed at me. "Denise, he's messed up. He thought he deserved more and was willing to do whatever it took to get it."

Denise stared at me for a moment, then said, "It's not ever going to make sense—what happened to Lewis."

I didn't know what to say. No matter what I added or how much Denise learned, it wouldn't bring back Colonel Pershall.

She blinked a few times, then roughly pushed away from the counter. She sniffed, then said, "How about some tea? It's bottled, not brewed, but it's the best I can do with the movers coming tomorrow," her voice forcefully brisk. She opened an ice chest and pulled out two bottles of Snapple.

"What's going on with Carrie?" I asked, to change the subject. "Is she still on base?"

"Not for long. Her hand is still healing, but she's become quite an online celebrity. She's blogging about her activities and recovery. She wants to move, too, to San Francisco. She found a job at a new antiwar organization. What was the name? Women Against War and Aggression, that was it. I have to wonder if they've realized what their acronym is."

"And I thought the military picked awful acronyms."

"I know! I don't think she'll be able to move out of state for a while. The charges against her aren't going away anytime soon."

Carrie had been charged with possession and manufacture of an explosive device, aggravated assault, and reckless conduct. Faye, the distraught woman I'd met on the night Carrie got hurt, had gone to the police and received immunity in exchange for her testimony against Carrie.

"Well, I guess she can blog from anywhere," I said as I checked my watch. "Oops! I better run. I have to pick up Nathan. I love the sweater and will wear it this winter even if it doesn't get below forty degrees." I put my Coach bag on my shoulder, tucked the box under my arm, and picked up the bottle of tea. "What are you doing for dinner?"

"Meeting Bonnie and Rich."

"So you're dining with our local writer?"

"Yes. It's amazing to me that he didn't want anyone to know he was a writer. In fact, it's amazing to me he was able to keep it to himself for so long. Now that it's out in the open, it's all he can talk about. Bonnie says if she hears the word 'agent' one more time, she's going to forward his mail to another address."

"So what's he going to do?"

"Oh, stay in the air force, for now. It pays better than writing, apparently. He still hasn't had any bites on his book. Bonnie'll keep pushing him, but now that his secret is out, he seems less inclined to follow her marching orders."

"They are a pair. Will he get the commander slot?"

"Nope. He's lined up a job in D.C. It's a good background for his writing—that was his reasoning—and Bonnie can't argue with the assignment because it's at the Pentagon."

"And it was his idea?"

"Yes. We'll see if it's the first sign of his newly apparent backbone or simply an aberration. People rarely change overnight. Now, go on. Long good-byes are terrible things."

I had to agree, so I didn't linger. Once in the car, I tried not to think of how much I'd miss her. Who knew what kind of person the next squadron commander's spouse would be? Would she try and revert to the traditional way of doing things? Would she like the idea of book clubs and playgroups?

My cell phone rang and the strains of "We Are Family" filled the car.

When I answered, Mitch said, "Just checking to see if Back to School Night is tomorrow or next week. The squadron wants me to pick up a night flight tomorrow."

"Next week, so there's no conflict there. Nice ringtone, by the way," I said.

"You like that one?"

"I do. That one's a keeper. It's perfect."

Tips for Busy, Budget-Minded Moms

Organizing routines that you only have to do once a year

Winter

- Sort holiday decorations, removing any broken or outdated items, then store in labeled bins until the next season.
- Check after-Christmas sales for discounted items. Create a gift storage area—a high closet shelf is ideal—to save money and time. You'll be one step ahead when Mother's Day or Father's Day is near or when birthday party invitations arrive. You can also stock up on greeting cards. Store them in card files: Children's Birthday, Adult Birthday, Sympathy, Get Well, etc.
- Clean out files and sort paperwork for taxes.
- Sort winter clothes, thinning items that you don't want/need.
- Sign up for summer camps.
- Fill out applications for schools and scholarships. (This may need to be done up to a year in advance, so check with your intended school for application deadlines.)

Spring/Summer

- Prep grill and lawn furniture for summer.
- Clean out school homework papers, saving a few items for memory boxes.

Fall

- Sort summer clothes, thinning items that you don't want/need.
- Plan and reserve holiday travel for fall.
- Store patio equipment for winter.
- Clean gutters.
- Prune bushes and trees.
- Fertilize lawn.
- Winterize home by bringing in water hoses, covering outdoor faucets, and draining underground sprinkler systems.
- Update contact lists for Christmas card/e-mail lists.

Acknowledgments

As always, thanks to Faith Hamlin. I don't know what I'd do without your steady guidance and confidence. Michaela Hamilton launched Ellie's story and my writing career. Thanks for your on-the-mark editing and endless support. I'm thrilled to have the opportunity to grow as a writer and continue Ellie's story. Many kudos to the team at Kensington Books. You're all so easy to work with and the books always look amazing when they arrive on the shelves.

I have to send out a huge thank you to the librarians, the booksellers, and the readers who support my books. I'm delighted that so many people enjoy reading Ellie's adventures. My writer friends, particularly the Good Girls and the Deadly Divas, help me stay on track when the word count seems overwhelming.

And for my family and friends, you're the best. Thanks to John and Edwyna Honderich for being first readers and a terrific publicity team. Thanks to Jim and Jan Rosett for embracing me and my writing. Thanks to Glenn for, well, everything. I couldn't do it without you. And, to Lauren and Jonathan, thanks for being my inspiration and reading me the comics when I get too serious.

Center Point Publishing

600 Brooks Road ● PO Box 1
Thorndike ME 04986-0001 USA

(207) 568-3717

US & Canada:
1 800 929-9108
www.centerpointlargeprint.com